"I don't want this any more than you do, but it looks like there is no choice."

For him to be that…fatalistic about even the thought of marrying her hurt more than she'd ever admit. Lorelei shook her head. "With a proposal like that, how can I say no?"

She forced herself to calm her rapid breathing as she tried to make sense of what was happening. Sean was agreeing to marry her. For so many years, she'd longed for a moment like this between them—now she deplored it. It didn't mean that he loved her. It simply meant that he was doing his duty. Logically, it was the best option. Emotionally—it just felt plain awful.

At least she didn't love him anymore. That would have sealed the hopelessness of her fate.

A wry smile touched his lips. "You look like you've been assigned a fate worse than death."

She nodded slowly. He seemed to think so. Why shouldn't she? "Maybe I have."

Books by Noelle Marchand

Love Inspired Historical

Unlawfully Wedded Bride
The Runaway Bride

NOELLE MARCHAND

Her love of literature began as a child when she would spend hours reading beneath the covers long after she was supposed to be asleep. Over the years, God began prompting her to write. Eventually, those stories became like "fire shut up in her bones" leading her to complete her first novel by her sixteenth birthday.

Noelle is a Houston native who is currently a senior, double majoring in mass communication with a focus in journalism and speech communication. Though life as a college student keeps her busy, God continues to use her talent for writing as a way to deepen her spiritual life and draw her closer to Him.

The Runaway Bride

NOELLE MARCHAND

Love Inspired

Recycling programs
for this product may
not exist in your area.

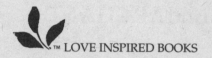 ™ LOVE INSPIRED BOOKS

ISBN-13: 978-0-373-82925-5

THE RUNAWAY BRIDE

Copyright © 2012 by Noelle Marchand

www.LoveInspiredBooks.com

Printed in U.S.A.

Bear with each other and forgive one another
if any of you has a grievance against someone.
Forgive as the Lord forgave you. And over all these
virtues put on love, which binds them all together
in perfect unity.
—*Colossians* 3:13–14

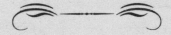

Dedicated with love to my sister by blood,
Ashley Marchand, and my sisters in spirit,
Cynthia Rouhana and Erika Gutierrez.
Also, to my mother, Juanita Marchand,
for her continued encouragement.

Chapter One

Peppin, Texas
August 1887

"Lorelei Wilkins, will you take this man to be your lawfully wedded husband, to live together after God's ordinance in the holy estate of matrimony? Will you love, honor and keep him, in sickness and in health: forsaking all others, keeping only unto him so long as you both shall live?"

Lorelei's eyes widened as she stared silently at Reverend Sparks. Did he have any idea how formidable those words sounded? If she was making a mistake, it would be irreversible. Yet, he stood there waiting. Waiting—just like the man beside her who'd gone through the trouble of slicking back his hair, shining his boots and donning a fancy shirt. She glanced at her groom. Lawson Williams swallowed nervously.

"I…" Her gaze slipped to Lawson's best man. Sean O'Brien's green eyes watched her carefully. He was probably wondering if she was going to prove that his suspicion about her had been right all along. Hadn't he secretly warned Lawson not to court her? Some secret.

She'd heard the words he hadn't intended for her ears two years ago, and they reverberated in her thoughts even now.

"You're making a mistake. Lorelei isn't the kind of girl you can count on. She's always been flighty and insincere. If you aren't careful, you'll end up with a broken heart."

She turned back to Reverend Sparks. "Will you repeat the second question?"

Nervous laughter spread through the church behind her, but she listened carefully as he repeated. "Will you love—"

He continued, but that one word was all she needed to hear. Would she love Lawson, as a wife should love her husband, for as long as the two of them lived? She couldn't do this to herself, and she certainly couldn't do it to Lawson…because the answer was no.

Shaking her head, she took a halting step backward. Gasps tore through the air as she lifted her white skirt and ran down the aisle she'd just marched up. The doors of the church burst open with a bang, and light flooded the sanctuary as she tripped quickly down the stairs onto the lawn. Gasping in quick hard breaths, she only escaped a few feet before she heard footsteps behind her.

"Lorelei!" a strident voice called.

She ignored it. Pressing the back of her hand to her lips, she felt the lump of her engagement ring. A hand caught her arm. "Lorelei?"

She swung around to face her intended. "I can't. I can't do this. I'm so sorry, Lawson."

His handsome face noticeably paled. "What do you mean you can't do this? We're getting married today. Right now."

She swallowed. "It isn't right."

"What are you talking about?" Painful silence lingered in the air until he stepped toward her. "I thought you loved me."

"I do love you, Lawson, but not in the way a woman should love the man she's going to marry. I wish that I did," she said sorrowfully, then tilted her head to survey him carefully. "Do you love me like that, Lawson? Can you honestly tell me that you do?"

He turned away from her and dragged his fingers through his hair before he met her gaze again. His answer was halting, almost inaudible. "No."

She pulled in a deep breath and tugged the ring from her finger. "Then this shouldn't belong to me."

His eyes filled with resignation as he took it from her. He allowed her a curt nod before he walked back toward the church where his best man waited on the steps. Her gaze caught only briefly on that figure before she turned away.

She'd barely made it to Main Street when her delicate white boots began to pinch her feet. She allowed herself a grimace as she leaned against the wall of Maddie's Café and rustled through the satin overlay and layers of tulle to reach her shoes.

"If you wait here, I can get the buggy and drive you home."

Her heart stilled at the sound of Sean's voice. She gritted her teeth. "No, thank you. I'll walk."

"Now, Lorelei—" His deep voice drawled.

Her blue eyes lifted to meet his suspiciously. "Why are you here?"

"Lawson asked me to see you home."

Frowning, she rooted around for the other shoe. "I don't need anyone to see me home."

He lifted an imperious brow, and she barely kept from rolling her eyes. She knew what that meant. Sean was Lawson's best friend. If Lawson asked him to see her home, then Sean would see her home out of respect for his friend's wishes even if he couldn't stand her. No doubt he saw it as his duty, and if that was the case Sheriff Sean O'Brien would never back down.

"Fine," she bit out. "We'll walk." She handed him her boots a little too forcefully, then lifted her skirts out of the dust as she crossed Main Street. It lacked its usual bustle since most of the town was still at the church waiting for word about her wedding. Still, there were plenty of folks around to gape at her, so she darted into the alleyway behind the post office to hide from their curious eyes. She ignored her companion as she led him through the alleyways to the residential area of town. Finally, Lorelei stopped on the stairs of her family's porch and faced Sean to murmur, "Thank you for walking me home."

He frowned and crossed his arms as he surveyed her. "I think you're making a mistake."

He always did. A vague cloud of disappointment settled over her at his disapproval, but she'd come to expect it. For so long she'd waited for her feelings for him to change. They had. They'd gone from a desperate unrequited yearning to a hollow ache. She wasn't sure that counted as progress. She hid her feelings with an impudent tilt of her head. "And I'm supposed to care what you think because…?"

His eyes flashed with annoyance at her decidedly rude tone. She didn't wait for his response. Instead, she stepped into the house and closed the door firmly behind her. Leaning against it, she lifted her shaking hands to cover her face as the impact of what she'd done finally began to settle in. She didn't regret her decision to call off the wedding. She just could not believe she'd let it go this far. At least she'd done the right thing in the end.

Of course, the town wouldn't soon forget the day a bride hauled up her skirts and dashed out of the church rather than finish the ceremony. Facing her parents when they arrived home would be hard. Facing Lawson in town in the days to come would be harder. And facing any more of Sean O'Brien's disapproval would be hardest of all. She shook her head. Somehow she had to get away from the memories, the murmurs and the men.

"Well, why shouldn't I?" she whispered to the empty house. She was already packed and ready to leave for the honeymoon to her great-aunt's house in California. The train ticket was in her reticule. There was no reason not to go. She'd change out of her finery, and if her parents weren't home by the time she was done, she'd just write them a note. Either way, she was leaving—now.

She could only hope that distance would do what time had failed to accomplish by ridding her of whatever feelings she had left for Sean O'Brien once and for all.

The late-afternoon sun burst through the nearby window to gleam off the metal star on Sean's dark green shirt. He heaved a sigh, then tapped his pencil on the paperwork in front of him to expend his frustration and anger. His mind kept replaying the scene that had taken place at the church that morning. How dare Lorelei walk out on his best friend like that? The couple had been together for almost two years, despite his original prediction that the relationship wouldn't last more than six months. He'd started to think Lorelei might not be as impulsive, unpredictable and flighty as he'd imagined. She'd proven him wrong—again.

He'd spent the past several hours sorting out the mess Lorelei had made of the wedding so Lawson wouldn't have to. Lawson had been abandoned by his parents as a child and forced to drift from town to town in order to survive. Sean's family had taken him in when he'd shown up in Peppin at age fourteen. Several months later, Doc and Mrs. Lettie had adopted him, but Lawson had stayed close to Sean and his family. They were practically brothers as far as Sean was concerned. His friend of ten years didn't deserve the treatment Lorelei had just dealt him.

Lorelei Wilkins had been a thorn in Sean's side since grade school days when she'd informed the whole school that they would get married one day. He'd been annoyed then, but by the time he'd turned nineteen the idea hadn't seemed so awful. Lorelei had become the belle of Peppin. She could have had any guy in town, but she'd made him think he was the one she wanted. Nothing had been said between them, but he'd started to plan for her. He'd left his family's farm and accepted the position of sheriff to save up enough money to provide for her. He'd even carved a pitiful wooden promise ring.

He'd waited for the perfect moment to express his intentions. Then, just when the time seemed right, she suddenly chose his best friend. She'd become Lawson's girl practically overnight, and Sean had finally gotten a glimpse of her true character—impulsive, unsteady and completely unreliable. He hadn't said a word to anyone about her betrayal. Instead, he'd pretended she hadn't just landed a punch to his heart that would leave him reeling for years.

He realized his pencil was tapping in cadence with the ticking of the nearby clock and threw it aside. He'd be better off pacing the streets than sitting at his desk. He was just pushing his chair aside when the door flew open. Richard Wilkins, the president of the town's only bank and Lorelei Wilkins's father, stepped inside with Lawson right behind him.

Sean's eyebrows lifted at the grim looks on the men's faces. He settled back into his chair, then motioned them to the seats across from him. He gaze bounced between their worried eyes questioningly. "What's wrong?"

Richard settled into his chair with a dejected slump. "Something has happened to Lorelei."

Sean frowned. "Is she hurt?"

"No." Lawson shook his head. "She's gone."

Sean's stomach dropped to his boots with a surprising amount of dread. He stared at the men. "You mean she's dead?"

Richard abruptly straightened in his seat. "Of course not, boy! She just up and disappeared while we were all shutting down the wedding and packing up the reception."

Sean sighed. That was exactly the kind of stunt Lorelei would pull in a situation like this. Nevertheless, he readied his notebook and grabbed a pencil. "She couldn't have gone far. How long has she been missing?"

Lawson shot a glance at Richard. "Well, she isn't missing exactly."

The pencil hovering over the notebook hesitated as he glanced up at the men across from him in confusion. "Then y'all know where she is?"

"No," Lawson said just as Richard said, "Yes."

Sean lowered his pencil in tempered exasperation. "Well, which is it?"

"My daughter has run away."

"You mean she truly ran away, as in she's left town?" At Richard's nod, Sean frowned. "Are you sure?"

"I'm sure because she left this." Her father handed him a folded piece of paper.

He studied the written note carefully. "She says she wants a new life for herself and is going to live with her great-aunt in California."

"Keep going."

"She begs you to let her go and—" he glanced up sharply to meet Lawson's gaze before continuing quietly "—and not to send Lawson."

Lawson nodded firmly. "That's why we chose you."

"You chose me," he echoed as a sense of foreboding filled his chest. "To do what?"

"To bring her back." Lawson swallowed. "Not to me, of course, but to her parents."

Richard cleared his throat. "I'd go myself but my wife says I'd just end up letting Lorelei have her own way like I always do. As much as I hate to admit it, the Lord knows Caroline is probably right. That's why you've got to do it."

Sean leaned forward to set his arm against the desk. "Listen, I'm sorry, but I am not the man for this job. I'll tell you what I can do instead. I'll send my deputy—"

Lawson laughed skeptically. "Jeff Bridger? He's the only man in town who's gotten lost walking down Main Street."

"His sense of direction isn't that bad anymore," Sean protested. "I've been working with him and he has definitely improved."

"I'm glad, but do you really think I'm willing to trust

that man to find my daughter, let alone bring her back? Besides, I think you're a little confused here." Richard's fierce gaze told Sean he wasn't to be trifled with. "This isn't about you, Sheriff. This is about my daughter, who, as a citizen of Peppin, deserves your protection just like everyone else. She has no chaperone. She has no supplies and hardly any money. She's a target for every charlatan from here to California."

Sean cleared his throat as he tried to regain control of the conversation. "I understand that, Mr. Wilkins, but I can't just leave town for several days to run after your daughter. I have a job to do here."

"Actually, that seems like a good job for Jeff." Lawson crossed his arms. "After all, the man can't get lost just sitting in an office, can he?"

"I guess not." Sean stared at the men before him with a mixture of bemusement and dread.

Lawson shifted forward in his chair. "Sean, I would go myself but you read the note. We both know it isn't safe for her out there. Why, she's never even traveled before. She needs protection. I know she and I aren't going to get married, but that doesn't mean I don't care about her. I'm asking you to protect her not only because she's a citizen of our town but for my sake, because I can't."

Sean pulled in a fortifying breath to push aside his misgivings. His voice filled with resolve. "I'll leave first thing tomorrow morning. It will take that long for me to pack and coordinate things with Jeff."

Relief painted Richard's face with a smile. Lawson reached out to shake his hand. Sean didn't bother to hide his frown. All he could hope was that he'd be able to head her off before she made it to California. It'd be a dandy of a fight to bring her all the way back to Peppin if she was already settled with her great aunt.

Nevertheless, he'd taken an oath to protect the people of this town, and it would take more than one particularly troublesome female to keep him from fulfilling that promise.

Lorelei eyed the gingerbread style white-and-green boardinghouse dubiously. She had no idea what she was going to do. She barely had enough money in her pocket to buy herself a meal and certainly not enough for the rest of the trip to California. She wasn't even close to the Texas state line—any of them. She still seethed when she thought of that horrible man on the train. How dare he take off with her reticule?

She had to own that it was partially her fault for being thoughtless. She should have hidden most of her money in her boot or corset instead of leaving it all in her reticule for some villain to ride off with. It wouldn't have been such a setback if the train went straight to California from Peppin. Unfortunately, she was supposed to transfer to another line. How could she do that when she didn't even have money for a ticket?

She needed help, and she didn't want to go to her parents for it. She was a grown woman on a trip of her own undertaking. She'd figure this out somehow, then write her parents from California to tell them exactly how wonderful her new life was. If this didn't work, then fine, but she at least had to try to do it on her own first. She entered the bustling boardinghouse and went over to the woman who seemed to be checking people in.

"Welcome! I'm Mrs. Drake and I have a room all ready for you. May I have your name please?"

"Lorelei Wilkins, but I'm not here for a room exactly—"

"Wilkins," the blonde woman repeated then smiled. "You're from Peppin, aren't you?"

"How did you know?" she asked with a bit of trepidation. Surely news of her wedding hadn't spread this far that fast.

The woman tossed a dismissive hand. "Oh, I've visited family in Peppin once or twice during the past several years. I heard of your family while I was there. Perhaps you know mine. My aunt and uncle are Joseph and Amelia Greene."

Lorelei easily placed the family connection. "Yes, I know them. My mother is friends with your aunt."

The woman's face lit up. "Isn't that wonderful?"

"Yes, it is," Lorelei said with a smile as she realized it probably wouldn't be wise to mention that Mrs. Greene also had a reputation of being the town gossip. "As I was saying, I've run into a problem and I hope you might be able to help me. I was taking the train to meet my elderly great-aunt in California—"

"California!" Mrs. Drake frowned. "That's quite a ways to travel alone."

"Yes, well, I placed my reticule in my lap where I was sure no one would dare take it, but when I awakened it was gone. I'm sure that man sitting across the aisle stole it. To think he got close enough to steal my money and I never even felt it!"

"How unnerving! I'm sorry, dear, but what can I do?"

"I thought perhaps you might let me work for you so I can pay my room and board. It would just be until I'm able to get more money somehow."

"I wish I could." Suddenly the woman froze with some sudden thought. "Do you like children?"

"What?"

"I know of a job for you if you like children but—

Oh, what time is it?" Mrs. Drake popped open her small pocket watch. "We just might be able to catch them."

"Catch who?"

"The children." The woman rounded the desk to survey her carefully. "Yes, I think you'll do perfectly. Is that your only bag?"

Lorelei glanced down at her traveling bag. "Yes."

"Good. You won't take up much room." Mrs. Drake grabbed her hat from the stand and opened the door. "Come on. We have to run to catch them."

Lorelei followed her out the door and down the porch steps at a trot to keep up with her rapid pace. "But, Mrs. Drake, I really don't understand. Where are we going? Who are these children and what sort of job is it?"

"I'm sorry. I get rather scattered when I'm in a rush." The woman darted across the street with Lorelei at her heels. "The position is with a traveling preacher and his wife. They are very good friends of mine. James takes his family with him on his circuit once every few months or so. They're going with him this time. Usually the young woman down the street goes with them to help see to the children, but her father is sick so she can't go. James and his wife, Marissa, couldn't find anyone else on short notice."

"So I'm supposed to replace their neighbor?" Lorelei asked breathlessly.

"Yes, if we can catch them. They were supposed to be leaving now," Mrs. Drake said. "Watch that hole in the road."

Lorelei veered away from the hole just in time to save herself from a sprained ankle. "You said he's a traveling preacher. Where are they traveling?"

"That's the beauty of it, Miss Wilkins. They're going

farther west. Not to California, mind you but— Oh, there's the wagon. Help me wave it down."

Lorelei lifted her free hand to wave at the retreating covered wagon. The little boy who was practically hanging out the back of the wagon waved back with a grin, then turned around. He must have yelled something to his parents because the wagon pulled off the road and stopped. Mrs. Drake caught Lorelei's arm and led her around the wagon to meet an attractive young couple. They listened patiently to Mrs. Drake's breathlessly halting explanation and introduction.

Marissa Brightly smiled down at Lorelei, though her brown eyes showed compassion. "I'm so sorry this happened to you, Miss Wilkins, but I can't help feeling this is all part of God's plan."

"It certainly is. We'd be delighted to have you join us," James said. "I know that you want to get to California as soon as possible, but we are heading farther west and would be glad to pay you a small salary. Once you have the financial ability to continue your journey, we would send you on with our blessing."

Marissa leaned forward. "Please, say you'll come."

Lorelei bit her lip for a moment, then smiled. "I suppose I will. I have nothing to lose and I think I'll enjoy traveling with you very much."

"Good," James said with a satisfied nod. "Let me help you into the wagon."

Lorelei thanked Mrs. Drake for her help, then followed James to the back of the wagon where the little boy she'd seen earlier peeked out from the large hole in the canvas. "Pa, is she coming with us?"

"She sure is," James answered as her traveling bag disappeared inside. "Move out the entrance so she can get in, Hosea."

Once inside, Lorelei glanced around to take stock of her surroundings and froze. "Are *all* of these children yours?"

"Yes. Starting with the oldest, there is Henry, Julia, William, Hosea and Lacy. Children, Miss Lorelei will be traveling with us. Mind her as you would your Ma and I. I'll leave y'all to get acquainted."

Each child lifted a hand when their name was called as though their father was taking attendance. They stared at her as she found a seat near the rear of the wagon on a cushioned wooden chest. She stared right back at them. Five children. She was going to be taking care of *five* children. She hadn't even had any siblings growing up. What was she going to do?

The wagon started abruptly, and she fell off her seat onto the wagon floor. A few stifled gasps echoed under the canvas roof as the children waited for her reaction. They looked so shocked that she burst out laughing. That somehow gave them permission to, as well. As they laughed, relief settled into her bones just as tentatively as she settled back on her seat.

She was on her way again after only a momentary delay. Although her trip had been a disaster in some ways, it had been successful in its main goal. She'd barely thought about Sean since she'd left Peppin and certainly wouldn't have a chance anytime soon, now that she was surrounded by five children. She tried not to wonder if he even cared that she'd left or what he thought about possibly never seeing her again. He'd probably been indifferent, or worse: relieved.

No, though the decision had been made on the spur of the moment, she knew she'd made the right choice in leaving. She only wished she'd made that decision sooner. If she hadn't wanted so badly to prove she wasn't a flighty, insincere heartbreaker, she might have done the right thing with Lawson a long time ago. She should have trusted her instincts from the beginning instead of spending so much time overthinking things. Usually her first thoughts on a subject were clearest anyway. She shook her head. That was in the past. She could finally look forward to a future without Sean's distracting presence. In the meantime, it seemed she had a job to do.

The chortles finally died down enough for her to ask, "Who wants to play a game?"

All five hands eagerly went up. She grinned. Her new life without Sean O'Brien was going to be a cinch.

There she was—Lorelei Wilkins. Sean slid from his mount, then put a calming hand on Jericho's nose to keep him quiet as they crept through the woods toward the banks of the river. He ought to walk right out into the open and give her a piece of his mind. That's what he'd been planning to do for the two days it had taken to find her. Now that he'd found her, he decided to take a moment to gather himself.

Through the green veil of leaves, he could see her peaceful expression as she sat innocently reading under a nearby weeping willow. He noticed the soft smile at her lips and the dark curve of her downcast lashes. For some reason only one thought came to mind—she hadn't married Lawson. Relief lowered his tense shoulders for an instant before he frowned. It shouldn't matter to him that she was no longer engaged. It *didn't* matter to him. The relief he felt at seeing her came only because it meant his task was nearly complete, and he'd soon be able to return home. Nothing more.

He gave a dutiful nod and began moving toward

her. Suddenly she tossed her book aside. The soft hum of a melody drifted through the air as she practically danced into the river. He froze, befuddled yet transfixed by the sight. Her well-trained soprano arched over the quiet woods into the first lilting verse of "Beautiful Dreamer." He was barely aware of leaving Jericho to walk quietly toward the woman wading in the thick expanse of river until he stood at its banks.

She hadn't noticed his approach since her eyes were closed, so he tipped back his hat and crossed his arms to stare at her. Now, this was a side of Lorelei he'd never seen. Oh, sure, she sang at church occasionally but never with such passion. He'd seen her smile a hundred times but never with such freedom. Apparently, a weight of some kind had been lifted from her shoulders…and placed squarely onto his. His jaw tightened in aggravation.

His horse neighed. Lorelei froze. Her lashes flew open. Their eyes met. He heard her breath escape her lungs in a startled gasp as she instinctively backed away from him. Her blue eyes changed from alarm to dismay, then she stepped back one too many times and disappeared into the clutches of the racing river.

Chapter Two

Lord, have mercy, it's Sean O'Brien! Water swirled above Lorelei's head as she tried to reconcile the man she'd just seen with the fact that she'd traveled all those miles to leave him behind. No, it couldn't have been Sean. It just couldn't. She'd been enjoying the first break she'd had after two days of caring for five exuberant children when she'd heard a sound like quiet footsteps. She'd ignored it, but then she'd heard that neigh. She'd opened her eyes never expecting to see *that man* standing on the bank of the river looking for all the world as though he'd been there for hours.

Her lungs began to hanker for air. Lorelei tried to swim to the surface to satisfy them. She also wanted to make sure her imagination wasn't playing tricks on her, but her heavy skirts dragged her downward, subjecting her to the twisting, turning pull of the current. She careened through the water and away from the bank. Panic filled her. She fought the urge to gasp in air, knowing it would only drown her. Her thoughts began to muddle together. *What a foolish way to die!*

Suddenly an arm encircled her waist. A body came alongside hers and pulled her upward. With one last thrust of energy, they surfaced. Lorelei gasped for air. She met Sean's vibrant green eyes as he held her tightly to his chest.

"Don't let go," he commanded abruptly. She was too spent to argue, so she allowed him to pull her to the riverbank. The water gave way to solid ground. They both collapsed on the grass-covered banks. She turned her face toward him and found that they were only inches apart, but she didn't have the strength to remedy the situation.

His arm lay across her stomach barring her from flight. He made no effort to remove it. Instead, they stared at each other as they both took in gasping breaths. A few days' worth of golden stubble covered the base of his jaw and met just above his mouth. A slight sunburn trailed down the bridge of his nose drawing more attention to his unsmiling lips. Hints of gold and light hues of green shimmered in his eyes like the sunlight reflecting off of a slow-moving creek. Despite the disapproval she found there, her heart gave a familiar thump.

What was he doing here? He couldn't be here of his own volition. That would be too unbelievable. More likely, he had been sent by her father to bring her home. Well, that was not going to happen. She would not stand passively by as he wrecked her plans. She glared at him.

The dashes of his dark gold brows lowered into a frown as he rose onto his elbow to look down at her with a maddening smirk and finally spoke. "The good news is you made it out alive. The bad news is you didn't get away."

"I wasn't trying to get away. You frightened me by appearing out of nowhere. I responded as any normal person would." Somehow she found herself lifted into his arms as he stood and swept her up to his chest. She kicked her feet. "Put me down. What are you doing?"

"You're in no condition to walk."

"Yes, I am. Put me down. What is wrong with you?" She could count on one hand the number of times he'd purposefully touched her. Now, he wouldn't let her go. She kicked her legs again. "I said, put me down!"

"Hold on, you wildcat—"

A warning shot rang through the air. Lorelei screamed. Sean froze, then whirled around to face his adversary. She peered through her wild chocolate-colored curls to get a glimpse of Pastor James standing broad-legged and determined. He cocked his gun again and aimed it at Sean. "You heard the lady. Put her down."

The tone of his voice was deadly. Not at all what she expected from the gentle man she'd gotten to know over the past several days. She bowed her head so neither man could see the smile that curved her lips. She allowed her body to completely relax even as she felt Sean's arms tense beneath her legs and arms. He carefully lowered her legs to the ground but trapped her against his side in a one-armed embrace entirely too close to be proper.

This man was determined to meddle with her head. She was too smart for it this time. She wouldn't let his protective instincts or plain orneriness put ideas in her head or a silly feeling like hope into her heart. He could hold her as uncomfortably close as he liked, but from the looks of James's rifle, this situation was about to become just as uncomfortable for Sean. She vowed to enjoy every moment of it.

* * *

Sean kept Lorelei tucked against his side so close he could feel her shaking. Was she shivering from her plunge in the river? The water hadn't been that cold. Perhaps she quaked from fear after nearly drowning to death. He glanced down at her and found the answer in her mirth-filled eyes. She was laughing at him.

He narrowed his eyes to stem her mirth, but that only seemed to increase it. She dropped her head so the preacher couldn't see her smile as her body continued to shake in silent suppressed laughter. Annoyance led his hand down to his revolver. It probably wasn't any good as water-soaked as it was, but it was nice to have some reassurance while staring down a shotgun. He widened his stance to stare at the man intent on defending Lorelei from him. "Look, I don't know who you are or how this is any of your business, but the only protection this woman needs is from herself."

That got her riled up. She gave a pretty fierce little growl for a woman her size and in her situation. He tried to fight back his smirk but wasn't quite successful.

"I am Pastor James Brightly and that woman is under my care. I insist you release her this instant."

"This instant, huh?" Sean glanced down at Lorelei. Her dark blue eyes stared back at him, making him realize there was a lot of sanity in doing just what the preacher commanded. He let go of her. She took a few wavering steps away from him but somehow managed to stand on her own.

The preacher waved his shotgun. "Now, be on your way."

Sean shook his head. "Oh, no. I've been searching for this woman for days. I'm the sheriff of the town where she lives. I'm not trying to hurt her, but I'm not leaving until she and I have a little talk, Preacher."

"Lorelei, is this true? Do you know this man?"

He met her gaze squarely. He watched her tilt her head thoughtfully as she considered her next step. He could almost read the thoughts running through her head. All she had to do was tell the preacher that little two-letter word. If she did, he'd be dodging bullets and receiving a nice little prayer for safe travel courtesy of the preacher. Her smile grew.

He frowned at her. "Oh, come on, Lorelei. I just saved your life. The least you could do is save mine."

Her expression changed to one of reluctant resignation. "I know him, Pastor James, but I'd also like to know what he's doing here."

Sean hid his relief when the preacher lowered the rifle to his side. Lorelei didn't bother to hide her disappointment when the two men shifted into a less combative stance. She frowned at him. "Well?"

"You know very well why I'm here." He shook his head like a wet dog, then pinned her with a look. "Your father and Lawson sent me to bring you home, and that's exactly what I'm going to do."

Lorelei stiffened. "Oh, no, you won't!"

"Oh, yes, I will." He stepped closer to her. "Do you have any idea how worried your parents are right now?"

"I left them a note."

"That only compounded their fears. They knew that you were traveling alone with very limited finances, no supplies and hardly any idea how to get to California, let alone reach your great-aunt's estate." He caught her arm, hoping to somehow transfer a little good sense. "Anything could have happened, Lorelei!"

She wrenched her arm from his grasp but lowered her voice. "Don't you think I've realized that?"

"Then come home with me."

She crossed her arms. "No. Not when I'm so close to getting away from—" she seemed to catch herself and changed the sentence "—getting to California."

"Have you looked at a map lately? You aren't even close to making it out of Texas."

Her hand made its way to her hip. "I will. Marissa and James are paying me a fair wage. As soon as I have enough saved up, I'll take the train."

"Alone? Haven't you been preyed on enough?" He nodded in response to her suspicious look. "I know all about your reticule being stolen. That just proves I'm right. A young woman traveling without protection will warrant the attention of every outlaw and charlatan from here to California."

"I'll be careful."

"That's not enough."

"Well, it will have to be enough because I'm certainly not leaving with you!" She flipped her wet hair away from her face and stormed off.

He'd nearly forgotten the preacher was still there until the man spoke. "Do you know why she ran away?"

"I know enough to say she should stop this foolishness and go home. Like I said, I'm Peppin's sheriff, it's my responsibility to keep the town's citizens safe—even when they're being too pigheaded to see sense."

James nodded patiently. "I understand that you're trying to do your duty, but that is her choice to make. You can talk to her about it, but you can't force her to return. In the meantime, you may want to think more carefully about trying to bring her back to the situation that was uncomfortable enough to make her leave."

Sean hid a grimace at the preacher's advice. There was nothing wrong with the situation Lorelei was in that she hadn't caused. His job was to find her and bring her home. Her parents were supposed to deal with her after that. Somehow he didn't think the esteemed Pastor James would find his reasoning particularly favorable, so he kept his mouth shut and nodded in agreement. He needed a place to sleep after all and a way to keep an eye on Lorelei since she had gotten into the habit of disappearing.

The leaves of the towering oak tree quivered above Sean's head as he placed his Stetson over his face. Four days he'd waited for Lorelei to come to her senses. It seemed as if she was just sliding deeper into her joyous little cloud of insanity. He could hear her now. She was playing with the children in the gurgling brook and having a wonderful time while he tried to cool his temper and not let the sound of her laughter set his teeth on edge.

He was glad James decided to give his family a day of rest from traveling. Sean was pretty tired himself. He figured this was the perfect time to craft a plan to change the mind of a stubborn young woman bent on getting herself to California. If he didn't figure out something soon, he'd be stuck trailing her halfway across the country.

The ground beneath his back seemed to sway slightly. He caught his breath. This couldn't happen. Not here. He needed to ward off the panic now before it got worse. Nevertheless, his heart began to quicken into a familiar staccato rhythm.

The first time he'd noticed that beat had been the night of the storm that had taken his parents' lives. At ten years old, he'd lain awake in bed listening to the wind howl past his window and trying to fight the sense of foreboding that gripped him. Somehow he'd known they wouldn't come back. The next morning brought news of the accident, and with it the entire world had turned on end for him and his two sisters. He'd tried to step up and be the man of the house, but at such a young age there was so much that he couldn't do to help his eighteen-year-old sister, Kate, manage the farm, besides try to keep eight-year-old Ellie out of trouble.

The next two years had passed with him in such a state of stress that he would lie awake at night listening to his rapid heartbeat pound in his ears thinking for sure it would burst from his chest. He never told anyone that, especially not his sisters. To them, he'd remained stalwart and dependable until his brother-in-law Nathan had stepped into their lives.

The burden had suddenly lifted from Sean's shoulders, and he'd thought that would be the end of the waves of panic that occasionally took over. It wasn't. Even now he could feel his breath shortening. It always did when he found himself in a situation like this where he could do nothing but wait. He forced himself to pray.

Lord, You know I'm trying to be patient, but I need to get back to Peppin. This isn't what I bargained for when I agreed to bring her home. Help me change her mind. It took a few minutes for his body to settle down. Relief filled him. He shouldn't have another one for a while now. He'd just go on as if it hadn't happened… like always.

He slowly felt himself leaning toward sleep. Suddenly a small fountain of water poured over the sides of his hat and settled around his ears before soaking into the ground. Letting out an exaggerated roar, he sat up. His Stetson tumbled to the ground, and Sean found himself face-to-face with a six-year-old. Hosea stood in what would have appeared to be paralyzed terror if not for the delight sparkling in his round eyes. His hand clutched a large tin cup now emptied of the water he must have carried from the nearby brook.

Sean quickly surveyed the situation and realized that, while Hosea may have been the culprit, he was only a small part of a much larger plot. Watching with just as much glee were the rest of the children and one very naughty nanny.

Time seemed to stop for the seconds it took Sean to slowly rise to his feet. Perhaps that was simply because all the children froze when he pinned them with a calculating stare. Then his gaze caught hers. His smile said one thing. William yelled it. "Run!"

Suddenly the world was a blur of motion. Hosea tried to make a break for it, but Sean was too fast for him. He scooped the boy under his arm like a sack of potatoes. Henry managed to evade his grasp, but Sean lifted William with his other arm and spun the boys around just enough to make them deliciously dizzy before he set them down. He repeated the process with Julia and Lacy.

Meanwhile, Lorelei casually meandered in the direction of the camp. She should have moved faster, but she couldn't help lingering to watch the sight before her. Sean was always so serious, so stern—it was fascinating to watch him grinning and playing with the children. It wasn't fair of him to look quite that…handsome. Not when she was trying so hard to ignore him.

Too late, she realized she'd missed her chance to escape. Her opponent caught sight of her and stalked toward her. He smiled predatorily. "Sending the children to do your dirty work, is that it?"

She widened her eyes innocently. "Now, Sean. It was all in fun."

"Was it?"

She glanced around for help, but the children had abandoned her to stagger laughingly toward camp. "Sean, don't…"

Sean swept her into his arms and spun her in a tight circle. She let out a small scream that lasted from the first rotation until he set her feet back on the ground. Her eyes finally opened to focus on his. The trees continued to sway perilously behind him. He gave her a pointed look. "There. Now, we're even."

"That's what you think," she muttered and tried to step around him, but he refused to release her.

"That's what I know. Unless you want me to haul you back to the Peppin jail for assaulting an officer." He gave a low whistle. "Now, there's an idea."

She glared at him. "Oh, why won't you just go away?"

He leaned toward her, meeting her challenge with his own. "You'd like that, wouldn't you?"

She pushed away from his chest, then wiped her suddenly wet hands on her skirt. "Yes, I certainly would."

"Tough." His green eyes captured hers. "You won't get rid of me until I drop you and your problems back in your father's lap. I gave him my word—and Lawson, too—which means I'm going to stick to you like glue."

"You mean fleas," she muttered as she brushed past him and walked back to camp. She wouldn't let it bother her that nothing short of a promise to her father and his best friend would tempt Sean to stick close to her. She hated being his *duty,* and he certainly didn't want her to be anything else, so the smartest thing for her to do would be to stay as far away from him as possible.

True to form, he followed her back a few minutes later and took a seat near the campfire to whittle as she helped Marissa prepare supper. She ignored him and was grateful when Marissa struck up a conversation. "Tell me more about Peppin, Lorelei. It sounds like a charming town."

"There really isn't much else to say," she said as she felt Sean's gaze resting on her. "It's small but not stiflingly so. The people are friendly and really care about you. There is always something going on, so you're hardly ever bored. You can just go to the mercantile or the café to find someone to talk to or about, in some cases. It's just a normal everyday Texas town. The only thing special about it are the people."

"It sure is a good town," Sean said wryly. "I guess that's why most people are content to stay right where they are."

Lorelei refused to meet his gaze. She'd never said Peppin wasn't a good town. It was her home. Nothing would change that. She'd only left to get away from Sean, and that hadn't done any good. Why, she could do a better job avoiding him in Peppin than she could in this wilderness. So it was decided. She was going home. She dreaded the victory she knew she'd see in Sean's gaze when she told him, but it couldn't be helped. She'd tell him tomorrow.

Sean ignored Lorelei's quelling stare as he propelled her through the evening shadows that painted everything in dark smudges of color. The Brightlys must have made very close ties with the people in this area. An inordinate amount of them were still around more than an hour after the service was over. Lorelei stopped short at the sight of the large crowd of people waiting to speak with the Brightlys. "I can wait until these people leave."

He shook his head. "I'm not going to give you that much time to change your mind. Besides, we'll both need our sleep. We're leaving at first light."

She rolled her eyes. "I know. You keep saying that."

"That's because I like the way it sounds," he said in satisfaction. Placing a hand on her back, he guided her forward until they took their place at the front of the line.

"You're going to get us shot," she whispered.

"This will only take a minute," he said loudly enough for the others in line to hear. "I'm sure the Brightlys won't mind talking to their children's nanny for a moment."

A short while later, with James and Marissa's undivided attention, he announced, "Lorelei has finally agreed to let me escort her home. We'll be leaving at first light."

"You're leaving?" Marissa asked in alarm.

Lorelei shot him a glance that told him exactly what she thought of his blunt way of telling the couple. "I'm afraid so. I'm so sorry! I know this leaves you in a lurch."

"We told you that you could leave whenever you liked. The problem is that the two of you would be traveling without a chaperone," James stated gravely.

Sean shrugged. "It isn't ideal, but it can't be helped."

Marissa shook her head. "You have to think about Lorelei's reputation."

"Her reputation," he echoed with frustration, then

glanced over his shoulder at the milling crowd that was shamelessly listening in.

"Maybe we should stay after all, Sean," Lorelei suggested, her determination wavering. "Just until we reach the next town with a train station. Then we won't have to worry about traveling unchaperoned."

"No," he said a bit too abruptly. "That could take days and days. We have to get back to Peppin. Perhaps one of the parishioners would be willing to act as our chaperone."

"I'll do it!"

Sean jumped in surprise at the quick response. He was still searching for the origin of that almost musical voice when a woman stepped forward to claim it. She didn't look anything like he thought a chaperone would. She was probably older than his mother would be if she'd lived but had pulled her mousy brown curls back with a girlish ribbon.

She stepped forward again which drew his gaze downward. His eyebrows rose. The woman was wearing pants or some female variation of them. Bloomers—Sean remembered his sister Ellie calling them. They were tucked into her high buckled leather boots.

Pastor James shifted uneasily beside Sean. "I don't think we've met, ma'am."

"The name's Miss Elmira Shrute. I've been traveling and came back to visit family." The woman's smile seemed friendly enough. "I'm about ready to head out though, so I can go with you. I assume the position would be paid?"

Sean glanced at Lorelei. Her reluctant expression turned doubtful. She cleared her throat daintily. "The little money I have, I'm going to need for traveling. Perhaps someone else would be willing…"

Her words were drowned out by a general murmur stating the opposite. Sean caught snatches of phrases like, "children to feed," "farm to run" and "pure foolishness." He grimaced.

Lorelei shifted slightly closer. "Well, what are we going to do?"

He glanced back at Miss Elmira. "I could pay you two dollars."

The woman grinned. "That works for me. When do we leave?"

"Sean, I'd like a brief word with you," Pastor James said as he took a step backward and led Sean away from the crowd. "I have to advise you against this. I've never met that woman before, but I know of her family. They don't exactly have the best reputation for being honest in their dealings with folks."

Sean frowned. "I appreciate your concern, but I'd be taking a chance with anyone I hired. Lorelei has agreed to go back with me, and I've got to get her moving before she changes her mind or gets a notion to take off on her own again. Miss Elmira may not be my first choice, but she is the only option."

"It's your decision and I respect that." Pastor James gave a reluctant nod. "Do what you have to do. Just keep an eye out for trouble."

They walked back to the crowd. Sean met Lorelei's inquiring look with an affirming one of his own. His shoulders relaxed from the tension he hadn't even realized was there. Things were finally going according to plan. Like Pastor James advised, he'd keep an eye out for trouble. It wouldn't be hard to do since he knew exactly what it looked like—a dark-haired beauty with the knack for getting under his skin in all the wrong ways.

***

"Lorelei, wake up. We've been robbed." Sean's words filtered through her consciousness, rousing her with a start.

Lorelei pushed the mass of dark curls from her face. Her hairpins had disappeared and Miss Elmira had refused to part with even one of her ribbons to help out a bedraggled fellow traveler. After two days of traveling, the woman had turned out to be as mean as she was peculiar. Lorelei realized Sean knelt at her side, so she propped herself on her elbow and frowned at him. "Was anyone hurt? Is Miss Elmira all right?"

"If I had to speculate, I'd say Miss Elmira is feeling pretty good right about now." He crossed his arms and glared out into the woods. "James was right about her. She must have taken off in the middle of the night, and my wallet went with her."

"*Miss Elmira* robbed us?" She glanced around to find her valise, but it was gone.

"Yes, and it's a little unsettling because she must have touched me to get my wallet and I never even felt it. In fact, I've never slept so deeply in my life. You don't think that tea she gave us…"

"At this point, I wouldn't put it past her," Lorelei said with a stifled yawn. "At least she left your horse."

He nodded. "She had her own horse. Besides, horse thieving is a hanging offense."

"What do we do? Should we go back to the Brightlys?"

Sean moved toward the fire he'd built and poured himself a cup of coffee. "I'm sure they've moved on by now. It would take longer to catch up with them than to simply keep going to the nearest train station."

"But we don't have any money!" She threw her bedroll aside and began to pace. "I suppose I could ask my father to wire us some once we get to town. That's probably the only option."

"I was kind of hoping you might say that," he admitted.

She sighed as she sank down onto a log across from him. "I can't believe I've been robbed twice since I left Peppin. What is *wrong* with this world?"

He glanced at her over his steaming cup. "An impulsive young woman ran off to California alone. That's what's wrong with the world."

She groaned. "You'd think there might be a grace period for fifteen minutes after I wake up, but no! You have to let me know you disapprove of me before I even have my coffee. I got that message a *long* time ago. Now, hand it over."

"Get your own." He nodded to the tin cup resting on the ground next to the coffeepot and ignored her rant. "At least she left us enough supplies to get to town."

She poured herself a cup, then blew away some of the steam. "I wish she'd left a letter of authentication, as well. 'To whom it may concern. This letter is to verify that in addition to my work as a thief I also dabble in conartistry—'"

"Conartistry?" Sean frowned, which was the closest thing to a smile she'd seen all morning.

She held up one finger and shook her head. "Let me finish. 'I also dabble in *conartistry* by convincing young men and women that I am an adequate chaperone before robbing them blind and leaving them alone in the wilderness. Therefore, let it be known that I exist and testify to my betrayed charges' good character.'"

He watched her carefully. "Do you always talk out of your head in the morning?"

"No, I usually try to talk out of my mouth. However, today there are extenuating circumstances." A quick glance at Sean's nearly smiling lips reminded her of why she'd dictated that letter in the first place. "What are people going to think when we show up without a chaperone?"

His green eyes flickered warily. "Hopefully nothing, but the less time we're alone in the wilderness, the better. It's time to pick up the pace."

Chapter Three

Lorelei paced in front of the Western Union office as she waited for a response to the telegram she'd sent her father. The anticipation she felt knowing she would soon hear from her family confirmed she'd made the right decision about going back to Peppin. Just the thought of seeing her home again suddenly made her so excited she couldn't get herself to sit down. Then again, she'd been sitting down—or rather, sitting *up,* on the back of a horse—for three days, and she wasn't about to do it again if she could help it.

For the past few minutes, she'd been testing out different walks. Originally, her purpose had simply been to stretch her legs. To her fascination, she'd discovered that it didn't matter how many different ways she walked past Sean. He simply would not look up from that piece of wood he'd been shaving with his pocketknife for the past half hour.

She literally waltzed by his bench. He still didn't notice, but a little girl with beribboned braids stopped to watch. Lorelei winked at her before the child's mother urged her on. The girl looked over her shoulder and beamed, causing Lorelei to do the same. Sean's horse neighed a welcome when she danced toward his hitching post. "Hello, Jericho. You know, you're much friendlier than your owner."

"Lorelei." She jumped at the sound of Sean's voice and turned to see him gesture to the seat beside him on the bench. She reluctantly sat down. He handed her the piece of wood and tucked his knife back in his pocket. "I made this for you."

A miniature replica of her stolen valise sat in her hands complete with tiny handles and a floral pattern. She stared at it blankly, then realized he expected a response. "This is nice."

"Thanks." He leaned back on the bench and covered his face with his Stetson.

She looked at it for another minute, then turned toward him to sharply ask, "Why would you do something this nice?"

"I was bored."

"You should be bored more often," she suggested.

He pushed his hat up slightly to meet her gaze. "Don't let it go to your head."

"Oh, I won't. I hate you. You hate me. Isn't that how this story goes?"

He turned to level her with his sincere green eyes. "I don't hate you."

She stared back at him. She believed him. In fact, she'd known it all along. It was just nice to hear him say it. For a moment she saw all the things that had once made her fall in love with him. She allowed a hint of a smile to reach her lips.

She could almost imagine that he began to lean toward her. The Western Union operator interrupted the tenuous moment by finally calling her into the building.

She immediately stood. Sean trailed after her because apparently that's what he did.

"Miss, your father sent the money with a message and special instructions."

"What was the message?"

"I love you and am glad you're safe," he read in a nearly monotone voice.

"Thanks, but I hardly know you," she replied calmly. The man looked up sharply and frowned. Sean turned away with a sudden coughing fit. She smiled weakly. "That was just a little joke."

Sean stepped up beside her again to ask, "What were the instructions?"

"I am to place all of the money in your care, sir. You are instructed to take care of Miss Wilkins's needs and your own from these funds. You are not to let the young lady run off under any circumstances."

"Papa, you didn't," she moaned.

The man surveyed her shrewdly. "He obviously doesn't trust you with the money, Miss Wilkins."

"Smart papa," Sean added with a smile.

She frowned at them both. "Now y'all are just rubbing it in. Sean, get the money from the man and let's get on with this."

"What now?" Sean asked once they left the building.

"We both need a change of clothes, food, a room at the boardinghouse and a train ticket for tomorrow."

Sean realized things had gone too far the moment the words *you hate me* came out of Lorelei's mouth. He'd nearly gotten the picture when she'd questioned why he was being nice, but it wasn't until later that the extent of their poor treatment of each other hit home. He wasn't perfect, but he held himself and others to a very high standard of behavior. Lorelei had failed that standard when she'd inexplicably walked away from their almost romance two years ago and again when she'd impetuously run from the altar and his best friend.

He did have legitimate reasons to dislike her, but *hate* seemed like such an unchristian word. If he'd learned anything by spending countless hours with the woman, it was that she possessed redeeming qualities. She had a funny sense of humor, she hardly ever complained and she didn't fall apart under pressure. He shouldn't discount those things entirely—but neither should he let them skew his view of her completely. Maybe there was a balance. The trouble was that he wasn't sure how to find it.

"Where is everyone?" Lorelei murmured as they waited at the front of the boardinghouse she'd visited before.

Sean glanced around, then spotted the bell on the counter and rang it loudly.

"Mrs. Drake," Lorelei exclaimed as the widow exited the kitchen.

The woman smiled as she glided toward them. "My dear Miss Wilkins, it's good to see you again. I guess you've given up your desire to see your great-aunt in California."

"Yes. I'll be catching the morning train back home." Lorelei gestured to him. "I think you've met Mr. O'Brien."

He nodded respectfully. "Mrs. Drake."

"We were hoping we might be able to stay here tonight."

"Certainly." Mrs. Drake turned to survey her keys. "I assume someone else will be joining you."

Sean tried to act as if he wasn't nervous. "No, ma'am. We'll just take two rooms, please."

"Do you mean that the two of you have been traveling alone?" Mrs. Drake's perplexed look changed to concern. "And for days, by the looks of you. I don't understand how Pastor and Mrs. Brightly would allow such a thing."

"We had a chaperone," Lorelei offered.

Mrs. Drake frowned. "I'd like to talk to her then. She needs to accompany you all the way home, not just part of the way."

"That isn't possible, ma'am." He decided to state the facts honestly and very calmly. "The woman who accompanied us from the Brightlys' camp ran off with all our money."

The woman was quiet for a long moment, then her gaze trailed to the package of new clothing he'd stacked on the counter. Before he could try to explain, her eyes lifted to his again. They boasted a hint of suspicion. "Let me guess. You were sleeping, and you didn't even feel this woman pick your pocket, isn't that right?"

Sean stared at her in amazement. "How could you possibly know that?"

"I've just heard that story somewhere before." The woman transferred her gaze to Lorelei. "Dear, I think you'd at least use a little originality."

Lorelei leaned forward earnestly. "Oh, but it's true this time, too."

"So the parcels in your hand just suddenly appeared?"

"My father wired us money."

"I see." The woman crossed her arms. "What did he have to say about your predicament?"

"I didn't tell him." Lorelei admitted quietly.

Her eyebrows rose. "No, I guess you wouldn't."

Sean felt it was time for him to step in. "Now, hold on. We aren't making this up. The Brightlys saw her leave with us."

She nodded. "Yet, she isn't here now. Do you remember where you left the Brightlys in case I write to them?"

He named the settlement.

Her eyes narrowed. "That's a five-day journey. How long did you actually have this supposed chaperone?"

He cleared his throat. "Really, Mrs. Drake, I appreciate your concern but I think this line of questioning is unnecessary. Chaperone or no chaperone, Miss Wilkins is under protective custody as per her father's request. Now, are you going to rent us two rooms or should we take our business elsewhere?"

The widow surveyed Sean skeptically for a moment. "Miss Wilkins, I'll place you on the second floor. Sheriff, your room will be on the first floor. No gentlemen are allowed upstairs after dinner."

"Thank you," Lorelei said.

Mrs. Drake gave a tight nod, then sent Sean a warning look. "If either of you need anything tonight, remember that my room is directly across from the stairs."

He barely refrained from rolling his eyes but noticed Lorelei gave Mrs. Drake a reassuring smile. He took his key, picked up Lorelei's packages and helped her find her room. As they walked up the stairs, he saw Lorelei bite her lip to keep from laughing. "You think this is funny, do you?"

She allowed her smile to grow. "Actually, yes, it is rather amusing. You made it sound like I was your prisoner. And you really ought to stop acting as though I'm a runaway. I'm much too old to be considered anything but an adult taking a trip, despite what my father or anyone else might say."

He frowned as he followed her around the corner. "When I say 'runaway' I am not describing your legal status."

She glanced at him over her shoulder. "Then what are you describing?"

"Your recent pattern of behavior," he said, then paused as she found her room and tried to unlock the door. "I still think you're just waiting for the first possible moment to get away from me."

"I am, but my efforts aren't doing any good. This door won't open." She turned the knob and banged her hip on the door, then winced. He planted his shoulder into the door and shoved. It groaned as it sprang open. She took her packages from him. "It was my decision to come back with you, remember? I've already told my father that I'm coming home. I won't run away. I give you my word on that."

He leaned against the threshold. "I think we all know what that's worth, don't we?"

It took her a moment to realize he was referring to her engagement with Lawson. When she did, pain flashed across her face. "How dare you? If you want to be mad at me because I left your best friend at the altar, then fine. Be mad, but you should really thank me for doing it."

He scoffed out a laugh. "Why would I thank you? You broke his heart."

She lifted a brow imperviously. "He didn't tell you that."

"He didn't have to. I saw the look on his face. He was stricken."

"He didn't love me, Sean. I know. I asked him. To be

honest, I didn't love him the way I should have, either. That's why I didn't marry him." She lifted her gaze to his. "He deserved better than a wife who isn't in love with him. He deserved better than me. Is that what you wanted to hear?"

Yes, but it didn't sound as wonderful as he thought it would. Not with that thread of pain running through the words and the self-deprecating tone in her voice. He met her gaze contritely. "I'm—"

"Save it," she bit out, then slammed the door in his face.

Thankfully the hinge made it close slowly enough that he could jump out of the way. He stared at the thick barrier between them. It always seemed to be there, whether visible or not. If it broke down, he wasn't sure how he'd handle it. It might not change anything, or it might change everything. He allowed his forehead to rest on the cool door for a moment. He couldn't lie to himself. Sometimes he wondered what might have happened if he'd fought for her even a little instead of just surrendering to someone else's claim. He'd never know. Maybe it was best that he didn't.

Sean helped Lorelei down from the train and onto the platform. She was immediately hailed by her parents who pulled her into a long hug. When her father stepped away, Sean handed him Lorelei's new traveling bag. The man gave a nod of appreciation but said nothing more. He seemed too moved at seeing his daughter to speak.

Sean returned his nod. He hesitated for a moment, then went to see about his horse. Once Jericho was secured, he looked for the Wilkinses again. He spotted them walking away. He watched them go, wondering if

Lorelei would turn to look at him or make any attempt to say goodbye. She didn't.

They'd both agreed not to lie if asked about the lack of a chaperone, but they weren't going to shout Elmira's deception from the rooftops, either. Lorelei had already told her parents they'd been robbed but hadn't mentioned when or by whom. Sean hoped that by not telling anyone, the subject would become a nonissue. And if that was the case, then this whole convoluted adventure of chasing Lorelei across Texas, bringing her home in spite of all the obstacles, spending every hour in her maddening, exhilarating company would be over. Relegated to the past and forgotten—like it never happened at all.

"What do you mean he hasn't responded?" a man's frustrated voice bellowed, snapping Sean out of his thoughts as he passed the telegraph office that was next door to the railroad station.

Sean stopped to watch the rough-looking older man who stood outside the door. The telegrapher shrugged casually. "I mean what I said. The message was picked up, but no response was given. That's all I know. Now, you can check again tomorrow if you like. Until then, I suggest you stop causing trouble and leave."

The man muttered a few unholy words, kicked the dust and walked away. Sean watched him carefully, then went inside to speak to the telegrapher. "Hello, Peter. What can you tell me about that man?"

"He says his name is Alfred Calhoun. He's been coming by every day for the last week. He sends telegraphs to a Frank Bentley down in Houston. They seem to be trying to coordinate a meeting of some kind. Near as I can tell, that Bentley fellow is coming here."

"I don't guess there's anything wrong with that."

"No. He's an odd one, though. I don't think he has a job. He seems to spend most of his time in the Red Canteen."

Sean nodded thoughtfully. "If you find out anything that concerns you or if you want me to help you handle him, just let me know."

"I will. I've been talking to Jeff about it and I'd planned to tell you when you got back in town. I'm glad you got to see the man in person." Peter finally smiled. "You find that Wilkins girl all right?"

"Yes, she's back with her family now."

"Wish I'd been asked to rescue her." Peter gave him a knowing smile.

"I wish you had been, too," he said with a parting grin. Peter was still laughing when the door closed behind Sean. He let out a sigh. All right, so that wasn't entirely the truth, but it was better to discourage any implication like that before it had a chance to take the form of a rumor. He only hoped that would be enough. The last thing he needed was for people to start asking questions. He planned to let this little episode in his life fade into the obscurity of nothing more than a faint memory. That was for the best. Wasn't it?

Chapter Four

Lorelei pushed the long strips of bacon around her plate with a fork, then glanced up at her parents. Her father sat across from her, hidden behind a copy of the Austin newspaper he'd managed to snag on his last trip to the city. Occasionally, his hand would slip from behind it in search of food. Her mother sat to her right unconcernedly drinking her morning tea as she planned out the day on a piece of notebook paper.

The silence was broken by the crinkle of newspaper. Lorelei tensed as her father folded the paper and set it aside. She braced herself when his gaze met hers. His blue eyes soon dropped to his coffee cup, which he carefully blew on before taking a long drink. She felt her shoulders relax. She lifted the bacon to her lips but could not force herself to eat it. She glanced up once more, feeling tempted to glare at her parents.

It was horrible what they were doing. They hadn't mentioned her running away once since she'd gotten home yesterday. At first, she'd assumed they merely wanted to give her time to rest after her journey. With breakfast nearly over and her father due at the bank in less than a half hour, there'd still been no mention of her actions. She knew that they were of such a magnitude that her parents couldn't and wouldn't leave the subject untouched. Why were they drawing it out? They must know the suspense was killing her.

"Lorelei," her mother began.

Her head shot up, and she prepared herself for battle.

Caroline smiled. "Would you pass me the salt, please?"

"Yes, Mama."

"Thank you, dear."

"You're welcome," Lorelei replied quietly.

Coffee cup drained, Richard stood. "Well, I suppose it's time I get over to the bank."

She watched dumbfounded as her father gathered his dishes and placed them in the sink before returning to the table to kiss her mother goodbye. "Have a wonderful day, you two."

"Shall I send Lorelei with your lunch?"

"That would be nice, if you don't mind, Lorelei," her father said, then leaned across the table to kiss Lorelei on the forehead. His beard and mustache tickled her skin in a familiar sensation.

"I don't mind." Tears pricked her eyes as she watched him turn away and grab his hat. She blinked them away resolutely. He couldn't leave without talking to her. Surely she deserved a lecture or something. She stood. "Papa, where are you going?"

He turned with a perplexed look on his face. "I'm going to the bank."

She gave an exasperated sigh. "I know that. What I mean is…well, I know you two want to talk to me. I'd rather you just say what you need to say now rather than drag it out by waiting until later."

He seemed confused. "What is it you wanted to discuss, Lorelei?"

Her mouth fell opened then closed. "I ran away."

"Yes," he agreed.

"Isn't that something you want to discuss?" she asked.

"Not particularly," her father said.

Lorelei looked to her mother for help, but the woman lifted her delicate brows in confusion. "Well, what would you like us to say, dear?"

She sat down in disbelief. "This is ridiculous. Don't you want to tell me how impractically and irresponsibly I behaved? How dangerous it was for me to travel alone as I did? How flighty it made me appear to everyone? How awful it was of me to leave you two wondering and worrying?"

Her mother took a sip of tea. "Is it necessary?"

She glanced to her husband who looked down at Lorelei thoughtfully. "I don't think so. She seems to have learned her lesson."

Lorelei looked from her mother to her father and back again. With a groan, she buried her face in her hands. "Did I just give myself a lecture?"

"I'm afraid so," her father said with amusement in his voice.

She frowned at him. "You planned this, didn't you?"

He smiled. "Goodbye, Lorelei."

As the door closed behind him, her mother smiled. "Dear, we spared you the lecture because we know you. We know you've already recognized what you did was wrong because you're here. You came back to us. Don't think for a moment we weren't worried or upset while you were gone, because we were both of those things and more."

"I really am sorry."

"We know that." She reached over to place her hand over Lorelei's. "Why did you leave? What happened that day?"

She sighed. "There I was in a beautiful white dress with one of the best men in the world standing beside me at the altar, and I couldn't do it. I couldn't—even after I spent all that time convincing myself that I could. I knew it wasn't right." She paused to take a deep breath. "It all was my fault because my whole life I was foolish enough to fancy myself in love with the one man who has never cared I existed."

"Sean O'Brien," her mother said softly.

Lorelei stared at her. "You knew. This whole time you knew?"

Her mother laughed. "Of course, I knew. You're my daughter. How could I not know?"

She froze. "Does Papa know?"

At her mother's nod, Lorelei groaned and buried her face in her hands.

Her mother pulled at her hands. "Come now, it isn't that bad."

Lorelei dropped her hands to the table. "That's what I'm afraid of. That everyone knows how I felt about him." *Including Sean.*

"I don't think that's the case. It's common knowledge that you had a crush on him as a girl, but then Lawson began courting you and everyone assumed you let it go."

"I almost convinced myself I had until that day. Suddenly, I realized I couldn't do that to Lawson. I couldn't go into our marriage halfhearted, knowing I couldn't love him as he deserved to be loved. It wouldn't have been right."

"I hope you know how proud I am of you for doing

that. It would have been much easier to let things continue as you'd planned," her mother said. "But why did you run away?"

Lorelei shrugged. "I just hated the thought of having to deal with all the gossiping, the speculation, the people whispering behind my back—or saying to my face—that I'm a silly flirt who broke Lawson's heart."

Her mother looked surprised. "Did someone actually say that?"

A long time ago, she thought to herself, and glanced away. "Never mind that. But all of it made the prospect of getting away for a while and starting fresh somewhere new seem awfully tempting. I had everything already packed and ready to go. It…" She smiled weakly. "It seemed like a good idea at the time."

The smile quickly faded as she continued. "But if I thought I could run away from being judged, then I was wrong. Sean tracked me down, and ever since I've had to live with his constant disapproval day in and day out. That's when I realized how foolish I'd been, and decided to come home."

Her mother nodded, then asked, "So where does that leave your feelings toward Sean now?"

Lorelei shook her head. "If I learned anything while I was gone, it's that I'm done with Sean O'Brien. I'm finished waiting for him to look at me with anything more than a frown on his face. I think I've allowed his dislike of me to shape who I've become. That's part of the reason I wanted a new beginning away from here and him."

"I see." Her mother took a sip of her tea thoughtfully. "Perhaps what you are searching for is a new perspective, dear, not an entirely new life."

"Maybe so." Lorelei sighed.

It wouldn't hurt to try, and it was much more practical than any step she'd taken so far. She smiled. A new perspective... That sounded perfect. She had no idea what perspective she needed but whatever it ended up being would be better than the one she had.

Lorelei smiled a greeting at the bank tellers as she breezed through the lobby with her father's lunch basket in tow. Her steps faltered as she neared the open door of the manager's office. Gathering her courage, she knocked lightly. Lawson glanced up from the box he was packing. He paused in surprise at the sight of her before giving her a welcoming smile. "Come on in."

She surveyed him carefully. He didn't seem to be upset with her, but she hadn't seen him since the wedding. She decided to tread lightly as she stepped inside. She placed the basket on his desk, then turned in a slow circle to survey the moderately sized room. The room had been stripped almost completely of his personal items. She turned to face him as the weight of guilt settled on her shoulders. "You're leaving the bank?"

"I resigned a few days after the wedding."

"I'm sorry."

"For what?" he asked curiously.

She crossed her arms and leaned her hip against the desk. "Well, it's my fault you're leaving, isn't it?"

He shook his head. "No. I'm just ready to move on, that's all. I've been inquiring about a few other jobs. Most of them are out of Peppin."

"I still feel responsible."

"Don't." He closed the box, then met her gaze seriously. "While we're at it, let's get something else straight. You already apologized to me about what happened at the wedding. I'll admit I was hurt but not as deeply as you might have thought because you were right. I didn't love you the way I should have. I knew something was wrong, but I'd made a commitment and I didn't want to be the one to walk away from it. I'm glad you did. It was the right thing for both of us."

She stared at him. "You mean it?"

He nodded. "I hope we can go back to being friends now and that you know if you ever need anything you can call on me."

"Thank you, Lawson. Hearing you say that means so much to me. I hated thinking that I might have hurt you. You've been such a wonderful friend. I wouldn't want to lose that."

"Well, you aren't. You're stuck being my friend so you may as well like it," he teased. Then, looking at her closely, he offered her his handkerchief. "No tears in my office and it's still my office until I take this box out."

She smiled and dabbed her watery eyes before handing it back with her thanks. "I'd better bring Papa his lunch. I guess I'll see you around."

"I'm sure you will for a little while at least."

"Are you all right?" her father asked a few moments later as he cleared his desk to make room for the food. She told him about her conversation with Lawson, and he shook his head. "He's a good man and a good manager. I wonder what sort of work he'll go into next."

"That reminds me," she said as she laid out a plate with her mother's baked chicken, green-bean casserole and corn. "On my way here I stopped to talk to Mrs. Cummings at the millinery shop across the street."

He stared at her in confusion. "How did what I say remind you of hats?"

"She was looking for someone to come in a few

hours a week to help her, and I told her I'd like to take the job. Isn't that wonderful, Papa?"

Richard frowned up at her from his dark leather chair. "No, it is not. Why should you want a job, Lorelei? What will my customers think if my own daughter has to work outside the home? I'll tell you what they'll think. They'll think their money isn't safe here."

She lifted an eyebrow and closed the basket. "As if they had anywhere else in town to put it."

He waved his fork. "That is beside the point."

"Well, I don't see why they'd care one way or the other," she reasoned. "Besides, I need something to do besides embroider with Mother."

Hope sprang within her when her father quieted for a moment. "If it's work you want, you are always welcome to work here."

She almost laughed. "Doing what?"

"Why, you could be a teller."

"Papa, I don't want to be a teller."

"I'd much rather you work here."

She grimaced. "I'd much rather not."

"It's a perfectly respectable place. I can watch you," he rationalized.

"It's a perfectly boring place and I don't need to be watched."

He looked at her in wavering contemplation, and she gave him her best and most pleading look. Finally, he sighed. "I have a feeling this is going to be like the rose garden you tried to start and that bakery idea you tried to get a loan for and the—"

She titled her head. "And the wedding I didn't go through with?"

He stilled. "Now, I didn't say that, did I?"

She fiddled with the lace on her dress and tried to

keep the tears from blurring her eyes. "Well, why don't you? Isn't that what you're thinking? I can start something but I don't finish it well, do I?"

"You can do whatever you set your mind to, Lorelei. When you like something well enough, you stick to it. Look at your music lessons. You've been playing the piano—very beautifully—for years. I guess you just try out more things than most and there's nothing wrong with that. If it's all right with your mother, then I don't mind."

"Oh, thank you, Papa." She smiled and slipped around the desk to give him a quick hug. "I'm certain I'll like it, and I'll stick to it no matter what."

"That'll show them." He winked.

She chatted with him for a few more minutes before exiting his office and walking right into a conflict between Mrs. Greene and her father's secretary. Neither party seemed to realize they were blocking the hallway. The man looked positively flustered. "But, ma'am, you don't have an appointment and Mr. Wilkins is having lunch. Why don't I direct you to a teller? I'm sure one of them will be able to help you."

"I'm sure they will *not*." Mrs. Greene's face seemed to grow redder by the moment. "I insist on seeing Mr. Wilkins right now. I have been entrusted with a letter for him and I aim to see he gets it."

Lorelei spoke up to try to diffuse the situation. "It's all right, Alexander. Father is finished with his lunch. I'm sure he'd be willing to see Mrs. Greene."

The young man stepped aside to let Mrs. Greene pass. The woman's gaze shifted to Lorelei, who smiled pleasantly. Mrs. Greene didn't return the gesture. She just stared with an appraising eye. Lorelei had the strangest feeling that she'd been weighed and found wanting. Mrs. Greene brushed past her to enter her father's office without waiting to be announced. Lorelei grimaced, then glanced at Alexander. He shook his head. "I'd hate to be your father right now. She has one mean bee in that bonnet of hers."

"I'm sure he'll be able to handle it." She said goodbye to him, then waved at the other tellers before she stepped back onto the sidewalk.

It was surprisingly good to be back in Peppin. She hadn't realized how much she'd missed her family and the entire town until she'd returned. Not that she hadn't noticed the curious looks and quiet whispers she garnered. Despite that small discomfort, it was good to be home. She'd decided her mother was right. She needed a new perspective. She was not going to allow herself to be distracted by old desires or thoughts anymore.

"Lorelei." She glanced up into Sean's green eyes as he tipped his Stetson to acknowledge her in passing.

I should have used the alleyways, she thought with an inward groan. She gave a small nod in return. She waited until she crossed the street to glance back for one final look at what never could have been.

Chapter Five

The door to the sheriff's office flew open, banging against the inside wall and allowing a burst of sunlight to paint the room. Sean's hand hopped to his gun. He rose so quickly from behind his desk that he sent his chair toppling to the floor. The door swung closed behind the man who scanned the otherwise empty room. After seeming to establish they were alone, Richard focused on Sean with narrowed eyes.

"Mr. Wilkins, what can I do for you today?"

Richard strode toward him with fire in his eyes. "Sean O'Brien, I ought to tear you limb from limb. No, I ought to lock you up in your own jail cell, scoundrel that you are."

"Hold on just a minute, sir. Those are some pretty strong words." He righted the chair without taking his gaze from the advancing man.

Richard pressed his fist on the top of Sean's desk. The man paused to catch his breath, then his blue eyes locked with Sean's in anger. "Did you think I wouldn't find out? She is my only child. I trusted you. I put her well-being in your hands. You were supposed to protect her but all you did was expose her to slander."

A chill crept down Sean's spine. "I'm not sure what you mean."

Richard's eyes narrowed as his voice turned steely, and he tossed a piece of paper on the desk. "Don't lie to me. You can read it for yourself."

"A letter?"

"Yes, it's from a Mrs. Drake. She writes in stunning detail how the two of you arrived *alone and unchaperoned* at her boardinghouse." He glanced down at the letter. "She says she tried to discover the reasons for this moral gaffe but you were hostile toward her while telling an incredibly dubious and conveniently difficult to disprove tale of being abandoned by your chaperone at some point during your five-day journey to town. She insinuates that you and Lorelei…that you… Well, it is quite obvious what she believes had been going on between you two. I want to believe it isn't true but if it is, so help me…"

"It isn't true." He wavered. "Well, not entirely."

"What does that mean?" Richard took a deep breath and seemed to calm down a bit, though his grim expression didn't change. "Can you prove this woman wrong?"

"Yes. No." Sean swallowed. "Not completely and not immediately. Listen, this can all be explained, but first I think it would be best if Lorelei were present during this conversation."

Richard held Sean's gaze for a long moment, then with a short nod he agreed, "Then send for Lorelei."

Lorelei hurried down the raised wooden planks of Peppin's sidewalk at a pace polite society would frown on. She could already feel herself starting to perspire. She would arrive at the sheriff's office looking flushed and wrung out. Not that she was trying to impress anyone at a time like this. Surely, something must be dreadfully wrong for her father to summon her through a messenger. His tone in the note had been abrupt, almost harsh. It was so unlike him that she was worried that something was seriously amiss. Had he been robbed? Threatened? Attacked? What disaster could have struck that required him to turn to Sean?

Her anxious thoughts hastened her steps the last few feet into the sheriff's office. Surveying the room, she noticed Sean sitting at his desk with her father seated comfortably across from him. Both men stood as she entered but remained oddly silent.

Obviously nothing was wrong with her father's constitution. He even had a bit of color in his cheeks. She paused a moment to catch her breath before venturing farther into the silent room. "Papa, whatever is the matter? I thought something must have happened."

"I'm afraid it did." He looked sterner than she'd ever seen him.

"What did?"

"That." He pointed to the desk.

Her confused gaze lingered on her father a moment before she followed his finger to the object on the desk. "A letter?"

"From Mrs. Drake."

"Mrs. Drake?" she echoed in confusion.

Sean's hand briefly touched her arm, drawing her gaze to his for the first time since she'd entered the room. His eyes were filled with what seemed to be concern and caution. "Lorelei, it seems that Mrs. Drake was concerned about our lack of a chaperone during our trip and decided to write your father about it."

"Oh, no," she breathed before she could stop herself. Her eyes widened as her mind raced through a thousand scenarios of how the next few minutes might play out. Very few of them were good. Her eyes collided with Sean's inscrutable gaze before she turned to her father. "Obviously Mrs. Drake must have misunderstood the nature of my relationship with Sean."

Sean nodded. "I was about to explain that to your father when we decided to send for you. Perhaps it would be best if we all sat down."

Once they all pulled out a chair, a moment of silence echoed through the room as everyone seemed to calm down and collect their thoughts. Her father let out a tired sigh. "Start from the beginning."

Sean leaned forward slightly in his chair, not enough to heighten the mood, but enough to call attention to himself. "Sir, when I finally met up with Lorelei she was traveling with a preacher, his wife and their children. After four days with them, I convinced Lorelei to come home to Peppin with me. The couple took umbrage with our leaving to travel in the wilderness by ourselves for a few days and insisted we find a chaperone. One of the local women offered to chaperone us for a wage, which we agreed upon. We set off with her in good faith, but we were only two days into our trip when she ran off with our money and Lorelei's valise. We considered turning back and rejoining the preacher and his family, but by that point, we thought they'd probably moved on, and that it would be faster to push on to town rather than trying to track them down. We finished the trip alone."

"In the wilderness, alone for a few days, you say?"

"Yes, sir."

The man looked as if he'd aged a few years since entering the office, but he nodded. "I see. Continue."

"Well, that's it."

"What do you mean 'that's it'?"

Sean shrugged. "There's nothing more to tell."

Lorelei pinned her father with her blue gaze and a raised eyebrow. "Were you expecting more, Papa?"

"Don't be smart with me, young lady," he said even as his skin appeared to flush a bit.

"In defense of my honor as a gentleman and Lorelei's as a lady, I would like you to know our behavior was circumspect on the trip home. She slept on one side of the campfire and I slept on the other." He met Richard's gaze. "I mean this as no insult to your daughter's sensibilities, but I want you to know I never touched her."

"All right, I get the point and I appreciate you making it." Richard shook his head. Rising to his feet again, he began to pace. He turned to face them. "I understand what happened wasn't your fault, and I believe you when you say you began the trip with a chaperone. *I* do, but I'm afraid that Mrs. Drake's account…"

"It's embellished, to say the least," Sean said.

"Perhaps so." He agreed. "That isn't the only thing that concerns me. This letter was hand-delivered to me by Mrs. Greene. She is aware of the contents and was quite adamant that I do something to fix the predicament."

"No wonder she glared at me in the bank," Lorelei muttered.

Sean grimaced. Mrs. Greene and his family didn't have the best history. After his parents' death, she'd taken it upon herself to guide their orphaned family on the straight and narrow. Unfortunately, that somehow translated into her being rather harsh and overly critical in her judgment of them. She was hardest on Ellie but wasn't particularly fond of Sean, either. He cleared his throat. "Surely you can just explain to her that there has been a mistake."

Richard shook his head. "I suggested that idea in my office, but she stood by her niece's account and painted a picture of the incident that whipped me into a fury. Sorry about that, Sean."

"It's understandable, sir. I reckon I'd act the same way if I had a daughter."

He stopped pacing to face them. "Even if we could prove your chaperone abandoned you, the fact remains that you traveled alone for days in the wilderness."

"It wasn't our fault," Lorelei insisted.

"No, but can you imagine the scandal? It could easily be construed that you two had some sort of affair only days after you were supposed you marry another man. If word gets around about this…" He shook his head and sat back down.

"Knowing Mrs. Greene," Sean interjected, "she may have already told everyone."

"I asked her to let me deal with this my own way first. She promised she'd keep quiet until I speak to her again but vowed that if I didn't hold you accountable she'd make sure the town would."

Sean clenched his fist. "What does that mean exactly?"

"We don't want to find out." Richard turned to Lorelei. "I need to talk to your mother about this. We'll decide together what to do."

"But, Papa—"

He shook his head. "I think its best that you go on home. I'll be there shortly."

Lorelei watched her father for a long moment, then left without a glance Sean's way.

Richard turned to him. "Come to our house for supper this evening. I'll know what to tell you then."

Without waiting for a response, the man left. Sean stared at the door for a long moment, then sighed. There was nothing left for him to do but straighten the chairs and prepare himself for that evening. Waiting—his least favorite thing to do. He needed something to occupy his time. He glanced around, his gaze landing on the Bible at his desk, and suddenly the choice seemed obvious. He'd read his Bible and maybe even say a little prayer. He could only hope it would help.

"I know we are all anxious to address the issue foremost on all of our minds," Richard Wilkins began, then glanced at her and Sean as if to be sure they were listening before he continued. "I won't keep the two of you in suspense any longer."

Lorelei glanced at Sean to gauge his reaction. His gaze was intent on her father's face as if it might give some hint to the outcome of her parents' decision. Certain she wouldn't be able to swallow another bite of her blueberry pie, Lorelei placed her plate on the small table that rested between Sean's chair and where she sat on the settee. Her mother and father sat side by side in chairs across the room, letting Lorelei know that they were unanimous on whatever decision they had reached.

As if reading her thoughts, Richard said, "My wife and I spent quite a bit of time in thought and prayer about this matter. We ask that you both refrain from commenting on what we say until you have heard us out completely. Is that understood?"

"Yes, sir," Sean agreed.

Lorelei nodded. Settling back in the settee, she clasped her hands nervously in her lap.

"You both have good reputations and I think you know that in a town of this size reputation is everything." Leaning forward, he looked at them intently. "It affects everything from who speaks to you on Sunday to who will do business with you. It's a precious commodity."

Her mother nodded gravely. "I know this will be difficult to hear since the two of you did nothing wrong, but I'm afraid there will be no way to avoid a scandal should any of this come to light. It's in your best interest to try to head that off if possible."

Richard smiled wryly. "I'm afraid I'm not giving either of you much of a choice. I'll not have my daughter's name bandied about as a common trollop. We've already seen with Mrs. Drake that people will turn the facts into whatever sordid scenarios their imaginations lead them to believe. What's worse is that the story would grow with each telling, and, believe me, people would tell."

Lorelei's stomach clenched as her father's gaze narrowed onto Sean. "I'm giving you six weeks."

"Six weeks, sir?"

"Yes." Richard straightened, his jaw firmed. "You have six weeks to court my daughter. At the end of those six weeks, I will expect a proposal."

Chapter Six

Lorelei gasped in shock at her father's ridiculous statement. He couldn't mean it. He just couldn't. "You cannot be serious."

Caroline sent her a warning look. "We certainly are."

Sean leaned forward in his chair. "What about Mrs. Greene?"

Her father shot a glance at his wife. "I think we may have figured out how to handle her. My plan is to try to get the woman on our side in this. We'll thank her for bringing this to our attention, assure her of our intentions to see you two married and ask her to help."

"I think she's done quite enough to help," Lorelei scoffed, feeling her shock give way to anger at the situation. "What else could Mrs. Greene do?"

"Amelia has been a friend of mine for ten years," Caroline said. "I think if I appeal to her sense of decency, she'll help us preserve your reputations by staunching any negative gossip and correcting it with our own messages. From what Richard has told me of his confrontation with her, I believe her concern is to see that the proper thing is done. If the two of you marry, that should satisfy her."

Sean shook his head. "Good luck with that. She doesn't exactly love the O'Briens."

"I think she'll do this favor for me."

"So you want him to propose in six weeks if Mrs. Greene is merciful. I suppose you expect us to fall in love in six weeks, as well." Lorelei shook her head at the hopelessness of their predicament.

"I expect you to try," her father replied. "Whether you do or not should be between you and only you. I want the town to think this is a perfectly normal romance. There will be fewer questions that way." He glanced at Sean. "Do I have your word on that?"

"Before I agree to anything, I have a few questions of my own." Sean shot to his feet and began to pace. "How could people think our courtship is normal when Lorelei was supposed to marry my best friend less than two weeks ago? People might think we'd been carrying on behind his back."

"Your dislike for each other has been rather apparent the past few years. I doubt anyone would believe that."

Sean crossed his arms. "Then why would they believe these silly rumors?"

"They aren't rumors," Caroline answered gently. "We're looking at the facts here. Y'all did spend days alone together in the wilderness."

Mr. Wilkins picked up where his wife left off. "Sean, the two of you could let all of this come to light. If you're right and no one believes the allegation, your reputations might weather the storm. If people do believe it, you'll still end up married because the town would see to that. The only difference is that you'd also be publicly disgraced. My wife and I would like to spare you that, but it means you'll have to cooperate. Will you let us help you?"

Sean met Lorelei's gaze for a long moment. She watched his emotions battle in his eyes until defeat won out. He gave a short nod. Lorelei's fingers bit into her palms. "You're really agreeing to this?"

"I don't want this any more than you do, but it looks like there is no choice."

For him to be that…fatalistic about even the thought of marrying her hurt more than she'd ever admit. She shook her head. "With a proposal like that, how can I say no?"

He sank onto the settee beside her. "I didn't mean for it to sound that way, Lorelei. It's just that this is so much bigger than us. It isn't only my reputation I have to consider—any gossip that's spread about me would reflect badly on my family, too. I can't do that to Ellie or Kate, not when it's my fault for letting this situation occur. I knew the moment Miss Elmira went missing that this had the potential to blow up in our faces. I'd like to control the explosion however I can."

She forced herself to calm her rapid breathing as she tried to make sense of what was happening. Sean was agreeing to marry her. For so many years, she'd longed for a moment like this between them—now she deplored it. It didn't mean that he loved her. It simply meant that he was doing his duty. Logically, it was the best option. Emotionally—it just felt plain awful. At least she didn't love him anymore. That would have sealed the hopelessness of her fate.

A wry smile touched his lips. "You look like you've been assigned a fate worse than death."

She nodded slowly. He seemed to think so. Why shouldn't she? "Maybe I have."

His jaw clenched, and he stared at her for a long minute, then stood. "I think I'd better go. Thank you for dinner, Mrs. Wilkins."

"You're quite welcome."

"Goodbye, Lorelei." He couldn't even seem to make himself look at her before he turned away to search for his hat.

Once the door closed behind him and Caroline rejoined them in the parlor, Lorelei let the silence close in thick around them. Both of her parents were waiting for her reaction. It took a few moments to gather her thoughts. "Maybe I should go to California after all. If I leave, this might all blow over."

"And leave Sean to deal with this alone?" her mother questioned with obvious disapproval.

Richard sat down on the settee beside her and took her hand in both of his. "Running away is what got you into this problem in the first place. It won't solve anything. Besides, didn't you just tell me this morning that you wanted to prove the town wrong about you? This is your chance."

"No, there has to be a way out," she muttered desperately. "We could hire a detective. We could find Miss Elmira."

"To prove that she left you to travel for several days alone?" Caroline shook her head sorrowfully. "Darling, there is no other way."

"No other way," Lorelei breathed, then glanced at the door Sean had walked out of moments before. "He'll hate me for sure now. If not now, then in ten or twenty years."

Richard frowned. "Why would he hate you?"

"I've taken his every chance at happiness, just as he's taken mine. Oh, how will we bear it?" Her parents protested, but she tuned them out with a quick shake of her head and fled to her room. Her desperate gaze flew to her large window. Opening it, a warm breeze washed over her along with the scent of the wild roses that she only bothered to tame when the mood struck her.

She knelt before the window and stared down into the garden. It would be so easy to climb down the trellis, slip into the night and leave her troubles behind—but she'd tried that before. Her father was right. It hadn't worked. In fact, it had only made her problems worse. No, this time she would have to take responsibility for what she had done instead of trying to run from it. Marrying Sean, a man who could never love her, was a high price to pay for her impulsive mistake, but what choice did she have?

She'd show Sean and the whole town. She'd see the courtship and the marriage through to the bitter end, but she wouldn't be foolish about it. She'd keep her wits about her. She wouldn't let any remnants of her child-ish feelings make her silly enough to love a man who would never love her back. She'd end up chasing after something she'd never be able to catch. The only way to keep her heart safe would be to keep even the slight-est fragment of love from taking root. That's exactly what she planned to do.

Sean closed the Wilkinses' gate behind him with a decided thud, then stuffed his hat on his head and clenched his jaw. He just couldn't wrap his mind around the fact that after all this time he was actually going to court Lorelei Wilkins. If this was some sort of divine joke, he didn't find it funny. He shook his head. "This is not part of the plan."

He'd planned to settle down in the next few years but not like this. Not to her. He'd wanted to find a stable, mature, sensible wife he'd be able to count on. Lorelei was flighty, impetuous and a dozen other things he'd wanted to avoid in a life partner. She was the one woman in the world he was sure he could never trust. The woman who'd trampled on his heart and his best friend's. She'd single-handedly managed to take his stable, carefully thought-out life and turn it into complete upheaval. His hands slipped into clenched fists. His heart began to race.

"Sean, where's the fire?"

He stopped short, then whirled toward his friend's voice, feeling a mixture of dread and relief. "Lawson."

Lawson tipped back his Stetson to look at him. "Where have you been? My parents have been out on a doctor's call all day. I got tired of my own company so I went to the café. I was going to rope you into going with me, but I couldn't find you."

"Sorry," he mumbled. Glancing away to survey the town's quiet streets, he debated whether or not to tell Lawson what had happened. How could he not? Lawson had a right to know as his best friend and Lorelei's former fiancé. He swallowed, realizing he might have just gained a wife and lost a best friend. He cleared his throat. "I hope you didn't wait for me. I had dinner with the Wilkins family."

Lawson's mouth dropped open. "You don't say? Well, no wonder you were running like you saw a skunk and looked like you swallowed a porcupine."

Sean shook his head. "Where do you get those sayings?"

"I don't know. They just pop into my head. Are you going to tell me what happened at the Wilkinses' or am I going to have to guess?"

Sean shook his head. "You couldn't guess this. I'll tell you, but I think you'd better sit down."

Lawson frowned curiously then lifted his chin in the direction of the Williamses' house. "Well, come on then. Ma made a pitcher of sweet tea and there are a couple of glasses left. We can sit on the porch."

A few minutes later, Sean clutched the sweating glass of sweet tea tensely as a heavy silence settled between him and his best friend. He'd done his best to explain the circumstances of his predicament and the events that were about to take place. Lawson had listened intently, but his expression remained inscrutably thoughtful. Finally, when he thought Sean couldn't bear the silence another minute, a wry smile pulled at Lawson's lips. "I think your mischievous youth has come back to haunt you."

The glass nearly slipped from Sean's hand. "Is that all you have to say?"

"What did you expect me to say?"

"I had no idea." He set his drink on the table next to him, then slumped in the wicker chair in a strange mixture of relief and confusion. "I thought you might yell at me."

Lawson was the picture of nonchalance as he propped his arm on the back of the wicker bench. "Why would I yell at you?"

Sean sat up in disbelief. "She was your fiancée!"

"Right. She *was* my fiancée."

"If you'd hit me, I would have called it fair. I almost wish you would. I'd hit myself if it were me."

Lawson's smile spread. "Now that would be something to see."

Sean rested his forearms against his knees. "Listen, stop being glib about this. I thought you loved her."

"I thought I did, too…for a while." He rubbed his chin thoughtfully. "Now I think I just loved the idea of being loved by a girl like that. You know what I mean?"

"No," he said dryly.

"Let's just say that when she left me at the altar a little part of me was relieved. I wasn't happy at the time because it was mighty embarrassing for both of us, but if we'd gone through with it…" He shook his head at some imagined outcome, then met Sean's gaze again. "How is Lorelei reacting to all of this?"

"She's no better off than I am." He frowned. "Worse probably and she let me know it."

"That's what I don't get about this whole thing. Lorelei and I never argued. We got along perfectly. I thought that meant we were in love, but now that I know we never were, I'm inclined to think there just weren't any strong feelings there at all. Not even enough to make us bicker." He crossed his arms and tilted his head suspiciously. "You two, on the other hand, can't seem to be in the same room for longer than a minute before you're shooting invisible bullets at each other. It makes me wonder."

Sean narrowed his eyes as he slowly asked, "It makes you wonder what?"

Lawson smiled. "Guess."

Sean's eyes widened. He cleared his throat and looked away. "That's impossible."

"Sure it is," Lawson said sarcastically, then ignored Sean's protests to ask, "When is this courting business supposed to start?"

"I don't remember if Mr. Wilkins gave a specific date besides the engagement, but I'd like to give Lorelei a while to cool down. I could use some time, too."

He pulled in a deep breath and rubbed his hand over his face. He groaned. "What am I going to do?"

Lawson shook his head dubiously. "You, my friend, are going to marry *Lorelei Wilkins*—your nemesis since you were ten years old. God help you both."

Sean stared at his friend. "What would I do without your encouragement?"

Lawson shrugged. "I've been wondering that myself, but I figured it would be best if we don't find out. I'll be sure to include it in my letters if I ever find a job out of this town."

"Thanks, Lawson. That would be just dandy." Sean slumped down to rest his head on the back of the chair and stare thoughtfully at the boards of the porch roof. He needed to think practically. If he was going to get married, he needed to find his own place. There was no way he could bring a wife into the one-room cabin he'd rented in town. Just around the corner from his office, the space served him well as a bachelor, but it was no place to start a family.

As if detecting the vein of his thoughts, Lawson cleared his throat. "I know this is supposed to be a secret, but what are you going to tell your family?"

"I don't know," he murmured quietly. "Nothing yet I suppose. I need time to think about this."

His family... His shoulders tensed under the load of a new thought. He was the only one of his siblings who would carry on the family name. With that came the responsibility of continuing his parents' legacy. Theirs had been a love match for sure. He'd wanted that for himself one day, but the way things were shaping up it didn't look as if he was going to get it.

He should have listened to Pastor James. For once, he'd been impulsive and agreed to let Elmira chaperone them even against his better judgment. That decision had gotten them into this mess. If he'd been more patient, he might have managed to convince another parishioner to chaperone them. Or, maybe someone from the next settlement would have gone back with them. He sighed. He'd learned a long time ago that maybes didn't change anything. Only hard work, logic and methodical planning guaranteed results. He'd need all three if he intended to improve anything about the situation he was in.

Lorelei couldn't contain her restlessness any longer. She abruptly set her embroidery on the settee beside her and stood. *If I have to push this needle through that cloth one more time, I'm going to toss this cushion out the nearest window.*

Her gaze landed on the large family Bible sitting on a nearby table. Maybe reading the Psalms would help. She wandered over to the Bible. It opened to the bookmarked page near the back. Before she could turn the page, a verse caught her eye. *"If a man says, I love God, and hates his brother, he is a liar."* She paused for a moment to allow those words to sink in. *"For he that does not love his brother whom he has seen, how can he love God whom he hath not seen? And this is the commandment have we from him. That he who loves God must love his brother also."*

She read the last part of the verse again and frowned. Wasn't there something between love and hate? If there was, God didn't seem to be all that concerned with it. The commandment was pretty simple. Love God. Love your brother.

"Wonderful," she murmured.

Her mother glanced up from her embroidery. "Did you say something, Lorelei?"

She shook her head, then narrowed her eyes thoughtfully. "You can love someone without being in love with them. Right, Mama?"

Caroline shrugged. "Sure you can. Why?"

"Never mind," she said. She wasn't even sure she was ready to go that far when it came to Sean. It was too dangerous to let herself love him in any way, and she just wasn't ready. She smoothed her skirts nervously, then set her shoulders decidedly. "I think I'll take a walk."

Her mother gave a slow nod before glancing toward the window where stylish blue drapes filtered the muted sunlight. "You'd better take an umbrella. It's likely to rain."

Lorelei walked to the curtain and peered outside. "It looks sunny enough to me."

"Nevertheless," her mother said significantly.

Lorelei turned from the window to quickly make her way upstairs. She donned a hat accented with deep blue ribbons and black lace. It perfectly matched her blue dress with the black ribbon detail that ran across her hips before floating artfully down the back of her dress. She hurried back down the stairs and paused just inside the door next to the umbrella stand.

Her hand reached for her father's overly large, overly green umbrella, then strayed to the dainty black parasol just beside it. A quick glance over her shoulder told her that her mother wouldn't notice, so she pulled it from the stand, then she set out on her way with a hurried good-bye. She opened the parasol and set it on her shoulder.

She pulled in a cleansing breath of fresh air as she passed the few remaining houses on the street. Her home had been stifling in the days since her father's alarming edict. She'd hardly allowed herself to think about the impending doom the courtship represented, let alone the man who would help bring it about.

The only bright spot on the horizon was that her mother had somehow convinced Mrs. Greene to agree to the plan they'd devised. Lorelei had listened at the top of the stairs while her mother soothed Mrs. Greene's bluster until the woman promised to help spread the rumors of the new romance, with the caveat that she'd take her niece's story to the judge if the wedding didn't happen as scheduled.

And so, her fate had been sealed over cinnamon scones a week ago. She shook her head in frustration. Sean had not shown up once since that evening or done anything to seek her out. If he didn't want to spend time with her, that was fine. She didn't exactly want to spend time with him, either, especially knowing he was being forced to do so. For that reason, she crossed the street toward the mercantile rather than continuing across the street where she'd have to pass the sheriff's office.

She stopped to peer into the display window of the millinery shop. She saw Miss Cummings speaking to a costumer. The woman had shown her around the shop on Monday when Lorelei had arrived for her first day of work. Since it was only Wednesday and Lorelei was not scheduled to work again until Friday, Miss Cummings only waved at her. She returned the gesture before moving on.

As she passed the seamstress shop, a young gentleman exited the mercantile and caught her gaze before offering an appreciative smile. Lorelei nodded politely but did not stop at the friendly invitation in his gaze. Though she hardly gave the stranger a second thought, his actions somehow reminded her that, despite all of her best efforts, she would be forever bound to a man who could not stand her.

A small cry of dismay escaped her lips, and she glanced around to make sure that no one heard the traitorous sound of her inner turmoil. She searched for something to distract her from her sad thoughts. Her gaze landed on the church's spire not far off of Main Street. Perhaps she would find some relief in the sanctuary.

Her feet began to hasten their steps. She waited for a wagon to pass, then hurried across to the same side of the street as the church. She stepped onto the sidewalk just as the café door opened. Sean stepped out. Her steps faltered when she met his gaze.

Sean watched Lorelei's eyes widen in alarm as he reached out to steady her. Her stormy dark blue eyes turned cold the instant before they dropped from his. She turned to continue on her way. For a moment, he was tempted to let her go. Then with a silent sigh, he turned to follow her. "Lorelei, wait!"

Taking her elbow in his hand, he pulled her to a stop as he stepped in front of her. Her affronted gaze met his as she tilted her head as though in deep concentration. "Is there a particular reason you've decided to cause a scene?"

He didn't have to glance over his shoulder to know he was probably drawing curious stares from the patrons of the glass-fronted café. He leveled her with a quelling look. "As a matter of fact, there is. We need to talk."

"Well, there's no reason for us to stand in the middle of the street to do it." She eyed the café, then took off walking toward the church at a fast pace, leaving him to follow. She glanced up to frown at the large rain-drop that landed on her parasol with a definite plop, then transferred her frown to him. "Why now? I don't see how whatever we need to talk about can be any more important today than it was yesterday or the day before that."

Though she ended her speech with a polite smile, Sean easily recognized her dig at his not having approached her before. "I needed time to collect my thoughts."

She glanced up again as the clouds began to steadily drizzle large drops of heavy rain before she turned back to him. "You were avoiding me. Now I wish you'd allow me the same courtesy you gave yourself."

He caught the slight look of hurt in her eyes before she managed to hide it. Lawson's theory about her behavior teased at the back of his mind. Right now, with her deep blue eyes staring back at him, he could almost imagine it was true. "I wasn't avoiding you. I was trying to think this through and come up with a plan."

Her frown turned skeptical. "What kind of a plan?"

He was about to explain when the clouds burst open. The large raindrops turned into a deluge of stinging rain. He glanced around for cover and realized that as he'd been talking to Lorelei, they'd left Main Street and were halfway to the church. He looked over to find she'd stopped to gape at the sky.

She looked rather pitiful. Rain streamed from the corners of her tiny parasol onto her fashionable dress. She seemed unable to decide whether to turn back or go forward. His hand settled pressingly against her waist. "Come on, you're getting soaked."

She followed his lead as they hurried toward the church, but he soon noticed that she'd slowed as they continued their frantic trek. He realized that her heavy skirts were tangling about her legs and restricting her movement. Impulsively, he came to a stop. She glanced at him in confusion. "What's wrong?"

"Hold on to your parasol," he said, then swept her into his arms. Her gasp rent the air. He glanced down at the face close to his own. "Ready?"

He seemed to have taken her completely off guard. She shrank slightly away from him in his arms but gave a small nod.

"Hold on tight," he urged.

Her arm slipped around his shoulder. He took off at a fast clip toward the church. He hid a reluctant smile as her drooping parasol slowly lifted to cover both their heads. It kept the rain from his face, which helped him to see, so he supposed it might have a slight purpose after all. He carefully mounted the church's stairs, pausing at the door only long enough to open it. He stopped just inside the foyer to let Lorelei's feet slide carefully down to the floor, keeping his hold on her waist to make sure she caught her balance.

The sudden silence of the church after the hammering rain rushed around them, stilling them both. He took the moment to survey the woman he was supposed to marry. Her wide dark blue eyes stared back at him framed by thick black lashes that swept downward demurely at his perusal. His gaze followed their movement downward over her angular nose that softened into a rounded tip before his eyes fell to her nearly-too-full-to-be-fashionable lips.

He hadn't allowed himself to notice it in so long that he'd nearly forgotten—Lorelei Wilkins was beautiful. That was why she hadn't been on the Peppin marriage market long before she'd been claimed by his best friend. Sean had thought that claim was going to last forever. Apparently, he'd been wrong. It looked as if he'd be the one to claim her as his own through no real effort of pursuit. It seemed wrong somehow, but it couldn't be helped.

He had to make the most of it, and he'd better start now. He was beginning to realize the task might not be as dreary as he'd once imagined. That meant he needed to be careful. He couldn't allow himself to get confused about his goal. That goal was to convince the town that they were a couple so that they could save their reputations. This courtship needed to go according to plan not only for their sakes but also for their families'. It was his duty to see that it did, and Sean O'Brien never shirked his duties.

Chapter Seven

Lorelei's hand slipped from Sean's shoulder to his chest as she pushed him away. Avoiding his gaze, she shook out her parasol on the church's unfinished floor. She closed it with a snap, then sent him a glare. "Was that perfectly necessary? I would have made it on my own."

"It was 'perfectly necessary' and a thank-you will do just fine."

"Thank you," she muttered, though it was clear she didn't mean it. She turned to glance around the church. The sanctuary doors stood open, but not a sound echoed through the halls of the church beyond their own. "It looks like we have the place to ourselves."

He walked forward to survey the sanctuary, then gestured her inside. "We might as well make ourselves comfortable until the storm moves on."

She averted her gaze knowing she certainly wouldn't be comfortable trapped anywhere with this man. Her grip tightened on her dripping parasol. She wanted to leave and leave now. Realizing that would be impossible, she schooled her features into a neutral expression. "I've never seen so much rain come through so suddenly."

"Well, summer is on its way out, and autumn is coming through like a steam engine. I'm sure we'll see plenty more of these squalls in the next few weeks." He watched her in concern. "You're shivering."

She forced herself to stop. "I'm fine."

"Nonsense. There should be a blanket around here somewhere."

She was cold, so she didn't keep him from leaving to find one. Once he was gone, Lorelei lifted her sodden skirt to step onto the small stage, then dripped toward the piano. She carefully traced her finger along its smooth wood. She'd spent countless hours practicing on the instrument since she was fourteen.

Her parents had donated the piano as a gift to the church with a request that Lorelei be allowed to play the instrument as long as it did not interfere with church functions. Since then, the instrument had provided her with an outlet for her emotions. She suddenly realized how sorely she'd missed playing it the past few weeks.

She heard Sean's boots ring on the wooden floor and stepped down from the platform to meet him in the aisle. She took the blanket he offered her. Wrapping it around her shoulders, she managed to give him a grateful smile and a whisper of thanks through chattering teeth. He grinned. "That wasn't so hard, was it?"

She sent him an ungrateful look.

He chuckled. "It's too late now. You can't take it back."

"I wasn't going to," she said, then settled into one of the pews near the back. She tried to ignore the fact that he took the seat beside her. She scooted a bit farther away under the pretense of fixing her blanket, but he angled his body so that he could see her face. It looked as if he was settling in for a long talk. She sighed. "We should check the weather."

"I just did." He pointed to the small windows that let light flow into the church. "It's still raining."

"Oh."

"No need to worry. We have plenty of time to talk."

She burrowed farther into her blanket. "I'm not worried."

"First off, I'd like to apologize."

Her eyes widened in surprise. "For what?"

He sighed wearily. "All of this is my fault. If I had taken the time to think, I never would have agreed to let Elmira chaperone us. It was a bad decision."

A slight smile teased the corner of her mouth. "Thank you for apologizing, but if I hadn't run away, we would never have needed a chaperone."

Sean seemed to think about this for a minute, then frowned and nodded. "You know what? You're right. It is your fault." He grinned when her mouth fell open, then continued seriously. "However, ultimately it was my responsibility to protect your reputation, and I failed at it. At least this courtship will give me a way to rectify the situation."

She stared at him thoughtfully. "Duty means a lot to you, doesn't it?"

His gaze shot to hers. "I live up to my responsibilities, if that's what you're asking. To do that, I learned I have to think things through and live life deliberately. Perhaps you'd do well to learn a similar lesson."

"You know, you have the oddest talent of saying something nice right before you say something rude."

He frowned. "What did I say that was nice and what did I say that was rude?"

"Never mind," she said, shifting slightly away from him.

He shook his head in confusion. They listened to the drum of the rain on the roof for a few moments before he spoke again. "I've been thinking. We really don't have a lot of time to convince people we're falling in love. I reckon this is as good a start as any."

"Start for what?"

"Our romance."

Dread settled in her stomach. She swallowed and met his gaze. "How do you figure that?"

"I carried you in here, though I doubt anyone saw us, to a rather secluded yet entirely respectable place to find shelter from the storm. It's the perfect starting point for us to further our acquaintance," he said thoughtfully, then nodded. "It makes for a good story."

"It isn't real."

"It certainly isn't a lie. I'll tell people I found myself charmed by your beauty, and you can tell them my unexpected kindness helped you see me in a new light."

"That isn't a lie?" She sent him a doubtful glance, then shook her head. "I don't know about this."

His arm slipped to the back of the pew, and he leaned toward her intently. "You don't know about the story or you don't know if you're ready to play along?"

She shifted away nervously. "Both."

"Listen, we're supposed to make this as believable as possible. That means you have to commit to this. If that's going to be a problem, then maybe we should just come clean and let the town do with us as they please."

"No," she protested. "I said I'd do it and I meant it."

He leveled her with a measuring stare. He nodded slightly. "All right. We'll take this one step at a time. Just follow my lead and do as I say. We'll be fine."

Her eyes narrowed. "What do you mean 'do as you say'? I hope you know I have no intention of—"

The door to the church opened, and excited chatter erupted from the foyer. She sprang to her feet as Sean rose next to her. They both turned toward the door together. She swallowed as she recognized a few of the women considered to be the pillars of Peppin society. When Mrs. Rachel Stone, Mrs. Amelia Greene and Mrs. Susan Sparks caught sight of them, their chatter slowly died.

Mrs. Stone, the retired sheriff's wife, was the first to speak. "Well, hello, Sean, Lorelei."

Reverend Sparks's wife surveyed them with concern. "Are you two all right?"

Sean glanced down at her and smiled. "Perfectly."

She felt herself blush from the regard his warm smile implied. The warmth in her cheeks only heightened as she caught the women's speculative looks. She was overcome by the need to explain. "I was on my way here and ran into Sean. The rain came pouring down so unexpectedly! We ran in here to find shelter."

The thoughtful quiet that descended on the group was disconcerting. She glanced to Sean for help. He reached down for the blankets they had abandoned. He held them out to Mrs. Sparks. "I'm afraid we soiled your clean blankets, ma'am. We were soaked and cold, so I borrowed them."

Lorelei reached for the blankets. "I'd be happy to have them washed for you."

Mrs. Sparks took her blankets and smiled. "No need. I keep them here for people who find themselves in need of them."

"Thank you," Lorelei said, then sent a sideways glance at Sean. "Well, I suppose I should go."

Mrs. Stone shook her head. "Don't leave on account of us. We just needed to gather a few things from the storage closet."

"We were only waiting the storm out," she said as she began to edge toward the door.

"It's almost over now," Mrs. Sparks added. "Be careful out there. The rain has caused a dreadful amount of mud. I'm practically covered in it."

Mrs. Greene, who had remained quiet the whole time, finally spoke up. "We all are, except you, Ms. Wilkins. How do you reckon that?"

Lorelei realized the ladies' dresses and even Sean's boots were all six inches covered in mud. Her skirt alone remained pristine…if somewhat damp. Her eyes widened. She glanced at Sean who had the gall to look amused. She sent him an impatient glare before turning to face the ladies. She lifted her chin and raised her brows slightly to give just a hint of daring to her words.

"There is actually a very simple explanation. Despite my protests, Sheriff O'Brien was kind enough to carry me into the church. He saved my new skirt," she said, turning to Sean with a half-gracious smile, "which of course leaves me eternally grateful."

A smile pulled at his lips. "As I said before, Miss Wilkins, no thanks is necessary."

Lorelei almost ruined the whole thing with her disbelieving laugh, but she quickly turned it into a delicate set of coughs. Sean stepped closer. "Sounds like you could use a strong cup of tea for that cough."

"You're right. I think I'd better get home." She turned to the women with a smile. "It was wonderful to see you."

They each nodded to her. Mrs. Stone tilted her head

as she looked at Sean. "Perhaps you ought to see Miss Wilkins home."

Lorelei shook her head. "That's hardly necessary."

"Now, now," Mrs. Sparks said. "Those mud puddles can be dangerous."

Sean smiled. "Would you mind, Lorelei?"

"I suppose not."

The women moved toward the storage closets, but Mrs. Greene held back to whisper, "I'll take it from here."

They murmured their thanks to her, then made a quick exit. Sean stayed close to her side as they walked across the muddy grass toward the sidewalk. Her heel sank into a deep mud puddle. They had to pause for her to yank her foot out of it. "They weren't kidding about the mud."

Sean smiled wryly. "Mrs. Greene is extremely observant. I'll give her that."

"I can't believe she thought to ask about my skirt."

"It's a good thing she decided to be on our side in this. I don't know how your mother managed that, but I'm grateful." He led her toward the sidewalk. "At least, we won't have to tell people the story of our being at the church alone together. By this afternoon, the entire town will know."

She sighed. "If not the surrounding counties."

"We'll just have to make the most of it," he said.

Dread settled in her stomach. It had begun. There was no turning back now.

But she would be fine. She would! She just needed to maintain her boundaries. She lifted her skirt to step carefully from the dirt to the sidewalk, and his hand supportively caught her arm, then immediately released it. Her gaze met his for a moment. They had barely made it away from the measuring eye of the women in the church, and he'd already slipped back into his normal demeanor. He looked closed off again. Distant. Slightly disapproving. In other words, the same as always. Yes, she'd definitely have to work on keeping up her boundaries. She doubted she'd have to worry about him maintaining his.

Sean intercepted Kate's skeptical gaze as she stood across the churchyard talking with her best friend, Mrs. Stone. He felt a dull heat crawl up his neck and forced himself to refocus on what his brother-in-law was saying. He could easily guess what story Kate was hearing. He didn't have long to wait for a confirmation. Kate walked across the grass to stand beside Nathan. She met Sean's gaze questioningly. "Well, is it true?"

Nathan's arm slipped around Kate's waist. "Is what true?"

She glanced up at her husband, and Sean was grateful to watch her face soften into a smile before she turned to Sean again. "There's a rumor going around that our little brother might be taking an interest in Lorelei Wilkins."

Surprise lit Nathan's eyes even as a cautious smile pulled at his mouth. "Is that right?"

Sean shrugged. He couldn't outright lie to his family, but this wasn't the place to tell them about his true relationship with Lorelei. For the time being, it would be best to talk around it. "You know how unreliable rumors can be."

Kate pinned him with her thoughtful gaze. "So are you saying you aren't interested in her?"

He flew to where Mrs. Greene held court with a

few of her cronies. He swallowed. "No, I'm not saying that exactly."

"I don't understand." Nathan tilted his head skeptically. "What does that mean?"

Sean cast about for something to say that wouldn't be an outright lie. Squaring his shoulders, he settled for a portion of the truth. "It means I've realized that Lorelei Wilkins is a beautiful, intelligent, maddening woman."

Kate exchanged a glance with Nathan before turning back to Sean. "This sounds serious. What are you going to do about it?"

He shifted uncomfortably and glanced around the churchyard until he spotted Lawson joking with a few of their friends. Nathan must have followed his gaze because he quietly asked, "Have you mentioned this to Lawson?"

Sean nodded. "He seemed fine with it."

Kate bit her lip thoughtfully. "Well, it has only been three weeks since the wedding. Maybe it would be best to take it slow."

Suddenly, Ellie appeared at his side. "Take what slow?"

"Sean is thinking about courting Lorelei," Kate supplied.

His little sister's eyes widened for an instant, then she smiled knowingly. "I'm not surprised."

"You're not?" they all asked in various degrees of surprise and confusion.

She eyed Sean as if he'd been living under a rock. "I always thought Lorelei liked you more than she liked Lawson. Don't you remember? When we were children she had an awful crush on you. She always said she was going to marry you when she grew up. Then you were mean to her and she left you alone."

"That's true," Kate agreed.

He frowned. "Sure it is, but that was a long time ago."

She shrugged indifferently. "Maybe so, but then you liked her before she started courting Lawson."

He narrowed his eyes. "What makes you think that?"

"You're my brother," she said as if that explained it all, then added, "Also, I'd catch you staring at her every once in a while and you'd always stand a little taller when she walked in the room."

"I did not," he protested when Kate's eyes flew to Sean's, and she bit her lip to keep from laughing.

"You did." Ellie nodded and continued to stare at him as if concentrating on a puzzle. "Oh, and you were really depressed once she and Lawson starting courting. You tried to hide it, of course, but you were still living with us so I noticed. Right now, your face is turning red. The only reason you'd be embarrassed would be if it were true—"

Nathan tried to hide his chuckle as Sean held up a desperate hand. "Ellie, please stop talking. I get it. Thank you."

She sidled closer to him. "I could help you, you know. I'm a very experienced matchmaker."

"Ellie," Kate groaned. "I don't think this family can survive another round of your matchmaking."

"Nonsense! It's because of my matchmaking this family has survived. Need I remind you of how you met Nathan?"

A general groan filled the air.

Ellie took that as a yes. "If I hadn't convinced Sean we needed to mail order a husband for Kate—"

"—and then proceeded to marry us by proxy without my knowledge," Kate reminded with the lift of her chin.

"Y'all never would have had the chance to meet," Ellie continued as if Kate hadn't spoken.

Nathan gazed down at his wife with a smile. "Or fall in love or really get married or have three beautiful children."

Kate grimaced as her shoulders gave a little shiver. "Now, that's a scary thought."

"See?" Ellie poked Sean in the side, causing him to jump. "Don't worry, big brother. I can help you, too."

"Please, don't." He ignored her calculating smile to ask Nathan, "So I have your approval if I decide to court her?"

"I'm not sure you need it, but you have it." Nathan smiled. "You have always been a responsible person. We trust you."

Maybe you shouldn't, he immediately thought. He looked at Ellie, Kate and Nathan. They looked so cautiously hopeful and so unsuspecting of what was really going on. He could tell them now. He *should* tell them now, but he didn't want to utter the words that would shatter their perception of him. He'd spent most of his life convincing everyone that he was the strong, dependable one who had everything figured out. Now he was the one who'd messed up, and there was no way to fix it. Finally, Kate left to round up her children and the moment was lost.

Sean had almost forgotten his offer to help out the telegrapher with his problematic customer when Peter stepped into his office the next afternoon. Sean motioned to the chair across the desk from him. "That fellow giving you trouble again?"

Peter nodded, then shook his head. "Not exactly. I just thought you should know I found out the reason the other fellow hasn't responded to any of Calhoun's telegrams. He was a wanted criminal who was caught and placed in jail. He's been accused of murder and robbery."

Jeff rose from the deputy's desk to join them. "That sounds like your customer is keeping some pretty bad company."

"It sure does. I found out today that the man escaped from jail. That marauder, murderer and outlaw is on the loose, and he already has a contact here. He may be headed this way. You've got to protect the citizens of Peppin."

Sean was quiet for a moment, then he nodded. "That's my priority, Peter. I don't have any jurisdiction outside of this town, so I can't keep that man from traveling toward us on the rail line. Should he come here, I promise I'll arrest him. Unless that happens, the only thing I can do is keep my eyes open."

The man nodded. "I guess that's all I can ask."

"I'd like to see a wanted poster of the outlaw. Can you ask them to send one to me?"

"Certainly."

"Let me know if you come across any other evidence, and I'd be happy to take a look at it."

"Oh, don't you worry." The man grabbed his hat to leave. "I'll let you know the minute I hear anything slightly suspicious."

"Do you think this is serious?" Jeff asked as he took the seat Peter had just vacated.

"I don't know, but we need to treat it as such." Sean went over the notes he'd taken while talking to Peter. "We need to find out more about this Alfred Calhoun fellow. If they were communicating, they might have been trying to coordinate something other than just an escape—especially since Calhoun clearly wasn't expecting his friend to be arrested. Otherwise, he wouldn't have been so angry that his messages had gone unanswered."

Jeff seemed to catch the direction of his thoughts. "I wonder if Calhoun has any other contacts already in town that might be of interest. If he does…"

"Then we may be dealing with a gang." Sean nodded, having already realized the danger. "In that case, there's only one target in town that's big enough to attract an entire band of outlaws."

"The bank," Jeff murmured.

A sober silence permeated the room. Sean leaned back in his chair to think. It made sense. The First Bank of Peppin was also the only bank in Peppin. Even people from the surrounding counties used the bank because Mr. Wilkins had a reputation for fair business practices. A lot of money went in and out of his doors which made it the perfect draw for undesirables. Now that he thought about it, Sean was surprised there hadn't been a threat on it before.

"What's the plan, Sheriff?" Jeff asked.

Sean smiled because Jeff knew he'd already have one. "I'll talk to Mr. Wilkins to find out how we can shore up any of the bank's vulnerabilities. We'll study that wanted poster when it comes in. We'll also keep an eye on Calhoun to see what he's up to."

If someone succeeded in robbing the bank, the community would be devastated and so would the Wilkins family. Oddly enough, the Wilkins family now included him. That made the threat personal. He might not always get along with Lorelei, and he didn't agree with her rather impulsive approach to life, but she was soon to be his wife. He wasn't about to allow anything to happen to her or her parents.

Chapter Eight

Lorelei caught in a short gasp, then let out a loud sneeze that exploded into the silence of the millinery shop. It sent scads of feather particles floating into the air, compounding her problem. She held her breath until the feathers settled back onto the worktable, then cautiously pulled in a small breath. When her nose didn't begin to itch, she turned back to the bonnet in her hands.

She eyed it carefully. Selecting a large peacock feather, she trimmed it down and attached it to the bonnet. A smile lifted her lips. *Perfect.*

She turned the bonnet around in her hands, then frowned. *Or not.* The hat was definitely missing something. As she glanced around the worktable for something to add, she heard the little bell above the door give its cheerful jingle to signal the arrival of a customer. Mrs. Cummings had gone upstairs for lunch, leaving Lorelei to face her first costumer alone.

She set the bonnet aside and dusted away the feathers clinging to her fingertips before hurrying out of the workroom. A cheerful greeting stalled at her lips, and she paused in surprise as she realized the customer was Sean's youngest sister. Ellie lifted one of the store's most elaborate hats from the shelf for a closer look. Lorelei allowed an amused smile to pull at her lips. She could hardly imagine Ellie wearing such an ornate creation.

Lorelei cleared her throat delicately. "Would you like to try it on?"

Ellie abruptly spun to meet her gaze with wide green eyes. "Oh, no. I wouldn't wear it. I'd like to think I am not as complicated as all that."

Lorelei met Ellie's self-deprecating grin with a smile of her own, then glanced around the shop searchingly. "I can find you something simpler. We have a straw bonnet that I think would suit you perfectly."

Ellie carefully placed the hat back on the shelf. "That's quite all right. You don't have to bother. I heard you started working here, so I just wanted to come in and say hello."

"Oh," she said, then wished she hadn't sounded so surprised when Ellie began to blush. *Honestly, though. What an odd thing for her to do. She's never sought me out before.*

After an awkward moment of silence, Ellie smiled. "You played so well on Sunday. Did it take you very long to learn the music?"

"I already knew most of the hymns from when I practiced as a child."

"I can't imagine." Ellie laughed. "When I was a little girl I never had the patience for anything like that. I was much more likely to be out with the boys finding some way or another to skin my knee."

She gave a cautious smile. "I remember seeing you climb a tree or two now and again."

"I haven't climbed a tree in years! It would hardly be proper now. I'm sure it would be much harder to manage in long skirts." Even as she said it, Ellie's gaze turned a bit wistful as if she was imagining herself doing that very thing.

Lorelei surveyed the young woman before her in knowing amusement. "I'm sure."

"Well, I'm much less rambunctious now," Ellie proclaimed, but the capricious look in her eye didn't lend her much credibility.

"I can tell."

Ellie laughed. "You aren't the least bit convinced, but never mind that."

The conversation lagged again, and Lorelei began to wonder if she should try to find some way to end it. She was sure Ellie had never said so much to her before. Ellie, Sean and Lawson had been the best of friends, and even when she'd been Lawson's fiancée, Lorelei had never tried to penetrate that bond. As a result, she'd never expected more than a slight acquaintance with Ellie, which was really too bad because she'd always admired the girl's exuberance.

Resolved to end the conversation, Lorelei smiled. "Well, thank you for the compliment about my playing. Are you sure I can't interest you in one of our bonnets?"

"Not this time, I'm afraid," Ellie said, then glanced around the shop for a moment before meeting Lorelei's gaze. "Actually, I did have another purpose for coming here. I've been thinking about having a get-together next Saturday. I was hoping you'd like to come."

"I don't know," Lorelei said in surprise.

Ellie's slim fingers touched her arm. "Please, say yes. I mean, I will understand if you had something else planned."

Lorelei shook her head. "I was just a little surprised you asked, that's all."

Ellie's lashes dropped toward her cheek. "Oh, don't say that."

Lorelei lifted her shoulder in a shrug. "I didn't mean anything by it."

Ellie met her gaze with sincerity. "I know you didn't. It's my own fault, you know. I never went out of my way to be friendly to you before. I'm sorry for that. I hope that we can leave that behind and be friends now."

Why? The question hovered on Lorelei's lips, but she couldn't quite bring herself to ask it. Her eyes widened as she suddenly realized what this must be about.

"I really do appreciate you telling me that, Ellie. I'd like for us to be friends, too." She glanced around the shop. Though it was empty, she leaned forward to slightly lower her voice. "I just don't want you to think that you have to be my friend or invite me places because of how things stand between your brother and I."

"You and my brother," Ellie repeated softly before her eyes widened, and she grinned. "You mean that you're going to let Sean court you?"

"Well, yes," she said slowly. "But—"

Ellie pulled her into a quick hug, then stepped back to meet her gaze. "That's wonderful. Of course we will be friends. There's no reason for us not to be."

Lorelei tilted her head to survey Ellie. She pulled in a slow breath as realization pulled at her mind. "He didn't tell you."

"Well, no. He hadn't told me yet, but he didn't really have to. I knew he was going to ask to court you. Now I really hope you'll come on Saturday. Please, say you will."

"I'll be there. What time?"

"Four o'clock. I'm so glad you're coming," Ellie exclaimed and honored Lorelei with a resplendent smile.

Lorelei returned it with a weak one of her own. *I can't believe he didn't tell them.*

Sean could hardly believe he'd convinced Lorelei to eat lunch with him at the café. Despite her earlier compliance, it was obvious from her cold glare that she had her own agenda for this outing, and it had nothing to do with furthering their pretend courtship. He could tell from the pitying glances he was receiving from those around him that they weren't fooling anyone. Everyone knew he was about to get raked over the coals. He might as well get it over with. "What has your bonnet all in a twist?"

"My bonnet is not in a twist," she said. Her hand lifted toward her pert little hat as though to make sure.

"Then why are you upset?" He lifted a hand to stop her protest. "Oh, I forgot. You normally glare at me like that."

She set her lips into a straight line, then leaned forward with a furious whisper. "You haven't told your family what's really going on. How do you explain that?"

He leaned toward her and tilted his head inquiringly. "How would you know what I have or have not told my family?"

She straightened in her chair. "Ellie visited me at the shop yesterday. It was obvious from our conversation that she didn't know. Why haven't you told them?"

"I plan to."

"When?"

When he found the courage to stomach the disappointment he'd inevitably see in their eyes. He wanted to spare them that. Who was he kidding? He wanted to spare himself. He'd grown up watching first his parents' marriage, then his sister's. Both had been love matches. Both had been filled with incredible tenderness. In short, they were nothing like the distant marriage that beckoned him into a future with the beautiful but almost hostile Lorelei Wilkins.

Even as those thoughts tripped through his mind, Lorelei's hand came to rest gently over his. Instinctively, he turned his hand over to hold it. Her gaze met his as she whispered, "Sean, you need to tell them before they find out like my father did."

Just like that, he read caring in her eyes—but not for him. Her concern was for his family, and he couldn't help but bristle at the accusation, from Lorelei of all people, that he was failing in his responsibility to the people in his life. He sternly lowered his voice. "Leave it alone, Lorelei. I'll tell them when I'm ready."

Her gaze dropped from his eyes to where her hand rested in his. Her face seemed to pale incrementally. He heard her catch her breath. She casually tugged her hand away. "I should go. I'm finished anyway."

"I'll walk you home," he offered.

"There's no need." She tossed him a smile he didn't believe and strode away. The door clanged shut behind her. Ignoring the curious gazes of the busy café, he stared thoughtfully at the vacant chair across from him. What was going on with that woman? She just plain didn't make sense. The way she acted…well, she either loved him or hated him.

If it was the first, he was on shaky ground because if she ever dropped the act he'd probably like her. Liking her meant he might forget the things she'd done and the choices she'd made that had hurt other people. However, that scenario was rather improbable despite Lawson's opinion. It was far more likely that after everything that had passed between them, Lorelei just didn't like him. He swallowed. He really didn't want to live the rest of his life with a woman who hated him, did he?

He needed to figure out how to have at least an amiable relationship with her. To do that, he needed to figure out Lorelei's true feelings for him. He would have to force her hand, and he knew just how to do it. First, he would walk over to the courthouse and see what had become of the old Hilson place he had his eye on. Then he'd plan a way to let his family know the truth.

Lorelei ignored the startled glances of a few strangers as she rushed down the sidewalk away from the café. She threw a wary glance over her shoulder, then slipped into the narrow alleyway next to her father's bank to wait for Sean to pass so she could continue undisturbed. She couldn't bear the thought of Sean pursuing her or forcing her to explain her abrupt response to him in the café.

She leaned back against the wall to try to catch her breath. It was hopeless to believe that Sean wouldn't have noticed her reaction to holding his hand. Even she was surprised by it. Though she knew it stemmed from nothing more than mere performance, she hadn't known how to react. His derision, impatience and scorn she could easily face without wincing, but she hadn't been prepared for her own weakness.

Oh, how she wished it hadn't affected her. She calmly reminded herself that holding hands could not cause a resurgence of youthful unrequited love. She knew better now. She'd made a decision to live her life with a new perspective, and nothing was going to change her mind. She nodded, feeling her unease slipping away.

She stepped farther into the shadows of the alleyway

as she heard confident steps pound closer on the sidewalk. She watched as Sean passed with a determined look on his face. She waited a few moments to be sure she'd avoided him. The sound of low voices reached her ear from deeper in the alley just as she was about to step back onto the sidewalk. They seemed to be coming from behind the bank.

"Don't tell me there's no back way in. Look! Not a door in sight. What kind of fool built this place?"

Another man snorted. "A fool didn't design this bank. There is only one door in and out. It faces the sheriff's office."

"It'd be a pain to have to blast through these walls. We'd need more power than we have now."

Lorelei stilled a gasp in her throat, then waited to hear the other man's answer.

"No sense in that. Besides, it isn't our way."

"Mighty tempting, though. I bet the safe is right along this wall."

"Let's not waste time. We've had a look at the place. Let's get out of here before someone gets nosy."

Lorelei's eyes widened. She scurried away as silently as possible. With a quick step, she was back on the sidewalk. She was preparing to hurry off when the heel of her boot caught in the seam of a loose wooden board. She tried to tug it out but it wouldn't budge.

Biting her lip, she glanced toward the alley. She saw a figure round the corner toward her. She leaned down so her hat would momentarily block her face. She hoped beyond anything that the man would just ignore her and step past without questioning her. His pace slowed to a curious tread as he drew nearer. Realizing her skirt hid her other hand from view, she shoved her reticule carefully along the ground. It stopped slightly away from her.

"What have we here?" a deep voice asked.

"Oh." Lorelei glanced up, affecting surprise. She slowly lifted her head to meet the dark eyes of a well-dressed, gentlemanly looking young man. He was not at all the rough drifter she would have expected from the conversation she'd heard.

She let her lips curl into a demure smile she hoped might befuddle his thoughts just enough for him to believe her. "I'm awfully sorry to be blocking your way, but I'm afraid my heel is stuck."

He glanced down at the sidewalk. "I see."

When he didn't say more, she lifted her skirt just enough so that she could see her heel then, endeavored to tug it out again. "I'm sure I'll get it out eventually."

"If you'll allow me?" he asked.

At her nod, he knelt beside her to pull the loose boards farther apart. She pulled her heel free and stepped to the side. "Thank you very much."

He smiled his welcome, then met her gaze with an appraising eye. "You would need to step just so to get caught by that board. Were you in the alley, then?"

"The alley? Why would I be in the alley?" she asked in confusion, then smiled. "I dropped my reticule, that's all."

She stepped to the side and gestured to the ground where her reticule lay. "If you would be so kind, Mr...."

"Smithson," he supplied. Bending down, he picked up her reticule and offered it to her. "You are?"

She took her reticule back, and, though she hated to tell him her name, she was sure he could easily find out some other way. "Miss Wilkins."

His eyes widened briefly. "Are you any relation to the owner of the bank?"

"Yes," she said, lifting her chin. "As a matter fact, I am. Why do you ask?"

He smiled. "No reason, Miss. I was just curious."

"Well, thank you for your help." She smiled again, so he wouldn't think her overly concerned. "Have a good day, Mr. Smithson."

"Same to you."

She gave him a parting nod, then stepped around him to walk along the front of the bank. She glanced sideways at the reflection in the glass to see if he followed her. She saw that he continued to watch her for a moment before he turned and went in the opposite direction.

A breath of relief filtered through her lips. She glanced across the street, debating whether or not to tell Sean what she'd heard. She shook her head. What proof did she have? The men hadn't mentioned any definite plans—but their intention was clear. She spared another quick glance behind her. Satisfied that she wasn't being watched, she walked across the street and entered the sheriff's office.

The last person Sean expected to see when he walked into his office was Lorelei Wilkins. Yet there she sat on the corner of his desk perusing his private files. He eyed her for a moment, then let the door close behind him with a bang. She jumped, and her eyes flew to his, then tracked his Stetson as it sailed through the air to land beside her on the desk. He lowered his chin to stare at her as he approached; tapping the mortgage papers he needed to fill out on his leg. "Where is Jeff?"

"I sent him to lunch. He said I didn't have the authority to do that."

"You don't."

"I know, but he was hungry. I assured him you wouldn't be gone long and if anyone needed anything, I'd send them to the café."

Sean shook his head. "Well, I hope you're here to apologize."

Her delicate brows lifted. "For what?"

He came to a stop in front of her. "Ruining our lunch—unless you can think of something else."

She braced her arms behind her, wrinkling more of his files in the process, and stared back at him. "I'm not here to apologize. I had every right to ask you why you hadn't told your family about us."

"Enough of that," he warned. "If you're not going to apologize, why are you here?"

She placed her hands in her lap and suddenly became serious. "I heard something when I was in the alleyway just now."

He frowned. "What were you doing in an alleyway?"

She shrugged guiltily. "That isn't important. What is important is that I heard two men plotting to rob the bank."

He paused for a moment to take that in. "Are you serious?"

"I wouldn't joke about something like this."

"Then please get off my desk."

She frowned. "That is not the response I was expecting."

His mouth twitched with a suppressed smile. "You're sitting on my notebook."

"Oh," she breathed and finally complied by sitting in the chair he pulled up for her. He grabbed a pencil to carefully record everything she'd heard and seen. Once she finished, he went over the notes he'd taken in silent contemplation. He closed his notebook and set it aside. "Lorelei, think very carefully before you answer the next few questions I ask you. Did he seem like he was suspicious of you?"

She thought for a moment, then nodded slowly. "I tried to ignore it but I definitely got that feeling from him."

"Never ignore your instincts in a situation like that," he advised. "What do you want to do when he contacts you again?"

"*When,* not *if?*"

He nodded and walked around the desk to pull up a chair beside her. "If he's smart, he'll try to figure out how much you really know about what they said. So that means you have two options. The first one is to wait until he approaches you and then play dumb like you did today. If he believes you the second time, you won't have to worry about it again. However, if he figures out that you know too much, you'll be in danger. And I've got to admit, if he didn't believe you this time, then he's probably not going to believe you later, either."

She bit her lip and fiddled with the folds of her skirts. "What's the second option?"

"The second option is to leave town. Visit your great-aunt in California, just like you planned to before. This Mr. Smithson wouldn't be able to go after you, not without delaying his plans for the bank, which he won't want to do. Once he and his friends are in custody, your father can send you word that it's safe to come home."

"No," she said firmly. "I'm not running away—not from this town, or my responsibilities, or bank robbers. Besides, what would Mrs. Greene say if I suddenly up and left?"

"If we explain the circumstances to her, I'm sure she'll understand."

"That's funny. I'm sure she won't."

"No," Sean agreed reluctantly. "She probably won't. But as sheriff of this town, I've taken an oath to protect its citizens—and keeping you safe is more important than keeping Mrs. Greene happy."

"This isn't only about keeping Mrs. Greene happy. If I left town, she'd tell everyone what happened and I might never be able to show my face in this town again. I left this town once, Sean. I know I wouldn't want to stay away forever. Besides, you have to consider your reputation, as well." She lifted her chin determinedly. "No, there has to be another way."

He crossed his arms dubiously. "Such as?"

Sean saw an idea spark in Lorelei's eyes, and his stomach sank as he realized what it meant. She was coming up with another one of her crazy, spontaneous, ridiculous ideas. And he was going to hate it, he was completely sure that whatever it was—

"I could go undercover," she said.

His jaw clenched in frustration. Yep, he hated it, all right.

"Oh, Sean, it would be perfect!" Lorelei continued, practically jumping from her chair to pace the floor in enthusiasm. "I'll pretend that I want to work with them, then they'll tell me all of their plans—I'd then tell *you* those plans, and we'd have the whole group identified and caught in no time."

"No," Sean replied.

She whirled to face him as though somehow surprised by his immediate refusal. "But this idea is the perfect solution and—"

"No."

"I'm sure I'd be able—"

"*No,* Lorelei. It's too dangerous. Don't you understand? It's my duty to keep you safe. This would be the complete opposite of safe."

"It's also your duty to protect the bank, isn't it?" she asked, tilting her head inquiringly. "And don't you think it's my duty, too? It's my town as much as it is yours—and it's my father's bank, which makes this personal. If you'll just trust me, I promise I won't let you down or—"

Sean honestly didn't intend to let the snort of disbelief slip out...but it did, and it stopped Lorelei in her tracks.

"Oh, so that's what this is really about," she said slowly. "You're refusing to let me help because you think I'm too *flighty,* too *insincere* to be trusted, aren't you?"

He shifted uncomfortably in his chair at the change in her voice. In an instant it had switched from that bright, overly enthusiastic tone to one that sounded cold, disappointed and downright...well...hurt. He suddenly felt about six inches tall. He didn't like that feeling at all or the way she suddenly seemed to withdraw into herself. He cleared his throat. "I never said that."

"Didn't you?" she asked pointedly, then perched on his desk a little too close to him for comfort, especially when she peered down at him with that fire in her eyes. "Well, Sheriff O'Brien, I am *not* leaving town and I am *not* going to play dumb the next time I see that man. If you don't trust me enough to let me help, then I suppose I'll have to do things my own way."

She got to her feet, and Sean felt a wave of pure panic wash over him as he grabbed for her arm. "Lorelei, stop! Can't you see that I'm just trying to protect you? Your idea is just too d—"

"Too dangerous—yes, so you said. But tell me, Sean, what would be more dangerous, the two of us coming up with a plan together to put the idea into practice, or me walking out the door right now and doing it all on my own?"

And she would, Sean was certain. Once she decided to act on an impulse, there was no stopping her. She wouldn't even pause to plan things out, either. She'd probably just trust it would all work out if she made things up as she went along. That didn't work in life, and it certainly wouldn't work in this situation. All he could do was try to figure out how to help her, and hopefully protect her.

"You are the most frustrating woman I have ever known," he muttered.

For some reason that made a smile blossom across her lips. She lifted her eyebrows entreatingly. "Does that mean..."

"Yes." He sighed. "You win."

To her credit, she managed to almost completely hide her victorious smile. "You won't regret it."

"I know I won't because we're going to do this together." He smiled ruefully before continuing, "I'll be with you, as you so nicely put it before, 'like fleas.' It also means that you'd have to stay with it until the end. Impulsivity could have no place in this. You'd have to stick to my plan."

He seated himself once more and was relieved to see her settle into her chair, as well. "I can do that, Sean. I know I can and I'm going to prove it."

He nodded. "All right then, Lorelei, I'm trusting you on this, and the whole town will be depending on you. If Smithson approaches you, let him know that you're wise to his plans, then tell me immediately. From then on, we'll take it one step at a time."

Chapter Nine

Sean watched his niece and nephew race across the field. Hope tossed her long dark mane of hair this way and that as she pawed at the ground, playing the role of a wild horse. Timothy was right behind her pretending to swing a rope like a true cowboy. Sean looked back at the picnic Kate had set up for Sunday lunch. Ellie lounged on the blanket beside him and was obviously daydreaming as she slowly finished the apple in her hand. Three-year-old Grace snoozed in Kate's lap, completely unaware of her surroundings while Nathan focused on finishing up a piece of his wife's delicious pound cake.

So this was it. This was the perfect time to tell his family the truth about his relationship with Lorelei. He glanced up at the cloudy blue sky above him to steady his nerves. *Lord, should I?* There was no message spelled out in the clouds, just an overwhelming sense that it was time to do the right thing. He cleared his throat and quietly announced, "There's something I need to tell everyone."

Ellie's eyes lost their dreamy stare as she met his

gaze. Sean looked from her to Kate who watched him curiously. Nathan nodded. "Go ahead. We're listening."

For the first time in a long time, he felt that God was with him. He pulled in a quick breath. "I accidentally have to marry to Lorelei Wilkins."

Shocked silence descended in uncomfortable thickness over his family. Kate recovered first. "Did you just say—"

"What does that even mean?" Ellie exclaimed in confusion.

"I'm really hoping I don't know what that means," Nathan said with a warning glance.

Sean held up a hand. "Hold on. Let me explain myself."

"I think you'd better," Kate urged.

"It started out innocently enough," Sean began, then quickly told them the entire story.

"Oh, Sean," Kate groaned. "What happens now?"

He glanced up to meet their gazes, then cleared his throat to ease the nervous lump that had settled there. "I'm supposed to publicly propose to Lorelei in a few weeks. In the meantime, Mr. Wilkins wants our courtship to appear perfectly normal so that no one else will find out what really happened."

"So that's the real reason you're courting Lorelei?" Nathan asked. "You two don't have feelings for each other?"

He smiled in wry amusement. "The truth is Lorelei can hardly stand me. She just agreed to it because her father didn't give her a choice."

Ellie stared at him. "Are you sure Mrs. Greene is helping you? I mean why would she do that?"

"I haven't seen any evidence to the contrary." He shrugged. "She's doing it for Mrs. Wilkins's sake."

She nodded. "Well, I can guarantee she isn't doing it for yours."

"You and Mrs. Greene need to stop expecting the worst of each other," Kate chided as she brushed a tear off of her cheek. "Sean, what I don't understand is why it took you so long to tell us this."

Nathan shifted closer to his wife to slide his arm around her and pull her into an embrace. "Don't cry, Kate. I'm sure Sean wasn't trying to hurt us."

She nudged him softly with her elbow. "I know that, Nathan."

"Then why are you crying?"

"Never mind," she said. "Let him speak."

Nathan looked as confused by the exchange as Sean felt. With a shrug, Nathan nodded toward Sean. "Go ahead."

"I guess I didn't want you to be disappointed in me."

"Don't be silly," Kate said as she adjusted Grace into a more comfortable position. "We wouldn't have been disappointed in you because of that. You're doing the honorable thing. The only reason I'm disappointed is because you didn't confide in us earlier."

"I'm sorry," he said, then realized something for the first time. "I guess I was disappointed for myself, too."

"Why?" Nathan asked.

"When I was growing up, I saw what a loving, God-centered marriage you guys had. It was the same way with Ma and Pa. I never said much about it, but I've always wanted to have a marriage like that. Now, I don't even have the smallest hope of it." Sean shrugged. "I guess I feel like I failed. I failed to continue Ma and Pa's legacy. I failed God by not allowing Him to lead me. I failed myself and I've failed Lorelei. That's a lot of failure for one man to admit to even to his own family."

Kate's eyes filled with tears. "Oh, there's so much wrong with that statement I don't know where to start."

Nathan met his gaze evenly. "You know, Sean, sometimes the desires we have in our hearts aren't just our own desires. I believe more than anything that God placed that desire in you to have a loving, God-centered marriage. There is a reason He hasn't taken it away yet."

Sean shook his head skeptically. "It's a sore temptation to give up hope after the mess I've made of everything."

"Never give up hope," Kate said. "No matter how much we might mess up, God never fails. Surrender the situation to Him. Trust Him to work it out and He will."

"That's easier said than done," he countered.

"No, it's the surrendering part that's easier in the long run," she insisted. "We were never created to carry the burdens of our lives alone. That's God's job, Sean."

But wasn't it his job, too? It was his life—shouldn't he take responsibility for it? Shouldn't he be able to come up with a plan to fix things? Surrendering it to God seemed like accepting defeat, admitting that he couldn't handle things on his own. He plucked a blade of grass and twirled it nervously between his fingers. "That seems so passive."

Nathan laughed. "It takes a lot more strength than you might think. Besides, once you are in God's will, He will show you how to be active with your faith."

"I guess that makes sense," he said, mostly because he thought that was what they wanted to hear. It still seemed like a pretty weak way to go about life to him.

Ellie cleared her throat delicately to gain his attention. "One last thing, Sean O'Brien."

He nearly groaned. "Yes, Ellie?"

She arched her brow threateningly. "If you call my

brother a failure one more time, I just might have to punch you."

He grinned. "I'll keep that in mind."

"Keep this in mind, too. I don't think you're failing at all."

"What would you call it then?"

She lifted her chin as though preparing for a fight. "I think it's romantic."

"Romantic?" he said with a look that told her exactly how preposterous she was being.

Her lips curved into a mischievous smile. "It certainly has the potential to be. Kate and Nathan didn't start off much better than you and Lorelei. That turned out well, didn't it?"

"What exactly are you suggesting, Ellie?"

"Just because Lorelei is playacting her way through the courtship doesn't mean you have to. We all know she liked you in the past. If she liked you then, what's keeping her from liking you now?" She pointed at him significantly. "Find that out and you could still stand a chance at making her fall in love with you."

He gave a dry laugh. "Not that I think what you're saying is actually right, but even if I did that, it might not bring *me* any closer to falling in love with *her*."

She narrowed her gaze. "Love is a choice, Sean. Don't let anyone tell you otherwise."

Nathan grinned. "She's right."

"Of course I am," she said.

Fine, so maybe love was a choice. But did he want to choose to love Lorelei? How could he trust her to be someone he could build a life with after all the things she'd done? But on the other hand, if he didn't let himself love her, what kind of life would they have together?

Maybe this was a case where he'd have to take a calculated risk.

"Listen, regardless of what I decide to do or not do, y'all can't tell anyone about this. Promise me you'll keep it a secret."

"It isn't our secret to tell," Nathan said.

Kate nodded. "We shouldn't mention it around the children, either. They'd be liable to let something slip without meaning to."

"I won't say a word." Ellie promised.

Kate smiled. "I'm glad you told us."

"So am I." It felt good to finally tell his family the truth. It was even better to realize that after the initial shock wore off, they were more than willing to support and encourage him. But accepting their support meant considering their advice, too. Could he do it? Could he surrender the whole situation to God?

I haven't been doing a great job of taking care of this situation so far, but I'm willing to ask for Your help, Lord. Isn't that the same thing as surrendering? If so, why did it feel as though panic was slowly tying his stomach in tight little knots?

Lorelei stepped down from the buggy without Sean's help and glanced at her surroundings. She couldn't understand why her father had encouraged her to travel unaccompanied with Sean to this abandoned old house just outside of town. Of course, since what the town had perceived as their spat in the café almost a week ago, her parents had been encouraging them to be seen in public more often...without fighting. So far they weren't fighting, but this wasn't exactly public. She pulled her shawl closer around her shoulders. "Why are we here?"

"This is our house, Lorelei."

She stopped walking to stare at him. "Our house?"

He continued looking at the house for a long moment. "Yes. We're going to live here after the ceremony."

She tried to form a coherent sentence, but her mouth would not move. She shook her head. "Are you serious?"

"Sure, I am. You didn't think I'd expect you to live in the one-room cabin I have in town, did you?"

"No," she admitted slowly. No, she hadn't thought that at all. She hadn't allowed herself to think that far.

He mistook her shocked silence for disapproval and turned a critical eye back on the house before he met her gaze. "I suppose you'd rather live in town."

"Yes," she breathed, since he seemed to expect a response.

Concern lowered his brow as he earnestly said, "I can't afford to buy a house in town. I know it isn't what you're used to, but I hope you understand that there is only so much I can offer you."

"My father—"

"He was kind enough to give us a low mortgage on this house. I won't expect anything more from him."

"Sean, don't you think you should have consulted me about this?" she asked incredulously. "Did you take me into consideration at all when you made this decision?"

"How can you ask that? Everything I've done so far has been for you or because of you." He pressed his lips together to keep from saying more. "Why don't we go inside? The house isn't as bad as you think. It will need some work, of course, but the building is sound. There is plenty of room and you'll be able to fix it up however you like."

A resounding "no" begged to dance from her lips.

He seemed to sense it for he lowered his chin to pin her with a look. "Lorelei, I trusted you when you said you'd help me with the bank robbery. Surely, you can trust my judgment enough to at least look at the house."

She let a few awkward moments of thoughtful silence pass between them. He smiled beseechingly. Finally, without a word, she moved forward. She stepped through the front door as he held it open for her, then cautiously walked into the house.

Light dove through the tall front windows to brightly illuminate the empty room. Dust lifted from the wooden boards at her feet and danced in the shafts of sunlight. A brick fireplace was built into the wall on her right. Its chimney stretched up the wall until it disappeared into the tall ceiling that housed the second floor. Sean left the door open behind them, allowing a breeze to filter through and stir the stale air. "This is the sitting room."

"It's a good-size room," she admitted.

"Did you see the fireplace? It will be nice come winter," he offered hesitantly.

She nodded. He seemed satisfied with her response to the sitting room, so he led her through the door into a much smaller space. It had a medium-size window and a small table for two. Sean announced it to be the dining room. She murmured something about it being adequate.

He led her into the kitchen. It had a large oven, but the stove seemed rather outdated. Sean seemed to notice her concern and mentioned something about replacing the stove. Suddenly she realized how like a shy little boy he seemed. He carefully watched her expression and waited for her approval over each feature of the house. She wasn't used to seeing him so unguarded.

She followed him back into the sitting room, then he led her up toward the stairs. As she climbed to the second floor she felt the shock of his announcement begin to wear off. Her feet slowed on the steps. This was going to be her home with this man.

Her heartbeat quickened in her throat. She glanced over the banister to the sitting room where she would probably spend hours in Sean's company. She imagined herself eating at that small table with him. She saw herself standing at the stove with Sean leaning over her shoulder to see what she was cooking, and her knees began to tremble. It was becoming too real.

They came to the landing of the stairs that ended in a wide hallway. Sean opened the door to one of the rooms on the left to let her peer inside of it. She slid through the doorway, careful to leave a few inches of space between herself and Sean. The room was moderately sized and the frames for two mattresses rested in opposite corners, but those could be removed to give Lorelei a nice sewing room or library. She heard the door slide open farther as Sean moved closer, and his voice interrupted her thoughts. "Eventually this would become the children's room."

Children. Her breath stilled in her chest as she realized what that implied. *I hadn't even thought about where we would live; I certainly hadn't considered he might want children. Why would he want to bring children into a relationship like this?*

She turned to find him striding directly across the hall to another room. He stepped inside and held the door open until she entered. The room was larger than the other with the same high ceiling. Large windows matched those on the lower floor, but drapes concealed the sunlight from their panes and left the room in dark muted tones. Sean turned toward her. His eyes glinted with determination and daring, yet his voice came out gently. "This will be our room, Lorelei."

Lorelei was grateful when Sean's tour ended moments later on the porch. His voice droned on in the background about how he planned to update the house, but she'd stopped listening to his words in the bedroom upstairs when reality had come crashing down around her. She braced her hands on the porch railing and pulled in a deep breath.

Foolish. Foolish. Foolish. I should have known. Of course, he would expect a real marriage and he'd want to have children. What man wouldn't? Why didn't I ever think that far? Why am I even surprised?

The truth was frightening. She'd been living in denial. The world she'd carefully constructed by avoiding her problem and stuffing her feelings as deeply within her as possible was nothing but sham. This was reality. A mirthless smile tilted at her lips.

How ironic that in running from a marriage with a man I couldn't love, I will find myself bound by that same union to a man who will never love me. Every day I'll have to live in his house, eat at his table, be the mother of his children and never know his love. What I spared Lawson in marrying me, I condemned myself to through my own willfulness.

She felt Sean's comforting but fleeting touch on her back and jerked away from him in surprise. He settled his forearms on the railing. "I didn't mean to startle you."

She refused to respond, but the silence worked against her fervent feelings. It lengthened between them until Lorelei felt her shoulders begin to relax and her fingers loosened their anxious clasp on the railing. Sean looked up from his relaxed stance to try to capture her gaze. "I know we said we'd pretend to court. I guess you thought we'd feign a marriage, too."

"I certainly did," she stated unapologetically. "I just don't understand why you'd want to bring children into a situation like this."

"That isn't something we have to decide today or even next year, but I guess I'm just hoping it won't always be like this." He turned to her. "As for feigning a marriage, we may not have much of a choice in this situation but we can choose to go about it the right way or the wrong way. The wrong way is letting this turn our entire lives into a lie."

She turned away from the truth of his statement to stare toward the fields. "What's the right way?"

"The right way is to do our best to fulfill your father's expectations while putting aside our past and trying to create a friendship, if nothing else."

She stilled. "Friendship?"

He stepped closer. "I know we were practically enemies as children, but when we grew up we were friends for a while, weren't we? What happened at the Harvest Dance a few years ago that suddenly changed that?"

She could hardly believe they were having this conversation now after so many years had passed—but wasn't that event what had fueled the last sparks of animosity in their relationship? She shrugged lightly. "You showed up with another girl. What was I supposed to think?"

"I did it as a favor to Chris. He was sick and didn't want Amy to miss out. Besides, I never thought you'd immediately start courting my best friend."

"You hadn't said anything definite up to that point. I thought it meant you didn't like me after all. Lawson saw that I was upset, though I wouldn't tell him why. He walked me home. He offered to be my beau." She smiled wryly. "Looking back, I think he just offered out of sympathy, but I said yes."

"Why?"

She confronted his intense stare with the truth. "I didn't think you'd care."

"I did."

"You cared." She turned away from his quiet words with a laugh. "Oh, sure."

He caught her arm and gently tugged her so that she faced him again. "Why are you laughing? Don't you believe me?"

"I believe you cared. You cared enough about Lawson to carefully explain all of my faults to him when he told you he wanted to court me."

His eyes narrowed. "Did he tell you that?"

"No, I overheard you. I was supposed to wait in the buggy, but I didn't." She'd wanted to see his face when he heard the news. She'd wanted to know if it would matter to him. He'd answered that question for her pretty quickly.

"You weren't supposed to hear that." His hand loosened on her arm. "I didn't mean it."

She wanted to believe him, but his every action after that moment called him a liar. She let out a sigh and shook her head. "That was ages ago anyway. What does it matter now?"

"You're right," he said seriously. "We're adults now. We should be able to put all of that behind us. Do you think we can?"

She glanced up at him to search his face and found nothing but sincerity. "I suppose we'd better. After all, I'm supposed to marry you and live here with you and possibly have your children. I should probably at least consider you a friend, first."

Relief at her agreement played at his features. He leaned his shoulder onto the porch post and nodded seriously, but a hint of amusement played at his lips. "I know. It's a pretty raw deal, isn't it?"

Was he trying to charm her? It was almost working. She leaned her back against the railing and shook her head in disbelief. "You have to admit it sounds a little crazy."

"It is," he agreed. "But, I think we can do it."

I guess I'll have to try the whole "love your brother" concept. She gave a nod of agreement. He gave her a hopeful smile as if he was truly inviting her into a friendship with him. Her heart gave a rebellious jump. She bit her lip and glanced away with one thought echoing through her mind. *He certainly is* not *my brother.*

Chapter Ten

Sean slid into the chair across from Richard as the man searched through his large mahogany desk. "This should explain all of the safety procedures we use at the bank. I go over this with each of my employees when they begin working for me."

Sean perused the paper he'd been handed. "I see you have information here regarding what to do during a bank robbery."

"Of course, but thankfully, we've never had to use it." Richard watched Sean carefully. "Is there a specific threat to my bank that I should know about?"

"Not at this time," Sean said. He couldn't pass along any specifics because he didn't have any yet. His investigation on Calhoun had only revealed that the man had a penchant for drinking and gambling. The telegrapher hadn't seen hide nor hair of the man since the news of Frank Bentley's escape from jail. There were no indications that the outlaw was heading to Peppin, but Sean continued to be watchful for any man who bore a resemblance to the wanted poster now hanging in his office.

He'd also surreptitiously learned as much as he could about Smithson after Lorelei's tip. From outward appearances, the man seemed above suspicion. He lived at Bradley's Boardinghouse. He'd seemed to have taken an interest in Bradley's eldest daughter, Amy, and was well liked by the other boarders. So far, there was nothing to connect him to Calhoun besides the fact that they both had rather vague sources of income. No one had mentioned seeing the two of them together, and there was no crime record for either man with the state.

Unfortunately, at this point a general warning was all he could issue. "I'm just asking several of Peppin's businesses to make sure that they have adequate security measures in place to ward off criminals. I don't want people to become complacent just because we haven't had trouble yet."

Richard nodded thoughtfully. "Now that you mention it, with that railroad coming through town, I'm surprised we haven't had more of an increase in crime during the last five years."

"Yes, well, the sheriff's department is always looking for preventative measures we can put in place to deter that kind of activity." He lifted the paper. "May I keep this?"

"Certainly."

He folded the paper and placed it in his pocket just as a knock sounded at the study door. Richard called for the person to come in. Lorelei leaned inside. Her eyes met his for an instant, then she glanced toward her father with a teasing grin. "Are you two going to sit here all afternoon? Sean and I are going to be late if we don't leave soon."

Richard sent Sean a wry smile. "I think that means she's finally ready to go."

Lorelei smiled and lifted one shoulder in a playful

shrug. "Well, a girl has to look just right for her first official evening as part of a couple."

Sean was surprised by the complete lack of sarcasm in her tone. Was she really committing to the friendship they'd agreed to? When she caught his gaze and properly read his surprise, a smile tilted at her lips. Lorelei hardly waited until they left the study to whisper, "Were you talking about the bank? Did you find out some new information?"

He shook his head. "Just safety procedures. Have you heard from Smithson?"

She handed him his Stetson from the hat rack. "No. I would have told you if I had."

He opened the door for her, then followed her out. "Maybe he believed that you hadn't heard anything after all."

"I hope not."

He sent her an exasperated look which only caused her to widen her eyes innocently. He shook his head as he closed the front door behind them. When she turned toward him, he didn't move but inclined his head toward her and looked deep into her eyes, hoping that he might be able to discern some of her emotions. Things between them had been going more smoothly since their truce at the house, but he couldn't let himself get complacent yet. Her behavior could be so hard to predict. He was half waiting for her to suddenly change her mind about their agreement. "Are you sure you're ready for this?"

She lifted her chin. "Entirely. Why? Aren't you?"

He suddenly felt more nervous than he had in a long time. He lifted his shoulders in a shrug and gave a curt nod. "I'm ready."

"Then let's go," she said. She turned away but not before he saw a slightly victorious smile tug at her lips.

He stifled a groan. As long as she cooperated they'd be just fine. Now, if he could only figure out what exactly she thought she'd just won.

Lorelei pulled in a deep breath of country air as the horses in front of her father's buggy trotted along the well-worn road toward the O'Brien farm. A satisfied smile settled at her lips. She'd done it. She had managed to be nice to Sean while being herself. Of course, it hadn't been entirely easy. She'd felt her heart nearly jump out of her chest when she realized he wasn't stepping away outside the front door, but she'd firmly reined in that silly impulse. So there. She could do this after all.

Suddenly Sean pulled off onto the side of the road toward the shade of an oak tree. She clenched the wooden seat in alarm as the wagon bounced over the uneven land. "What are you doing?"

He parked the wagon under the tree, then hopped out and rounded the buggy. "I just thought of something we need to do before we join my family."

"What is it?" she asked as he lifted her from the buggy to settle her on the ground in front of him.

"This." He reached out to take her hand, and she immediately tugged it away. "You always withdraw from me when I touch you."

"I don't *always,*" she began, then stopped herself when she realized they both knew he was right.

"We need to be comfortable with each other. People notice when others are on edge. You, Lorelei Wilkins, are definitely on edge. We have to fix that."

He held out both of his hands to her in a silent challenge. She looked at them for a moment, then placed her hands in his. He seemed to wait for her to withdraw. When she didn't, he clasped her hands and let them fall casually between them.

"Much better," he murmured. "By the way, if I happen to say something you think is funny, go ahead and laugh. Or if you're happy, smile. Don't hide what you're feeling from me or others."

"Are you abiding by these rules, too?" she asked, wondering how long he was planning to hold her hands. She was pretty sure this was a test and refused to be the first to pull away.

He winked. "Sure, but you have to say something funny first."

Her heart jumped in her chest at his wink, dislodging an almost reluctant laugh in the process. He nodded in approval at the sound. "You should probably know my family has very little sense of personal distance. They also tend to hug a lot, so expect that."

"It might take me a while to get used to it," she admitted. "My family doesn't particularly emphasize that sort of thing. Neither did Lawson."

"I've noticed that your family is more formal than mine. Lawson has always been that way. I think it has something to do with whatever happened before he came to Peppin." He finally released her hands and stepped back. "Now you reach out to me. You can't hold my hand. We already did that. Do something else."

She stared at him blankly as butterflies began to dance in her stomach. She didn't like this game. She tucked her hands into the pockets of her skirt. "I can't."

"You can." He smiled in what must have been an attempt to put her at ease. It only increased her nervousness. "You're overthinking it."

She pulled in a deep breath. "You said your family hugs a lot."

He nodded.

"All right then," she breathed. Stepping forward, she reached around him to give him a light hug, then immediately stepped back.

He chuckled. "What was that?"

"A hug."

His chuckle changed into a full-grown laugh. "That was the poorest excuse for a hug I've ever experienced."

She stared at him in shocked amusement, then shook her head. "When I see your family I'm going ask them why you're so mean. Just you wait and see if I don't."

"Tut, tut. Friends, remember? Try it again."

She crossed her arms and just looked at him.

He grinned. "I'm sorry for laughing. Show me you forgive me."

She let out a long-suffering sigh as she realized he wasn't going to leave well enough alone until she complied. It had nothing to do with how nice it felt to laugh with him or have him smile at her like that—even if it had scarcely ever happened before. She slipped her hands around his waist, intending only a slightly prolonged repeat of her last hug. But just as she was about to step away, he swept her into his arms, nearly lifting her feet off the ground. She stumbled slightly as he set her back on her feet, then murmured in her ear. "That's what I call a hug."

"For goodness' sake. Do your sisters do that, too?" She threw back her head to see his face. He was already bending down, so they found themselves so close their noses nearly brushed. His eyes captured hers, causing them both to still. She swallowed. She could have sworn his eyes dropped to her lips, then immediately danced away. He released her. "No. Not exactly. We'd better get going. We don't want to be late."

Sean couldn't help stealing a sideways glance at Lorelei as the buggy approached his family's farm. She'd hardly spoken since their hug. Perhaps that was for the best. He wasn't sure what to say, either. He'd wanted to make sure she was comfortable with him before they faced their first test as a couple. He hadn't planned on the sudden vulnerability their closeness unleashed in her eyes. In that moment, he'd wanted to assure her that everything would be all right. That he'd never hurt her. He'd wanted to kiss her.

He pulled in beside the other vehicles and set the brake with a bit more force than necessary. *Keep yourself in check, O'Brien. You can be her friend. You can protect her. You can even marry her, but don't start letting your heart get in the way of your head. Remember who she is and what she's like. If you let yourself care for her too deeply, she'll only let you down.*

Ellie must have spotted them coming because she hurried across the yard toward them. As soon as he helped Lorelei down from the buggy, his little sister embraced her in a hug. "I'm so glad you could make it."

Lorelei managed to give her a decent hug in return. "Thank you! So am I. I hope we aren't late."

Ellie waved away her concern. "Oh, don't worry about that. There is no real time structure to this. We just wanted to give everyone a chance to socialize with each other."

Ellie promptly turned to give his chest a playful little punch in greeting. He absorbed the harmless blow by pulling his sister into his arms for a quick hug. "Is everyone here?"

"No, we're still waiting on a few others to arrive."

Lorelei glanced at Sean then cleared her throat. "Ellie, there is something Sean needs to tell you."

He placed a stilling hand on her shoulder. "It's all right, Lorelei. My family knows the truth about us."

Ellie nodded. "We certainly do. I told him I think it's romantic."

Her gaze flew to him in surprise. "Romantic?"

"There's no accounting for taste," he said with a shrug.

Ellie only smiled in response to their protests. "Lorelei, now that you're practically family, you're welcome to come here anytime you like. There's always plenty to do. We can go riding, wading, anything you like."

"Thank you, Ellie. Maybe I will."

"I hope so."

Sean and Lorelei followed Ellie through the few people who stood outside the house in groups of twos and threes. He felt tension rise in Lorelei's shoulders as they drew nearer to the door. His hand landed in a proprietary touch near the back of her waist. She stiffened for a moment but managed to relax by the time they stepped into the house. He glanced around and was relieved to find that since the house was crowded no one seemed to notice that they entered together. He smiled wryly. *Honestly, did I expect the entire room to stop what they were doing to gasp and stare?*

Someone called Ellie's name. The girl sent them an apologetic smile and promised to return quickly before she set off across the room to a group of young women. It took him a moment to realize that he was practically pushing Lorelei along because she'd stopped moving forward almost completely. He glanced down to find her worrying her bottom lip as she scanned the crowd with a slightly lost look on her face. He pulled her closer to ask at a volume only she could hear, "Are you all right?"

She straightened. "Yes. I just got a little intimidated for a moment. I haven't seen some of these people since the wedding. Now I'm showing up here with you only a month later. What will they think?"

"We can't control that. We can only control what we do. We said we were ready. Now we have to prove it. All right?" He waited until she nodded before he ushered her toward the kitchen. "Come on. Let's find Kate."

Sean immediately spotted his cinnamon-haired older sister laughing with Mrs. Lettie as the two finished preparing the food. He snuck up beside his sister, then darted around her to kiss her cheek. Kate jumped, then grinned at him even as she shook her head in exasperation. "What if I'd accidentally stabbed you with my knife?"

"You would have sewn me right back up. Isn't that right, Mrs. Lettie?"

The doctor's wife who'd been their mother's closest friend barely glanced up from playing with her three-year-old honorary grand-niece. "I learned a long time ago not to get drawn into sibling squabbles."

Kate set aside her knife to welcome Lorelei with a smile. "Lorelei, Ellie told me you were coming. I'd hug you but my hands are a bit messy. I'm glad you came."

"Thank you for inviting me," Lorelei said graciously, then greeted Lawson's adoptive mother, Mrs. Lettie Williams, with an easy familiarity. "Is there anything I can help with?"

"There isn't much left to do, but if you want to wash your hands and put on an apron I certainly won't stop you." Kate nodded over to where a spare apron hung on a hook. "Sean will tie it for you, won't you, Sean?"

Before he could respond his nephew tugged at his arm. Sean glanced down, then sent Kate a sly grin. He caught the boy by the waist and threw him up into the air before catching him and setting him safely on the ground. The little boy let out a whoop of joy and begged Sean to do it again.

"Later. Right now, I want you to meet someone." Sean looked up from the child to meet Lorelei's gaze. "This is my nephew, Timothy. Say hello, Timothy."

The boy grinned at Lorelei and leaned back onto Sean's leg. "Hello, Timothy."

Lorelei laughed. "Hello, yourself. I'm Lorelei."

Sean poked his nephew slightly in the ribs. "That's Miss Lorelei to you."

He watched as Lorelei tilted her head conspiratorially to capture the boy's dark brown eyes. "How old are you, Timothy?"

"I'm seven," he stated proudly, then pointed across the room at the little girl sitting on Miss Lettie's lap. "That's Baby Grace. She's little."

Lorelei nodded. "I see that. She's your sister, right?"

"Yes, ma'am." The boy stepped away from Sean to get closer to Lorelei. "I have another sister. She's with Pa. Her name's Hope. I think she's four."

Sean placed a hand on Timothy's dark brown hair, and the boy looked up at him. "Hope is five."

"Right," Timothy said then looked back at Lorelei. "Hope is five but I'm seven."

"I remember."

"Do you want to play with me?"

Lorelei hesitated, then glanced at the other adults in the room as though to ask if it was all right. Kate shook her head. "Timothy, Lorelei just got here. Why don't you give her some time to talk to the grown-ups, then maybe she can play with you later?"

"Yes, ma'am," he agreed but whispered loudly to Lorelei, "There's a bunch of us kids outside. You can play with us when you get bored with the grown-ups, all right?"

She nodded seriously. "That sounds like a good plan."

Ellie breezed into the kitchen just as Timothy left. "The girls want to get a closer look at your dress, Lorelei. Will you come with me?"

Lorelei lifted the apron in her hand. "I can't. I promised Kate I'd help with the food."

"Oh, that's all right. You go on." Kate urged, then turned to Sean with twinkling eyes. "I'll make Sean help me. He can wear the apron."

"I'll help but I'm not wearing the apron," he warned as Lorelei and Ellie left. As he washed his hands in the sink, he suddenly became aware of the palpable silence in the room. He glanced over his shoulder to find that Miss Lettie had left him alone with his sister. "What?"

"I like her."

He dried his hands on the apron, then put it away. "I'm glad. That's a slightly different Lorelei than the one I'm used to."

"In what way?"

"She's nicer, friendlier..." He shrugged. "Did you see how well she got along with Timothy? Her eyes just sort of came alive."

She handed him a knife to help her cut up apples. "I noticed that. Maybe she seems different because she's in a different setting. Or, maybe you were just slightly wrong about her."

He spared her a quick glance. "Maybe."

Chapter Eleven

Lorelei deftly tied a wide piece of bright blue ribbon into a dainty bow, then pinned it onto the crown of a wide-brimmed straw bonnet. This hat would be just perfect for Ellie. Lorelei smiled as she thought about the hours she'd spent with Sean's family on Saturday. They'd been so warm and welcoming. By the time she'd left, she'd become much better friends with both of Sean's sisters. She'd taken a tour of the horse ranch from his brother-in-law, Nathan, and even had had time to play with his nieces and nephew.

It made sitting in the back room of the millinery shop seem almost boring by comparison. It was Monday and her day to work, so she needed to stop daydreaming before she fell behind on her quota. She stashed her bright white handkerchief in her dress pocket before she made her way from the workroom to the front of the store. Mrs. Cummings glanced up with a smile when Lorelei entered. "Watch the front, Lorelei. I'm going to make a deposit."

"Yes, ma'am," Lorelei agreed as the woman tucked a small mound of money into her reticule and hurried out the door.

Lorelei turned her attention to the window display she had been working on. She paused to survey the assortment of hats in the window before she placed the one with the blue ribbon near the middle. Just as she hoped, the bright blue ribbon added color to the display and made the entire window more attention-grabbing.

She smiled, feeling a sense of accomplishment. She'd managed to keep this job for more than a week. That was longer than she'd tended the rose garden. What's more, she was actually good at this, which was why her bakery idea hadn't exactly taken off. She was committed to keeping this job if only to prove that she could.

The bell above the door chimed, and Amy Bradley walked in on the arm of none other than Mr. Smithson. Lorelei steeled herself with a smile as she welcomed the young woman who had been her good friend in school. Though the two had drifted slightly apart since then due to Amy's responsibilities at her family's boardinghouse, they tried to maintain their friendly ties whenever it was convenient. After inquiring about Lorelei's parents, Amy introduced her to Mr. Smithson. The man greeted her politely before recognition sparked a gleam of curiosity in his brown eyes. "Miss Wilkins and I have already met."

Amy sent Lorelei a confused glance. "You have?"

"Well, yes," Lorelei said blithely. "He helped me free my heel from that broken piece of sidewalk by the bank. I didn't know he was your Mr. Smithson at the time."

Amy blushed mightily and gave a subtle shake of her head. Lorelei quickly turned the conversation to another subject entirely. "As you can see, we sell a large variety of ready-made hats for men and women. However, we do encourage that you personalize the hat to better reflect your personality. We can do that by making subtle changes to the ready-made hats or we can help you design your own."

"That sounds fun."

"It really is." She glanced at Mr. Smithson, who was studying her intently. "We don't offer to design hats for men, but we do have a specialty catalog you can look through if you'd like. With the railroad coming through town, shipping is quick once we take the measurements and send out the orders."

He agreed to look at the catalog while Amy attempted to try on nearly every item in the store. Lorelei attended to her, sensing the young woman might actually be looking to buy something. Every now and then Lorelei would glance back over to where Mr. Smithson stood and find him already looking at her in that unnerving way of his. If his attentions were any indication, he had not been convinced by her act outside the alley. That meant she had to take control of the situation, just as she and Sean had planned.

She didn't have much time. Mrs. Cummings would be back from the bank in a few minutes. She needed to do something now. Amy was having trouble deciding between two hats, so Lorelei left her alone to think and moved closer to Mr. Smithson. She gathered her courage to set her plan into motion. "Is there anything I can help you with?"

"Perhaps," he said without looking up. "I think you know more than you're letting on."

She swallowed. "About men's hats?"

He glanced up in amusement but said nothing more.

Lord, help me to do this right. She glanced nervously at Amy who was busy trying on a third hat in one of the store's mirrors. She gave Mr. Smithson a significant look and hoped the right words would follow. "As a matter of fact, I do tend to see and hear more on some subjects than you would imagine. With my father being the president of Peppin's bank, hearing something about that would draw my interest."

"I thought so." He shot a glance toward Amy as the young woman moseyed over.

Lorelei smiled at her, then turned her attention back to Mr. Smithson. Feeling more in control of herself and the conversation, she continued, "I think fashion, especially hats, communicate a lot about a person."

"What do you mean, Lorelei?" Amy asked with a curious tilt of her head.

"Take, for instance, the bowler hat Mr. Smithson came in wearing." She dared to lift it from where it rested on the countertop to survey it carefully. "It's different from the Stetson most men around here wear, so it tells others that he's a stranger. It also shows that he's a businessman." She tilted her head thoughtfully. "You're a man with a plan, aren't you, Mr. Smithson? I'd bet the plan is going to involve a lot of money."

He sent Amy an amused glance that hardened when he looked at Lorelei. "You saw that in my hat, too, did you?"

"Certainly," she said. "It was easy to tell that from the quality of the hat."

Amy shook her head. "Lorelei, you're a wonder. Tell her, Silas. She's exactly right, isn't she? Mr. Smithson is an investor."

"Really? What sort of investing are you doing in our little town? We hardly have much to offer other than land. You're rather late to invest in that. I'm afraid the railroad already passed through, and those who had land along the rail line cashed in long ago."

"I work for the railroad."

"Oh, a railroad investor," she said, challenging the legitimacy of his statement more for Amy's sake than anything else. "What exactly does a railroad investor do?"

"Really, miss. I'm just passing through." He turned to Amy. "Are you about done here?"

"Yes, Silas."

"I'll wait for you outside."

He brushed past Lorelei. They watched him walk outside, then Amy turned to Lorelei with a glare. "Honestly, Lorelei. What were you trying to do?"

She lifted one shoulder in a shrug. "Well, I wasn't trying to chase him away."

"That's for sure," Amy huffed.

She stiffened. "What do you mean by that?"

"Nothing," Amy said then amended, "It's just that if I didn't have it on good authority you and Sean were courting, I'd think you were trying to show me up with Silas."

"Goodness, no! I'm not the least bit interested in Mr. Smithson."

"Good," she said with a huff, then frowned. "Well, if you weren't flirting, what in heaven's name were you doing?"

"I was just letting him know that someone is watching out for you." She almost said "this town" but caught herself in time. "I don't trust him, Amy. Be careful."

"That's a fine thing to say about someone you only just met. Perhaps I'd better go." Amy placed the hat on the counter and hurried to the door. She stopped in the door to give Lorelei a wave that said they were parting as friends before she turned and almost ran into Mrs. Cummings.

Mrs. Cummings watched the girl leave before eying

the bonnet Amy left on the counter. "What was that all about?"

"A difference in opinions," Lorelei said as she turned to walk into the workroom. She eyed the table strewn with feathers and ribbon, then closed her eyes. Smithson knew that she was wise to him. That much was obvious. She wished she'd been able to gain a clearer idea of what he was going to do about it.

Lorelei sat down and tried to sort the supplies into some sort of order. Feathers began floating in the air. She pulled out her handkerchief to cover her irritated nose from that onslaught when something fell from her pocket onto the floor. She reached for the folded piece of paper. Unfolding it, she stared at the words printed neatly on a scrap torn from a page in the catalog. She smoothed the folds out of the paper as she read it just above a whisper. "Say nothing. Do nothing. I'll contact you."

Sean slipped the scrap of catalog paper Lorelei had given him during her lunch break into an envelope. He sealed it, then placed in it the slim file he'd collected on the investigation. He knew Silas Smithson was up to no good, but Lorelei hadn't been able to provide any description of the other man in the alleyway that day. Sean was sure it must have been Calhoun. Unfortunately, he couldn't prove that or anything else about this investigation. Hence the nearly empty file.

He locked the file in his equally empty bottom desk drawer and frowned. Regardless of the lack of evidence, Sean couldn't get rid of the uneasy feeling in the pit of his stomach. He was running out of ideas, and he was running out of time. Lorelei was his only chance to break open the case. So far she'd done admirably well.

He hated to ask more of her or place her in any more danger, but it was beginning to look as if that might be necessary.

Lawson provided a welcome distraction when he stepped into the sheriff's office. Sean stood to greet his friend and eyed the man's large suitcase. "I'd ask how it's going but I think the better question might be *where* are you going?"

Lawson set the suitcase down on a nearby chair. "I'm going to Austin. Nathan talked to one of his contacts with the Rangers and they're giving me a chance at a job."

Sean took a moment to process this, then gave a low whistle. "The Rangers? That's a great opportunity, but are you sure you want to go?"

He chuckled. "Would I be leaving if I wasn't sure?"

"Guess not." He leaned back onto his desk and crossed his arms. "How long are you planning to be gone?"

"At least a couple of months. I'll try to come back whenever I get a break." He smiled sheepishly. "Look at me talking like I already have the job."

"You'll get it," he said with quiet certainty.

"Thanks for that." Lawson shifted uncomfortably, then met Sean's gaze and held out a hand. "Seriously, thanks for everything."

Sean shook his hand. "You're welcome, but that sounds a little too final to me."

He shrugged. "Well, I've said all of my goodbyes, so I guess this is it."

"Have you seen Lorelei?"

"Yes, she wished me the best."

"So do I."

"I told her what I'll tell you." He grinned slyly. "I'd

wish the same to you, but you already have the best. You're just too stubborn to see it. You know I think she made the right choice, ending things between us. I hope you don't hold a grudge for my sake."

Sean made a noncommittal sound in reply. He wasn't quite ready to let go of that grudge yet, and he didn't want to lie to his best friend. Lawson shook his head at him but seemed to accept that. "I also made a deal with her," he continued. "One I'd like to make with you, too. I'll pray for you if you pray for me. How about it, Sean?"

"It's a deal." He held out his hand, and Lawson shook it firmly.

"I'd better go so I won't miss my train. Doc and Mrs. Lettie are waiting to see me off."

Sean nodded. "I know you'll do us proud but you're always welcome home."

"I'll make y'all proud." Lawson hefted his duffle bag onto his shoulder and paused at the door to tip his Stetson. Then he was gone.

Lorelei opened the door to the boardinghouse a few days later with a bouquet of yellow roses to make amends with Amy for their little misunderstanding at the millinery shop. She was also prepared to deal with Silas Smithson should she happen to run into him. She glanced around the large two-story's foyer for some sort of direction.

She followed a sign's instructions to ring the bell at the front desk for service. Amy appeared from around the corner. "Lorelei!"

"Hello, Amy. I'm sorry to bother you, but I wanted to bring by some of my roses. I hope you'll forgive me for the way I behaved in the millinery."

Amy took the flowers Lorelei extended to her with a smile. "Of course, I forgive you, silly. I thought we'd cleared up that misunderstanding already. Thank you for the flowers. They're beautiful. Now, I don't mean to be rude, but a whole bunch of new boarders just checked in and I've got to help Ma."

"Don't let me keep you." Lorelei received Amy's hug before the girl hurried off to do her chores. She opened the door and nearly ran into someone who was entering. She glanced up directly into the eyes of Silas Smithson. "Oh, excuse me."

His surprise gave way to a pleased grin. "Miss Wilkins, how fortunate. I was just thinking that I should visit you in the millinery and here you are practically on my doorstep."

Lord, help me to do this right if it's Your will, she prayed, though trepidation sent her pulse jumping. He followed her down the steps. She pulled in a deep breath. "What did you want to discuss?"

He tilted his hat to another boarder who passed them. "A present for Amy, of course. Don't let me hold you up. I can walk with you a ways."

She glanced at him in wry amusement. "Was that a joke? 'Don't let me hold you up.'"

He held her gaze, then looked around before steering her toward the quieter area of town by the courthouse. "Since you obviously know what I want, why don't you tell me what you want? I assume you want something. Otherwise, you would have already alerted the sheriff."

All right, Lord, here goes. She braced herself. "I want in."

"You want in," he repeated incredulously. "Tell me why you, of all people, would want anything to do with this."

She tried to dredge up some of the desperation she'd felt weeks ago. She found it really wasn't that hard, especially since she'd rehearsed it in front of her mirror. "I'm tired of the memories, the murmurs and the men. I want out of this town. This is going to pay for my ticket and my new life."

He scoffed. "Why not just ask your dear old papa for the money you need? He obviously has plenty of it."

"You really are new to this town, aren't you?" She laughed, then slowly transformed her face to a scowl. "I ran away from this town a few weeks ago. I got as far as the Texas border before 'dear old papa' got the sheriff to drag me back here kicking and screaming. He's not suddenly going to have a change of heart."

He gave her a skeptical glance. "Ah, yes. I heard you're on pretty good terms now with that same sheriff who brought you home kicking and screaming."

She sighed. "I'm just keeping Papa happy until I can make my move."

"You're willing to rob your own father for a ticket out of this quaint little place?"

She glared at him. "I'm not planning to rob him. You are. I see no reason why you can't cut me a small take of that big Peppin safe in exchange for some information."

That caught his attention just as she and Sean had thought it would. "You'd sell me information?"

She nodded as she tried to maintain her composure when she could hardly believe what she was proposing. She swallowed. She'd gone too far with this to back down now. "Yes, for the right price."

"What if I refuse?"

She stopped to look at him. "Well, Silas. Let me put it this way. I'm prepared to make this process easy for you or I'm prepared to make it a lot more complicated. There is no in-between."

He lifted a brow coldly. "I could kill you and be done with it."

Sean had thought of that, too. She was ready with an answer. "Sure, but that wouldn't get you any closer to robbing that bank. Besides, this is too small a town for you to get away with something like that. Are you willing to exchange bankrolls for a murder charge?"

"They'd probably just think you ran away again. No one would even look for you."

"Of course they would. Besides, I thought you were a gentleman. I doubt you'd want a lady's death on your conscience," she said. *If he has a conscience, which I can't be entirely sure of,* she realized but continued confidently, "Really, why go through all that trouble when having me on your side would make things so much easier?"

"All right. You're in at three percent. You won't get a penny more, so don't ask for it. You'll keep quiet and do as I say. Don't ask questions. I'll tell you what you need to know. Is that clear?"

She hid a frown at his command not to ask questions since her job was to do exactly that. However, she decided it was best not to push him on their first meeting. She nodded. "Completely."

He shook his head as if he couldn't believe he was agreeing to it, then he smiled. "Welcome aboard, Miss Wilkins. It's going to be quite a ride. I'll contact you again soon. Be ready."

"Be careful how and when you contact me, Mr. Smithson. I have a reputation to uphold," she reminded him. He nodded, then tipped his hat and left her to circle back toward the boardinghouse. She continued toward

Main Street alone. She paused across the street from the bank to stare at it while she gathered her thoughts. She shook her head and whispered, "Well, I did it, Lord. Now what?"

Chapter Twelve

A satisfied smile tilted Lorelei's lips as she followed Ellie through the woods the next day. Her spur-of-the-moment decision to take Ellie up on her invitation to visit anytime had resulted in a wonderful day and an exciting new friendship. She glanced down to survey herself and shook her head. "If my mother could see me now, she'd faint."

Ellie glanced back at her curiously. "What? Why?"

"Just look at me." She stopped to exhibit herself. "My hands are red from washing clothes. My fingernails are stained purple from picking blackberries. I have a bruise on my arm from falling off a horse. I'm drenched from head to toe because you pushed me in when we went wading."

Ellie rolled her eyes unsympathetically. "You tripped and fell in. That's hardly my fault."

"That's your story and you're sticking to it, but I'm not buying what you're selling."

Ellie wrinkled her nose at Lorelei, then lifted her chin to curb a smile. "You may as well admit it, Lorelei. You…had…fun!"

"I certainly did." She exchanged a grin with Ellie,

then looked more closely at the young woman and sing-songed, "You've been eating berries. Your teeth are purple."

Ellie's eyes widened as she guiltily pressed her lips together. "Well, don't look so smug, Miss Wilkins, so are yours."

"What?" She covered her mouth with her hand and groaned. "It's getting worse by the minute."

Ellie giggled. "Do you know what will make it better? A race."

Lorelei laughed. "You didn't even give me time to ask."

"First one to the house without spilling their berries gets to freshen up first."

"I don't know, Ellie— *Go!*" She rushed through the woods toward the house, keeping a careful eye on her bucket.

"Cheaters never win!" Ellie yelled from a few paces behind her. Lorelei lengthened the distance between them in long, smooth strides. She rounded the corner of the barn and stopped abruptly when she came face-to-face with Sean.

"Lorelei," he said in startled amusement.

She began to respond, then remembered to clench her lips together at the last second. She slowly became aware of the awful picture she must make. Suddenly Ellie shot past them with a triumphant laugh. The race! Lorelei sprang into motion once more with nothing more than a backward glance at her befuddled husband-to-be. She burst into the kitchen only seconds behind Ellie. Kate glanced up from her mending at their abrupt entrance but otherwise didn't bat an eye at their appearance. Apparently, this sort of thing wasn't un-usual around the O'Brien house.

"I won!" Ellie declared.

"No fair. I ran into Sean."

"You certainly did," Ellie said with a teasing purple smile.

Lorelei laughed. "At least I remembered not to smile. I guess that means you get first dibs on freshening up."

Ellie shrugged. "That's all right. I'm used to the grime. You go on. Anything in my wardrobe is fair game. Just keep in mind that you'll probably get dirty again."

She frowned. "I don't see how."

"Ellie seems to attract messes, so you can't go by her. Although it is good advice with three children running around here," Kate suggested. "Besides, you'll want to be comfortable at dinner."

"Oh, I wasn't planning to stay. I mean I don't want to put y'all out. I've been here most of the day already."

Kate set aside her mending to check on the stew she was cooking. "Don't be silly. Now hurry upstairs unless you want Sean to get a better look at you."

It wasn't long before she'd cleaned up and changed into a simple blue blouse and navy skirt. She helped Hope set the table while Kate put the finishing touches on dinner and Ellie kept three-year-old Grace occupied. Nathan, Timothy and Sean soon filed inside. Sean washed his hands, then nonchalantly meandered over to take the seat beside her. "I was surprised to see you here but Nathan says you've been here most of the day and even helped him with the horses."

She fiddled with her napkin. "I thought you were working."

"Today is my day off. I always come home for dinner."

Lorelei glanced from him to his sister. "Ellie didn't tell me that."

"No," he said with a chuckle. "She wouldn't."

Ellie pretended not to hear them, though she would've had to have been deaf not to as she slid into a chair across from them. "We just keep adding more chairs to the table."

"And more table to the table," Nathan added as he took his seat at the head of the table. "That's a good thing."

"It certainly is." Kate made sure her children were settled, then glanced at Sean. "Let's say grace."

Sean bowed his head. "Lord, thank You for the food and those who prepared it. We especially want to thank You for our unexpected company. Amen."

"Amen," Lorelei echoed along with everyone else, then glanced up at him. He smiled and handed her the mashed potatoes as dishes of food began circling the table. "What were y'all saying about chairs? I didn't quite understand."

Kate's gaze swept around the table. "When our parents died they left two empty chairs at the table. Nathan filled one when he came. Lawson filled the other while he lived with us. Since then we've been adding chairs. One each for Timothy, Hope, Grace, and now there's one for you."

It took a moment for her to gather her voice. "Thank you. I'm honored."

"I wish my parents could have known you," Sean said without looking up from his plate.

"They would have liked you," Kate said, but Lorelei couldn't glance away from Sean when he finally met her gaze.

"I wish I could have known your parents, too." she said softly.

Ellie smiled. "It's all right. You'll meet them one day."

Lorelei nodded, then sat back to watch the O'Brien family interact with each other and Sean. He seemed to drop the mantle of responsibility just enough to enjoy dinner with his family, but she could still sense his tension. Or, maybe that was from her being there. She glanced around the table, then looked down at her food to hide her rising emotions. She'd never imagined his family would be so open, kind and accepting. They all knew the truth about her relationship with Sean but they didn't seem to care.

Sean's left hand strayed behind her to give a comforting rub to her back without his family's notice. She glanced at him in surprise, then looked away as he drew his hand back. Who was this man? He was more relaxed. More gentle. More himself? She was starting to like him. That was fine. Like was a long way from love. Wasn't it?

The stars stretched across the expansive Texas sky above where Sean settled on the thick, moist grass an hour later. His hands cushioned the back of his head. He could hear the soft undistinguishable murmur of Ellie's voice as she talked to Hope and Timothy a good distance away. Lorelei stirred beside him. Her hand lifted, tracing out patterns he'd shown her in the constellations before she let it drop to her chest. He turned his head to look at her. "How long have you been here exactly?"

"My father dropped me off this afternoon. He was going to pick me up in an hour, but Nathan insisted he'd take me home when I was ready and that was the end of that," she answered softly. "I like it here. It's peaceful, simple, uncomplicated. Do you think the sky will look this big from our place?"

"It should." He turned to look at the sky again. He just couldn't get over how well she fit into his family. The children loved her because she played with them. Kate seemed to appreciate the way Lorelei was always willing to help out. Nathan obviously liked being able to explain his business and talk about his horses to someone who hadn't heard him say it all a thousand times already. Ellie seemed to have found a new best friend. As for him, well, he wasn't sure what he thought about it yet. He wasn't sure what he thought about her anymore for that matter.

"Sean?"

"Yes."

"I talked to Silas yesterday."

He smiled. "I know. I saw you in the courtyard out my office window."

"Oh." She sat up and hugged her legs to her chest. "I told him I wanted in. He let me on the team—"

"Into the gang," he corrected with a smile.

"—under the condition that I help out and keep quiet," she finished. "I convinced him that I wanted in for an opportunity to get out of this town. He believed me."

"That's funny. I would have believed it, too," he said as he sat up. "In fact it sounds—"

"Strangely familiar, I know." She smiled almost cheekily in the moonlight. "That's why it worked so well. Oh! The funniest part is that I told him you were just a pawn in my scheme to keep Papa happy."

"Oh, yeah. That's really funny."

She smothered her mirth but not before a laugh slipped out. "I'm sorry."

"You should be, but I don't think you are."

"He said he'd contact me soon."

"I figured." He heaved out a sigh. "Well, it's pretty obvious that you have to continue. Don't look so excited. You're going to have to abide by my ground rules since this is an official investigation. You'll have to let me know when he contacts you and the specifics of what is said. If he threatens you, you will let me know immediately. I reserve the right to pull you off the investigation at any time but especially if I feel you're in danger. Is that understood?"

"Yes."

"If you happen to think of this as a lark or a game or anything other than a life-and-death situation, you should shed those notions right now. We aren't entirely sure who or what we're dealing with, but we do know that Smithson is dangerous. You could get hurt or killed."

She met his gaze soberly. "I understand that."

He surveyed her for any sign of fear but didn't find any. He nodded. "Good. When you meet with him, there is certain information you can give and certain information you need to try to get."

"Shouldn't I write this down?"

"No. I want you to memorize it." He placed his elbows on his knees and leaned toward her. "If Smithson is working with someone else, and we know he is, then I can arrest him and his partner or partners before they ever set foot in the bank on the charge of conspiracy to commit an armed robbery. That means they agreed to carry out the robbery, then took some action toward doing so. We're looking for evidence in the form of things like layouts of the bank, the date the robbery is going to take place, getaway plans, anything like that. You can draw that material out by advising them on all of it."

She frowned. "But should I really tell the truth about that? What if they actually get away with it?"

"They won't because we won't let them," he said seriously. "Tell them the truth. We don't know how much information they already have, and we don't want to let them think you're double-crossing them in any way. We'll have to see how deep they let you into their plans. So far you've been pretty clever about all of this. Keep your wits about you, and I think you'll do all right."

She leaned back, bracing her hands behind her, and tilted her head. "Was that a vote of confidence I just heard?"

"It certainly was."

"My, oh, my. What an unusual day this has been. Maybe it's time for me to go home. I don't know how much of this I can take."

Neither do I, he thought at the sight of her smiling like that with the backdrop of a million twinkling stars. "I'll get the horses."

Chapter Thirteen

Lorelei became intensely aware of the hand Sean had tucked into the crook of his arm when Mrs. Greene's gaze landed there. Rather than pass them on the sidewalk, Mrs. Greene stopped to smile at them. "You two seem to be holding up admirably well. I'm sure this must be quite a strain on you to pretend feelings you don't have."

Lorelei's eyes widened, and she glanced around to make sure no one was in hearing distance. Relieved that no one was, she realized she had no idea how to respond to the woman's statement. She was grateful when Sean changed the subject. "We'd both like to thank you again for being so considerate about this."

"Well, as Mrs. Wilkins said, there's no way to prove you did wrong just like there is no way to prove you did right. I love telling a good story as much as the next person, but I'm not out to ruin anyone's reputation needlessly." She dabbed her handkerchief across her brow. "I'm still holding y'all to the wedding ceremony. If you don't go through with it, the deal is off."

"We know," Lorelei said quietly.

"Your courtship is getting more believable, but

something is still a little peculiar. I'd know that even if folks weren't telling me. You'd better fix that or people might start asking questions and I might not catch myself before answering." The woman's eyes strayed back to Lorelei's hand before she nodded a farewell. "Y'all have a good day now."

As soon as the woman passed, Lorelei released her hand from Sean's arm under the pretense of staring into the display window of Sew Wonderful Tailoring. She caught a glimpse of her reflection in the store's window and carefully smoothed a lock of hair back into place. Her moment of respite came to an abrupt end when Sean stepped up beside her. "I don't know what else to do to make this more believable."

"Neither do I."

"I'll think of something," he said before they continued on.

He'd invited her on this walk. In the spirit of their new, tentative state of truce, she had agreed, but she'd hoped Sean would make this a short venture. She didn't like the feeling of being on display. A sideways glance at his expression almost made her sigh in discouragement. He looked perfectly content to mosey along hardly making any progress. His slow pace might actually convince someone he wanted to spend every moment he could with her. She knew it was only part of the show. She just wished that fact didn't bother her so much. He touched her waist to indicate they should cross the street. "Have you had any contact with Smithson?"

"I haven't seen nor heard a word from him since last week. He's making me nervous. What do you think he's waiting for?"

"It could be any number of things," he said as he led her to the gazebo the town had built halfway between the church and the schoolyard. "He could be waiting for someone to arrive. He could have decided against going through with it, though that is highly unlikely. He could be waiting to see if you're serious enough to contact him again."

They slowly mounted the stairs to the empty gazebo. "So what do I do?"

"Give him a little while longer. We'll try to stick to our original plan, and if he doesn't come through, we'll figure something else out." He sat near the end of the wooden bench that followed the curve of the gazebo. His gaze strayed from hers to rest on the schoolhouse. "You've made quite an impression on my family. Almost a week has passed, and they're still talking about you, especially Timothy."

An unbidden smile rose to her lips. "They were sweet and Timothy was adorable."

"You seem to make a good impression on children, Lorelei."

"I guess I do," she said, thinking about her rapport with the Brightly children. "I can't for the life of me figure out why."

He frowned at her self-derisive comment. "I don't think it's too hard to figure out. You let down your guard when you're with them."

Her eyes flashed to his suspiciously. "What does that mean?"

"You're different somehow. Maybe it's because you know they won't hurt you. I've watched you. You suddenly become more charming and clever and interesting. Your eyes even start to twinkle."

She crossed her arms. "I think I should be offended by that comment."

"Don't be."

"Why are you telling me this?"

"Because I'm beginning to think you aren't exactly who you've presented yourself to be—at least, not to me."

She couldn't look away for a long breathless moment. Finally, she stood and turned away from him to lean against the gazebo railing that looked out toward the schoolhouse. She could almost see herself as a child slipping away from her friends in the playground to confidently tell the boy she loved that she'd marry him one day. It hadn't even crossed her mind that he wouldn't feel the same way. His disgust had taken her aback, and the schoolchildren's incessant teasing for weeks had kept the wound from healing as it should.

She'd learned a valuable lesson. Love wasn't something that should be boldly exposed but rather hidden away for protection. Somehow in hiding that she'd hidden away so much more. She'd hidden part of herself.

She suddenly realized Sean had joined her. He caught her arm to guide her away from the railing, so she faced him. He looked searchingly over her features. "I think I figured out what's missing from our courtship, Lorelei. It's you, isn't it?"

She allowed her gaze to drop to their feet.

He sighed. "Maybe that's for the best."

She glanced up in sharp inquiry.

He shrugged. "The woman I glimpsed playing with my nephew, having dinner with my family and racing across the barnyard with my sister wasn't just downright beautiful. She was practically irresistible. I don't think either of us are ready to handle that, are we?"

She tensed and stepped back. "No."

He picked up the Stetson from where he'd dropped it on the gazebo bench. "I think I'd better get you home."

* * *

Lorelei desperately tried to focus on her job to put yesterday's conversation with Sean out of her mind, but she'd discovered a problem. She couldn't breathe. At least, she couldn't breathe normally. She concentrated on pulling even breaths through her lips as she placed one hat aside to look at the request for another. Orders for hats had come rushing in after a few of her designs had been seen around Peppin. Lorelei took special care in designing the hats so they would live up to the expectations of the new customers. But it was hard to concentrate on sartorial brilliance when she could barely breathe. Mainly, she just wanted to live past her shift.

She glanced around the lonely workroom and sighed. "Lord, I so wanted to prove that I could stick to something, but this is just awful. The feathers are simply everywhere—in the air, on the table. I even find them in my hair when I get home. I don't understand. Really, I don't. They just seem to multiply."

She opened her eyes to stare at the fragments of feathers lying on the table. She had hoped that her body would get use to them after a while. Instead of getting better, she seemed to be getting worse. She hadn't noticed how much worse until this morning. She closed her eyes a moment to gather herself. "Well, so much for that."

Tucking her handkerchief back into her pocket, she marched the few feet to Mrs. Cummings's office. Mrs. Cummings glanced up from her books. "Yes, Lorelei?"

Lorelei opened the door farther and stepped in the room.

The woman's eyes widened. "Your face is remarkably red."

She reached up a hand to touch her warm cheek. "Is it?"

"Are you all right?"

"No. I'm afraid not. I can't tell you how sorry I am. I will have to leave early today." She took a moment to gather her breath, then shook her head. "I appreciate this opportunity, but I will not be coming back."

"I was expecting that."

"You were?"

"This is your last check." Mrs. Cummings took an envelope from her desk and handed it to Lorelei. "I was going to let you go at the end of the day."

"Oh," Lorelei breathed.

"Child, I've never heard anyone sneeze so much in my life." The woman gave a firm nod. "As wonderful as your work has been, I, for one, am glad you came to your senses. Promise me you'll go see Doc Williams right away."

"Yes, ma'am, I will." She didn't bother to smile. She gathered her hat and reticule from the workroom before hurrying out the door. It slammed shut behind her with a plaintive ring of its bell. She'd hoped the fresh air would help, but the air was humid and she felt even more uncomfortable.

"Lorelei!"

She glanced up from her boots at the sound of someone cheerily calling her name. She lifted her lips into a weak smile as Ellie fell in step beside her. "Ellie, I'm sorry. I've got to get to Doc's."

Ellie's large green eyes widened as they traced Lorelei's features. "Heavens, you look as if you might faint."

Lorelei shook her head. "I'll be fine. I'm just allergic to the feathers I've been working with."

"At least wait a minute to catch your breath." She

pulled Lorelei to a stop, then glanced around in a mix of frustration and concern. "Now, where did Sean go? There he is."

"Please," Lorelei said as kindly as she could while she removed Ellie's detaining hand and tried not to panic. She continued on by herself for a moment before a strong arm slipped beneath hers to offer support. She glanced up into Sean's concerned gaze.

"Let me carry you to Doc's."

She immediately shook her head. "It isn't that bad."

Ellie stepped up to the other side of her. "Please, Lorelei. We don't know what's wrong, but we want to help. Let him carry you. You'll get there faster."

She glanced toward the bank. "If Father sees—"

"He won't," Sean promised. "I know a back way that's shorter."

She nodded, then followed Sean off the sidewalk to the narrow alleyway behind the businesses with Ellie at her side. Sean immediately lifted her into his arms. Her arms instinctively went around his shoulders while embarrassment caused her to turn her face into his neck. She caught her breath enough to murmur, "I don't think this is necessary."

"A lot of things aren't necessary in life, Lorelei," he said quietly. "That doesn't mean you should do without them."

"Things like allowing others to care for you when you're in need," Ellie said firmly. Glancing over her shoulder at the two of them, she smiled. "And things like love. It may not be as necessary as the air you breathe or the water you drink, but a life without love is hardly worth living."

Lorelei lowered her brow in confusion.

"Ellie, this is not the time," Sean said with a bit of

exasperation. "Run ahead and tell Doc we're coming, will you?"

Ellie's eyes flashed Sean a silent message Lorelei couldn't quite decipher before she lifted her skirts to run down the alley.

"We're almost there. Just relax."

Lorelei closed her eyes and tried to do exactly that. It felt like the longest few minutes of her life. The tension in her chest refused to ease as she attempted to take easy breaths. Thinking about breathing seemed to make it more difficult, so she tried to think of something else. She lifted her face from Sean's chest to see if they were attracting any attention. Thankfully, they were now the only ones in the alleyway.

She slowly became conscious of the rapid thundering of Sean's heart beneath her fingers and swallowed. When exactly had her free hand slid over his heart? She stared at it for a long moment. Sean shifted her closer. She readjusted her arm around his shoulder. *Lord, please help me. I really can't breathe.*

Sean glanced down, distracting her with a rueful smile. "This is beginning to become a habit with us, isn't it?"

She lifted her shoulder in a hapless shrug. "Don't get—used to it."

He chuckled quietly. "No, I suppose not."

She closed her eyes as he turned a corner, then mounted the steps to Doc Williams's office. Ellie threw the door open for them. Doc led them down a hallway and into an examining room, then promptly commanded Sean to leave. One quick encouraging look later, Sean was gone. Lorelei glanced over at the doctor who had turned away to prepare her treatment.

"From what I've heard, you are having trouble breathing, is that right?"

"Yes," she exhaled.

"Runny nose, watery eyes, itchy nose and eyes," he rattled off as he examined her. "You, my dear, have a severe case of hay fever. Try breathing through your mouth calmly instead of gasping for breath. If you keep overcompensating, you'll hyperventilate. There's nothing to worry about. I'll give you some medicine and keep an eye on you for a while."

"It isn't serious?" she asked in disbelief. "But…"

"But what?"

But…when Sean held me I couldn't breathe. She swallowed. "Nothing, Doc. It was nothing."

Sean's thumb tapped a frantic rhythm on his denim-covered knee while he waited for Doc and Lorelei to emerge from the examining room. Ellie's hand covered his. He squeezed it gently, then glanced up at her. Her smile was reassuring. He leaned back in his chair and let out a pent-up breath.

"Don't be so worried. She's with Doc. If anyone can make her better, he can," Ellie said.

He glanced at her. "I know that. I've just never been good at waiting."

Her lips curved into a smile. "You're really starting to care for Lorelei, aren't you, Sean?"

The question settled into the air like the smell of kerosene at an explosion site. Sean grunted. Let it settle all it liked, he wasn't about to answer. "Do you really want to ask that question, knowing what you know?"

She winked. He shot her a glare. She gave him a saccharine-sweet smile, then picked up a catalog from a table. He sighed, then walked the window for some time alone.

"Lord, I can't make heads or tails of anything lately," he muttered in a barely audible voice to keep Ellie from hearing. "I don't know if it's me messing up my life or if You're trying to teach me something, but I've never been so lost or confused. Please help me out here."

He stood in quiet anticipation in the stillness interrupted only by Ellie's intermittent page turning. He waited for peace to overtake him, but instead panic filled his chest. His heart began to beat faster. His hands clenched into fists. He wanted to take it back. Those words he'd spoken were good in theory, but they came a bit too close to surrender. He wanted to believe that he could fix it on his own. Perhaps if he just tried a little harder to do…something….

The truth was he'd become so invested in his relationship with Lorelei that it was making him a little crazy. The more he thought about it and the more he played along, the more he really began to hate this game of pretend he and Lorelei were involved in. He hated wondering if the town would find his proposal too sudden and start asking questions he wouldn't want answered. But most of all, he hated the way he wasn't sure himself how real their courtship was, for him or for her. They'd been getting along so much better recently, but was the new cordiality real, or was Lorelei just keeping up appearances? And what about him? Were his feelings for her truly growing?

He probably shouldn't have told her that he found her irresistible when she wasn't acting like someone she wasn't. It was true though. He realized that they'd finally been able to create a friendship. But it wasn't enough. She wasn't the type of person he'd planned on spending his life with, but they were getting married. That meant he needed to do something that would start them on a path that would eventually lead to love. But would he end up on that path alone?

He closed his eyes against the dizziness and heard a door open down the hall. Grateful for the distraction, Sean glanced up to see Doc Williams walking toward him. "How is she?"

"She should be fine. I'm going to watch her for a while to make sure the treatment is working. She asked me to take her home after that."

Ellie slipped up to Sean and nudged him softly in the ribs. "I guess that's our cue to leave."

"I guess so." He reached down to grab his Stetson.

"Tell her we'll be praying for her," Ellie urged.

"I'll do that," Doc promised.

Ellie stepped up to press a kiss on Doc's cheek. "Bye, Doc."

Sean shook Doc's hand. When he would have let go, Doc held on. He glanced up to find the man looking at him carefully. "Actually, Ellie, I'd like to speak with Sean alone."

Ellie nodded. "I'll wait at your office, Sean."

Before Sean had a chance to respond, Doc released his hand and turned back down the hallway he'd just walked. Sean followed him in confusion. Doc motioned Sean into an empty examination room. "Sit down, Sean."

"What's wrong?"

Doc took the chair across from him, pulled out a notepad and looked him in the eye. "How long have you been having this panic problem?"

Shock stilled his rapidly beating heart for a moment before it resumed its quick pace. He shifted in his chair, then stared at the door. So that's what these episodes were called. He wasn't sure if he was more alarmed or relieved to know what they were. His gaze shot back to Doc's. "How did you know?"

"I felt your racing heart during our rather moist handshake, you seem short of breath and if the look in your eyes tells me anything, you are feeling an unexplained sense of terror or lack of control right now." He didn't wait for Sean's confirmation. "Do any other symptoms usually occur along with or instead of these?"

He swallowed. "Dizziness."

Doc marked it down, then nodded for him to continue. "When did you first begin to have these episodes?"

"After my parents' deaths."

Doc put down his pencil. "I'm not surprised, but I am concerned that you have not mentioned this to me before. Does your family know?"

"Should they?"

Doc smiled slightly. "It isn't fatal, if that's what you're asking. Telling them is up to you."

"Is there a cure?"

"That depends. Do you know what triggers them?"

Sean was thoughtful for a long moment. "Thinking about certain things like situations I can't control."

"A loss of control due to outside pressures," Doc muttered as he wrote in his tablet. He glanced up. "In that case, I would suggest you find someone to confide in. Talking about what's wrong rather than internalizing it, will probably help. Also, how often during those moments do you pray and surrender the situation to God?"

"I pray…sometimes." He swallowed.

"I see." Doc leaned forward. "In medicine we have vaccines. That means to keep someone from contract ing diseases such as smallpox we give them smallpox in a little dose. Once the body builds defenses against the small dose, it can fight off a stronger infection. In my opinion, the best vaccine for the panic you feel when giving up control is to give up control in small ways until you can do it comfortably in large ways."

Sean's smile was wry. "So to treat panic I need to panic."

Doc laughed. "Yes, because the point is to learn how to deal with that panic."

"If I do that, will I finally be able to overcome this?"

"With time, I hope that you will."

He wanted to overcome this, and if that meant he needed to give up a little bit of control, then maybe he could do that. The biggest source of stress for him was his relationship with Lorelei. What had he thought earlier? He needed to start them on a path toward love. That meant taking a chance. That was a form of giving up control, wasn't it? Perhaps it was time to be honest with himself and with Lorelei. He was tired of playing pretend. He wanted a real relationship with her. For once, he'd take a risk. He'd approach Lorelei and ask her to let him court her for real. Maybe, just maybe, she'd say yes. Perhaps that would help him shake this panic once and for all.

Chapter Fourteen

Sitting on the wooden bench of her parents' back lawn the next afternoon, Lorelei placed her pencil back onto the paper. It was the first time she'd ventured out of the house since Doc had helped her drowsily inside. Whatever medicine he'd given her had been enough to fell a horse. She'd slept her way past the effects of the allergy and the medication to awaken feeling healthy and strong again. Now that she didn't have a job and Silas Smithson hadn't contacted her, she figured she might as well try a new hobby. Obviously drawing wasn't going to be it. She drew line after line with her pencil, but no matter how many lines she drew, she couldn't come up with a flower.

A shadow suddenly covered her drawing pad. She frowned and glanced up at the sky for the offending cloud only to meet the shimmering deep green eyes of Sean O'Brien. She jumped. Her drawing pad tottered violently before diving into the grass. Glancing back up at Sean, she uttered a single slightly disappointed word. "Oh."

His lips stretched slowly into an amused grin. "That isn't exactly the kind of hello a man dreams about."

She couldn't help but return his smile. He watched her for a moment before he knelt in the grass to retrieve her things. She took them from him, then carefully swung her feet down and scooted to one side to make room for him on the bench. He sat beside her but angled himself so he could see her face. She shrugged in a delayed response to his statement. "Maybe not, but do you realize that I've seen you nearly every day this week?"

He angled his chin down and leveled her with a teasingly suspicious look. "Are you complaining?"

She lifted her shoulders while innocently placing a hand on her chest. "Complaining? Oh, no. I was just commenting about it, that's all."

He gave her an easy grin. "Yeah, well, I'm afraid you're going to have to get used to it, darlin'."

She narrowed her eyes, ready to tell him just who he wouldn't be calling darling. He unnerved her into silence by sliding his arm across the back of the bench and leaning toward her. She forgot to breathe when he met her gaze. He gestured toward the drawing pad. "What's this?"

"My failed attempts at drawing." She shoved the drawing pad toward him. He seemed to take the hint because he took the pad and moved closer to his side of the bench. She watched him look over her drawings.

"These aren't so bad." He held his hand out for the pencil.

She handed it to him, glad to see him engrossed in something other than staring at her, even if it was correcting her mistakes. She smoothed down the wrinkles in her dress. Finally, she grew impatient. "Don't tell me you came all the way over here just to look at my awful drawings."

"I might have troubled myself to walk all of those three long blocks between our houses just to look at your drawings, if I'd known ahead of time you were drawing, but I didn't." He flourished one last stroke of the pencil, then handed the drawing pad back to her. "They weren't awful."

She stared down at the paper in astonishment. "You fixed them."

"I moved a few lines."

"You must have." She brushed away a clump of small scarlet flowers that fell onto the page from the crape myrtle branches that stretched above them. "How did you learn to draw?"

"I sketch the designs for the furniture and wood carvings I make now and then. It's just a hobby." He shifted to face her. "Lorelei, I came here to say something, so I may as well say it. I want to court you for real."

She stared at him for a long moment. His words just didn't make any sense. She frowned at him and shook her head in confusion. "Whatever for?"

"Aren't you tired of putting on an act, Lorelei? If we were really courting, we wouldn't have to do that anymore. We would just have to live."

"What's wrong with acting?" she asked, setting her drawing pad and the pencil on the grass.

"Besides the facts that it's slightly deceptive and that neither of us are very good at it?" He laughed. "Well, I hate to tell you this, but I don't think we can even come close to convincing the town we're really a couple if we don't make this courtship legitimate. Remember what Mrs. Greene said?"

Leaning back into the corner of the bench, she sighed. "I remember."

"Peppin is too small to hide anything. How long do you think we can keep up a ruse like this before someone finds out? This way we may have to act like our relationship is progressing faster than it really is, but at least there would be a genuine relationship."

She could feel her heartbeat drumming through her veins. He was threatening to out-reason her. She couldn't let that happen. "I really don't think this is a good idea."

"Just forget about the town for a minute. Forget that we're pretending. Forget everything else and think about this." He took her left hand in his right and looked her straight in the eye. "We're getting married, Lorelei. We've already established that we're going to have a real marriage. Shouldn't we also have a real courtship?"

"No," she whispered as she removed her hand from his. "I don't want it to be real."

"Why not?"

"I just don't," she said urgently.

He dropped his head for a moment, then quietly asked, "Do you really dislike me that much?"

"Dislike you?" she asked in a breathless exclamation. She turned away from his disconcerting scrutiny to try to control her emotions. She had suppressed them for so long that they refused to be contained any longer. She stood. Pressing her lips together, she turned to face him. Once the words finally came out, she couldn't seem to stop the rest that followed.

"I never disliked you, Sean. I loved you once, or at least I thought I did. I let all of those silly emotions go. I moved on. I was even going to find a new life for myself in California, then you had the nerve follow me. Now, after everything I've gone through, you say that you want to court me for real because that will make things easier on you."

Her breath was coming in short gasps. She paused to catch her breath and tried to remember why she was telling him all this. *Oh, yes.*

"The answer to your question is no. No, Sean. I don't dislike you. Well, maybe I do just a little for good reason, but that's not why I don't want you to court me. It will just confuse everything and take the focus off what we're supposed to be doing—fooling the town into thinking we're falling in love."

She waited for shame and fear to follow that statement, but it didn't. Instead, she felt a burden lift from her soul only to be replaced by peace. There. She'd said it. She'd told him exactly how she felt and now she felt free. Finally, free from the secret that had weighed her down for years. It felt wonderful. It also left her feeling exposed.

Sean slowly stood and stepped directly in front of her. As the moment lengthened, curiosity eventually drew her eyes to his. What she saw there wasn't at all what she expected. She had no idea what emotions glimmered from those depths, but there was no trace of mocking or disgust. It wasn't until a slow half amused, half confused smile pulled at his lips that she knew she was in trouble.

Sean watched the blush in Lorelei's cheeks heighten incrementally. His amused smile grew even as he tilted his head to survey her in confusion. "Wait a minute! Did I just hear you say you love me?"

If possible, her eyes widened even more, and she shook her head. "No, you didn't. You heard me say 'I loved you.'"

He frowned, not seeing the difference.

"It was past tense," she carefully explained.

"Oh, I see." He nodded. "It was very clumsy of me to make that kind of a mistake. There is a very large difference in loving someone and having loved someone."

She frowned with a trace of suspicion. "I should say so."

"Then I take it back. You are an extremely good actress. I had no idea."

Her lips parted in surprise, though her brows lowered in suspicion. "You really couldn't tell? Not even when we were younger?"

He shook his head. She looked at him carefully as if trying to discern the truth of his statement. Obviously finding something wanting, she tilted her head and pinned him with a look before slowly asking, "Then why don't you look more surprised?"

For the first time during their exchange, he felt slightly uncomfortable. "Lawson recently guessed you might feel that way."

"Lawson guessed," she repeated thoughtfully, then shook her head. "Well, now you know he was right. I hope you also understand that I've refused to let you court me."

"Hold on. I think you've got something wrong. I'm not *asking* you to let me court you for real. I'm *telling* you. I'm going to court you for real."

Her mouth dropped open, then she narrowed her eyes. "You can't do that."

He hadn't planned on it—and even now he could feel an edge of panic deep inside at the thought of committing himself to a courtship when she wasn't willing to meet him halfway—but it was obvious that there would be no other way to end this standoff. He could see them thirty years down the road still at the same impasse. One of them was going to have to risk getting hurt, and since it clearly wasn't going to be her, it would have to be him.

He was going to romance this woman whether she liked it or not because he didn't know what else to do. Surely God would take it from there. He had to. There was no other way this would work. It was with that knowledge that he stepped out in faith. "I can and I will."

"I don't understand. You don't even like me. Why would you want to court me?"

He frowned. "I thought we went over that."

"Yes, and we agreed to be *friends*."

"We are friends, aren't we?"

She was quiet for a long moment—too long of a moment. She just stared at him skeptically with those large blue eyes of hers. She was making him uncomfortable on purpose, and they both knew it. A smile tipped his lips, causing her to try to hide one of her own. She glanced away. Her tone spoke of her long-suffering patience. "I guess."

"Think of this as the next step then."

"The next step to what?" She crossed her arms. "You aren't going to make me fall in love with you. You know that, right?"

He didn't want to examine why those tentative words cut right to his heart, but they did until he remembered. "You fell in love with me once before."

"Yes, but I've resolved not to be that foolish again," she said stubbornly.

He frowned. "What's foolish about loving someone?"

She straightened. "Well, everything! You're giving

someone the power to hurt you by becoming completely vulnerable."

"I don't want to hurt you, Lorelei," he said in frustration. "I just want to court you."

"Oh, no, you don't. You're like every other normal man. You want a wife who loves you, but that's hardly fair in this case."

"Why isn't it fair?"

"Because you aren't going to love me back!" She let those uncomfortable words settle between them for a moment before she continued passionately. "Oh, you may start to care for me, but as soon as you do you're going to think about Lawson and what I did to him. You're going to think about the Harvest Dance when I ignored you because I thought you betrayed me. Then you're going to remind yourself of all the little things you don't like about me—"

He gently clutched her arms. "Stop it, Lorelei."

"It's true. Tell me it isn't," she challenged. He couldn't and she knew it. She glanced down, but not before he saw the tears in her eyes.

"Lorelei," he began, but she shook her head.

"That's quite all right, Sean, because I'd be doing the same thing. You want this to be real, so fine. For you, it's real. But, I won't do it. I'll just keep acting." She gathered her things and headed inside. "Say hello to my parents before you leave. They love your visits. I'll be in my room if they need me."

She was right. He realized it then and there. She was right about him, and she always had been. He did tend to focus on her faults, but that was only so he wouldn't have to focus on all the things he liked about her. She'd been his best friend's girl for so long that disqualifying her had become a necessary habit. There. He'd admitted it to himself. His heart always had a weakness for Lorelei, and he'd never allowed himself to give in to it. Doing so would have meant betraying a friend.

Things could be different now if they let it. They needed their relationship to work now, not just in the long run. He would continue with his plan to woo her because it was all he knew to do. Hopefully along the way they'd both be able to set aside the past.

Lorelei picked up the large serving spoon covered in melted cheese and hefted a portion of casserole onto her plate. She wasn't sure who'd brought the dish to the church's potluck picnic, but it looked delicious. She was only vaguely aware of someone stepping up beside her in line before a low voice murmured in a teasing tone, "You're a hard woman to get a hold of these days, Miss Wilkins."

Lorelei carefully placed the spoon back in its place before she glanced up into the eyes of the man beside her. She smiled politely to hide her relief that he was finally making contact. "Hello, Mr. Smithson."

"Please, call me Silas." He returned her smile as they progressed down the line. "I was sorry to hear you quit your job at the millinery."

Lorelei exchanged a smile with one of the church ladies overseeing the buffet table. She carefully placed a sweet roll onto her plate. "I'm afraid it couldn't be avoided. It was literally making me sick."

He paused to take a large piece of her mother's pie. "I heard it had something to do with that. I hope that won't prevent you from helping me."

"I see no reason why it should." She glanced around at all of the innocent churchgoers milling about in groups.

"I thought you might say that." Silas led her farther away from the table where they were less likely to be overheard. "I hate to mention this, but your illness might have caused a problem. How am I supposed to contact you without raising suspicion?"

Her lips tilted upward in amusement. "You'd be doing fine now if you weren't frowning."

"How can you say that?"

"What's wrong with us meeting here?"

"It's a church, isn't it?"

She laughed. Maybe God had a purpose in allowing her to get sick after all. "Don't tell me you came to church just to talk to me?"

He glared at her.

"Did you have to sit through the whole sermon?"

"Yes, I did. I don't understand why you're so amused by it."

She shrugged. "I just thought it might have done you some good, that's all."

"Like it did you good? Just imagine what these people would think if they found out what you were really like."

She bristled at his tone but found his words achingly true. She was trying to deceive the town just as he was, only not with the same intentions. He wanted to steal the town's livelihood. She was just trying to protect her reputation. She glanced back at Mr. Smithson and realized he expected a reply, so she shrugged nonchalantly. "They'd never believe it."

"Well, it doesn't matter. I have to talk to you about something serious. Our old plans have been delayed, so we're creating a new plan. I'm going to need you to produce on that information you promised me."

"What do you need?"

He shook his head. "Not now."

"When?"

"Meet me Tuesday evening at 7:30 in the alley where we first met. We have a lot of planning to do."

She returned his nod as they went their separate ways. A few minutes later, Lorelei leaned across her mother's brightly colored quilt to snag a sliver of Mrs. Greene's famous cornbread from one of the three plates stationed in the middle. A few crumbs managed to drop from the moist cornbread before she captured it in her mouth.

Her father grinned at her from where he sat to her left. "Is it good?"

"Delicious," she said, finishing off the rest of the piece.

"Lorelei," her mother called softly. "I think you have a visitor."

She glanced up in confusion to see her parents smiling. Following their gazes, she turned around to see three-year-old Grace standing at the edge of the quilt. She held her hands behind the skirt of her blue-and-white dress while she watched Lorelei shyly. Lorelei's lips lifted into an amused smile. "Grace. Hello."

"'Lo." The girl smiled impishly, then pulled a bouquet of wildflowers from behind her back. "Yours."

Lorelei stared at the bouquet in surprise. "Are you sure?"

The little girl nodded so adamantly that a little red curl slipped from its place to dance around her shoulder. Lorelei heard her parents chuckle. She shot a helpless glance at them before she turned back to the girl.

"Thank you so much." She took the flowers from the girl. "They're beautiful."

The girl grinned, her blue eyes sparkling. She

dropped to her knees and placed her hands on her lap as though ready for a long chat.

"Did you pick these flowers all by yourself?"

Grace shook her head. "No."

"Did someone tell you to give them to me then?"

A smile blossomed on the girl's face. Her brow lowered earnestly as she said something that sounded almost unintelligibly like, "Unca."

"Uncle." Her eyes instinctively swept the picnic blankets laid out against the green lawn, searching for Sean. A moment later, her suspicious gaze connected with his. He was kneeling on one of the O'Brien family's picnic blankets, obviously having just sent off his little emissary. He caught her watching him, and a slow smile spread across his face. She shook her head slightly even as a reluctant smile teased her lips.

"Yes, I see," she murmured.

His smile and gaze were completely genuine, which meant he was really going through with his misguided attempt to court her. That didn't mean she was going to make things easy on him. Oh, no. If she had her way, things were going to become very interesting.

He was trying a new strategy on her, but he had no idea she had a strategy of her own. She was no longer an insecure child half-afraid of the attention she might arouse. She was going to guard her heart, but she was also ready to fight fire with fire. She glanced back to Grace. "I think I'm supposed to take you back to dear old Uncle."

The little girl gave a careless shrug and pointed to the flowers. "I like those."

Lorelei laughed. "Which one is your favorite?"

The girl pointed to a bright yellow one. Lorelei pulled

it from the bouquet and deftly shortened the stem before tucking it into the girl's hair. "There."

Grace beamed and carefully lifted her hair to touch the flower. "Pretty."

"Very pretty," she said as she stood, then glanced down at her parents. "I've been summoned."

"Go ahead, dear," Caroline said. "We're almost through here anyway."

Her father scooped up Lorelei's abandoned plate and winked at her. "More pie for me."

Lorelei pulled in a deep breath, then stood and extended her hand to Grace. "Let's go see Uncle Sean."

Instead of grasping Lorelei's fingers, Grace extended both arms upward in a sign that she wanted to be carried. She swept the girl onto her hip as she approached the other blanket and sent Sean a grin. "Look what I found."

"I knew I'd left her someplace." He stood to greet them with a smile.

Grace lurched forward and placed her hand on Sean's cheek in order to get his attention. "I did it."

"Yes, you did. You are such a good girl." He leaned forward to kiss her forehead. "I think your mama was looking for you."

Lorelei set Grace down, then watched as she raced the few yards to where Kate was talking to a few other women. "I talked to Silas."

"I know. I saw you. What did he say?" He listened as she explained about the meeting before frowning. "You did well, though ideally you should have tried to arrange it for a public place in daylight. That's my fault for not instructing you to do that. We'll go over what you need to say again before you meet him. I'll be present, but you won't see me. Do your best to act like I'm not there."

"Yes, sir," she dutifully agreed.

"By the way, did you like the surprise I sent you?"

Impulsively, she stepped forward onto her tiptoes to place a quick kiss on his cheek. "I did. Thank you. It was an adorable surprise, and the flowers were lovely."

She had the pleasure of watching him blush. He cleared his throat, then raised a brow. "That almost sounded sincere."

"I think it almost was," she said teasingly.

A suspicious smile played at his lips. "Why, Miss Wilkins, I haven't the slightest idea what you're up to, but I think I like this side of you."

She felt a pink warmth steal across her cheeks even as her heart gave a decided thump. For goodness' sake, what was wrong with her? It wasn't as if she'd never flirted before. Of course she had. She'd just never flirted with Sean. She covered the sense of panic bursting through her by tilting her head and sending him a mischievous look. "What makes you think I'm up to something?"

"Aren't you?"

She'd hoped to somehow even the playing field by unnerving him. It was the only way she could think of defending her heart from the onslaught of his unfeigned courtship. Perhaps she was overestimating her abilities. She'd hardly seen more than a fleeting flash of attraction in Sean's eyes. Still, it was too early to concede defeat yet. She swallowed. "So what if I am?"

"Nothing," he said as he casually stepped closer to her. "Just do me a favor, will you?"

She lifted her gaze to his questioningly.

He dipped his chin to capture her gaze more completely, then grinned slowly. "Don't stop."

Her breath stilled in her throat. Then again, there was the possibility that she was in *way* over her head.

Chapter Fifteen

Sean's fingers carefully followed the curving wood of the headboard for the bed he was making. As soon as he finished this, he would start on a set of new kitchen cabinets for Lorelei. The ones in his new place were hardly worth looking at. He was also planning another project. A wardrobe that he hoped might interest Mr. Johansen at the mercantile. It was a wild idea, but it might give him another source of income besides what the town allotted him.

He glanced up at the sound of the barn door swinging open and met Ellie's gaze with a welcoming grin. "Hey, I thought you were helping Kate with the mending."

She carefully settled on a chair he'd made for the kitchen. "We finished, so I thought I'd come out here to spend some time with my big brother. I can hand you tools or something."

Right. He shot her a wry glance. "What's on your mind?"

She froze in surprise for a moment before her green eyes began to sparkle and her lips pulled into an annoyed pout. "You think you're so smart. What if I had actually come out here to help you?"

He laughed. "Then you wouldn't have settled onto that chair like you were ready for a good, long chat." He grabbed a nearby chair and straddled it. "I'm ready for a break, so shoot. Just try not to make it fatal."

She rewarded his jest with a smile before she leaned back onto the chair and met his gaze seriously. "I was just wondering how things were progressing between you and Lorelei."

Glancing away, he shrugged. "I don't know, Ellie. I think we've made a lot of progress in some ways, but we're still at a stalemate."

"What kind of stalemate?" she asked gently.

He met her gaze. "As best I can figure, she doesn't want to love me because she doesn't want to get hurt."

"What about you?"

"What about me?" He rubbed his hands together to rid them of the dust from the wood. "I'm trying to love her—"

"Trying to love her?" she asked in amused derision. "No woman would want to hear a man say he is 'trying to love her.' What does that even mean? It sounds like you're telling her that despite her best efforts, you haven't been able to make yourself actually fall in love. That's just awful."

He sighed and crossed his arms over the back of the chair. "Well, Ellie. Would it sound any better if I said that there are lots of things that make her easy to love— but lots of reasons why it doesn't seem like a good idea? I've had a whole list of reasons why I shouldn't fall for Lorelei for years now. Even now that I want to move on and care for her, how can I just let go of that?"

A compassionate smile pulled at her lips. "Well, I think you should stop trying so hard to love Lorelei and just love her."

"That doesn't make sense."

"Sure, it does. I don't have to think about loving you, Sean. I just do." She glanced up to the rafters of the barn as if the words she sought were just out of reach. "It's like when you're trying to breathe. If you just sit there and think about it, you become so aware of it that it's harder to do. You just kind of have to surrender to it. You just have to trust that it will happen without you trying. Then it does. Don't worry about the reasons why you should or shouldn't fall in love with her. Just let it happen naturally."

He stared at his sister for a moment before letting out a short, low whistle. "That's a little too deep for me, Ellie."

She sent him an exasperated look. "I'm being serious."

"I guess you're right."

"I know I'm right," she said earnestly. "Sooner or later you'll figure it out."

He rolled his eyes. "So that's it? You just came out to impart wisdom, and now you're going to leave?"

She lifted her eyebrows. "As if you'd actually let me touch one of your projects anyway."

He grinned, knowing he usually didn't. "Get out of here."

She wiggled her fingers in a little wave, then flounced out the door. He shook his head. All right, so she made some good points. He'd made some progress so far by deciding to court Lorelei for real. She'd dropped the cool, unemotional act. The problem was she'd picked up another. Suddenly she was being warm and friendly. She'd even gone so far as to flirt with him more than once. He couldn't tell where the act ended and her real feelings and personality started. She wasn't playing fair anymore, but it didn't matter. He wasn't giving up on her or himself. Meanwhile, he'd do his best to ignore that whisper of fear—the one that told him it would be far easier to convince himself to love Lorelei than it would be to convince her to love him back.

Lorelei grasped her hat by its black ribbons and held it tightly in her hand as she stepped from the house onto the porch. She cast a careful glance to where her parents sat together on the porch swing. Her mother was the picture of peaceful contentment as she sat within the circle of Richard's arm. Her father lifted his book closer to his face to compensate for the rapidly fading light. Lorelei knew better than to attempt to sneak off, but she wanted to make her leaving seem as natural as possible. She breezed past them with a quick smile on her way to the porch stairs. "I'm going to meet Sean. I'll see you two later."

"Just a minute, Lorelei," her father's strong voice called out.

She tried not wince before turning around with an innocent expression. "Yes, Papa?"

"I just wanted to say that I'm proud of the way you're dealing with this courtship. You're handling it well. What's more, you actually seem to be giving Sean a chance. That shows great strength of character."

"Thank you. That means a lot. Our relationship has improved, but I'm still not interested in falling in love with him. That hasn't changed. He hurt me once before. I may have moved on, but I haven't forgotten."

Caroline sighed. "I hope one day you'll be able to, dear."

"Well, try to have a good time and enjoy yourself,"

Richard said. "If you come back after dark, make sure he walks you home."

"Yes, sir."

A few minutes later, she waited in the alleyway beside the bank for Silas to join her. She heard a sound in the alleyway and turned abruptly only to see Mr. Smithson making his way toward her. Her heart rate ratcheted up a notch from nervousness, but his grin was actually rather calming. "Well, what do you know? You're here."

"I told you I would come." A cool wind blew through the alley, sending chills across her skin.

"That you did." He stepped farther back into the alley. "Follow me around the corner. I've got a place all set up for this meeting."

Hoping Sean would be able to see her from wherever he was hiding, she followed him farther into the alley. Sure enough, as she turned the corner she saw a barrel set up against the back wall of The Barber & Bath House. A shadow opposite the barrel moved as she approached. Her steps slowed as she met the gaze of the stranger who straightened from where he'd been leaning against the wall. Silas stepped forward to shake the man's hand. "I didn't know you'd decided to come. How are you holding up, Calhoun?"

The man shook his head. "This waiting is bad business."

Mr. Smithson nodded. "Don't I know it? Calhoun, this is Miss Wilkins. She's going to help us make our wait as strategic as possible."

Lorelei stepped forward with a polite nod. "Mr. Calhoun, how do you do?"

Mr. Calhoun looked her up and down, then met her gaze for a long moment before he grinned. "It looks like we've got a real live lady present. I haven't talked to one of them in a long time. It sure is a pleasure. Evening, Miss."

She hid her smile, then glanced at Mr. Smithson for direction. He stepped forward, then lifted her carefully onto the barrel before she had a chance to react. Pulling a small pad and pencil from his pocket, he glanced at them. "Let's get to work. Lorelei, you may as well know I'm giving you information as needed. I'm guessing you'll do the same with us. The first thing we need to know is the location of the safe."

"Do you have a layout of the bank building?"

Calhoun handed her a piece of paper.

She looked at it for a minute, then frowned. "Is this it? It's just a big square with little notches for the tellers."

Calhoun grimaced. "We couldn't get past the lobby."

"I'll draw a better one for you." She took a pencil from her reticule, then turned the paper over and found herself staring at a telegram. On my way STOP Do not do anything stupid STOP. She glanced up at the men. "Does anyone have a blank sheet of paper?"

Silas took a small notebook from his coat pocket and tore out a piece for her. She folded the telegram and held it under the closed notebook he gave her to write on. She carefully drew a diagram of the bank complete with the back offices and hallways. She drew an X near the back wall. "The safe is all the way back here."

"Who knows the combination to the safe and where do they sit?" Calhoun asked with a greedy gleam in his eyes.

"Only my father and the manager."

Silas smiled knowingly. "Yes, but your former fiancé has left town so there is no manager."

Lorelei rolled her eyes at him. "This town talks too

much. I can't wait to get my ticket out of here. Speaking of which, how am I going to get my share of the money?"

"I'll stick around a few days after the robbery to keep from looking suspicious. I'll get you the money."

Calhoun edged toward her. "You two can figure that out later. Tell us about the safe, Miss Wilkins."

"The new manager is coming in from out of town. He'll be a good target because he'll be too new to care about anything other than not getting hurt. His office is right here. He won't get here for a week, though. Is that going to be a problem?"

"Not the way things are going with the boss," Calhoun said dryly.

She handed them the new layout and the notebook while nonchalantly tucking the pencil and the telegram in her reticule. "What else do you need to know?"

Sean couldn't help feeling a bit proud as he shifted into a more comfortable position to watch Lorelei act her way through the meeting. If he didn't know better, he might even believe Lorelei was really in league with the possible bank robbers for a percentage of the safe and a quick ticket out of Peppin. Trusting her to handle her part of the plan hadn't been a mistake after all. Of course, they'd gone over her role in this a hundred times, leaving no chance of a mistake, but she'd taken his instruction with relative complacency and already given him a big break in the case.

Calhoun was involved just as he'd suspected. Just from listening to their conversation, he almost had enough to charge both Calhoun and Smithson with conspiracy to commit armed robbery. He'd been planning on that very thing until Calhoun uttered one word that changed everything. *Boss*—their boss wasn't here yet.

That proved his suspicion that these two men weren't acting alone but as part of a larger gang that had set its sight on Peppin. Smithson seemed the highest ranked of the two men, but when it came down to it they were muscle men. If he wanted to keep this from happening to Peppin again or to another less suspecting town, he needed to go after the top. That made things infinitely more complicated.

Twenty minutes went by. It felt like an eternity, especially once the mosquitoes discovered his hiding place and tried to give him away. Finally, Calhoun slunk down the alley toward the saloon, leaving Lorelei alone with Silas. The two continued talking for a few minutes until Silas set her on her feet and walked off. Lorelei seemed to wait until she was sure the fellow was gone before she smiled, lifted her skirts and took off half running, half skipping down the alley away from Sean and toward their meet-up point.

He grinned at her obvious excitement at a job well done. He rose to his feet to leave, then immediately sank back into his hiding place when Calhoun appeared again. The man scanned the alley and seemed to catch sight of Lorelei's fluttering hem as she disappeared around the corner. The rough drifter started following her at a leisurely pace.

Sean surged to his feet and rounded the corner back onto Main Street. He had to catch up with Lorelei before Calhoun did and before Lorelei could find him absent, start calling out for him and give them both away. He saw Silas had nearly reached the boardinghouse and hoped the man wouldn't turn around to see him running down the sidewalk or at least wouldn't draw the connection from him to Lorelei. There were only a few folks on the street he had to avoid so Sean was certain he was making better time than Lorelei and Calhoun.

He rounded the hotel and slipped back into the alleyway skirting around the tall wooden fence that sectioned off the expansive garden of the hotel. Lorelei ought to come along at any moment now with Calhoun not far behind her. Sean tugged at the thin fence door that led from the alleyway into the garden. It opened easily. Relief filled him. He'd told Mr. Martin a dozen times if he'd told him once not to leave this gate open to the alley. Thankfully he hadn't listened. It would provide the perfect getaway if he could manage it.

The lanterns in the garden cast golden shards through the slats in the fence to warm up the murky twilight as he stalked silently along the fence. He positioned himself so he'd be within easy reaching distance of Lorelei once she turned the corner. He heard her accelerated strides as they approached. He timed it perfectly so that as soon as she turned the corner, his arm went around her waist and his hand silenced her startled scream. Her eyes were wide with alarm. They widened more as recognition filtered through them.

"Quiet," he whispered, then ushered her through the open gate mere feet away. He closed it and locked it behind them. She began to speak but he shook his head abruptly. He grabbed her arm to urge her to hide behind some tall bushes in case Calhoun got a notion to peer through the fence slats. They knelt together. Her eyes met his in confusion. A minute passed between them in silence until it was filled by quick uneven footsteps. They went past the fence gate then slowed to a stop. Calhoun rattled the locked gate, then a quiet curse punctuated the air. "Lost her. Fool woman."

Sean and Lorelei waited as the footsteps faded away. He helped Lorelei stand. She held on to his arm, tensely whispering, "He's gone?"

"I think so," he whispered back but wasted no time in paving a way through the bushes to distance them from the fence.

"Why was he following me?"

"Perhaps to see if you'd meet up with me." He jumped down the steep grade to the garden path, then reached up to lift her down.

She didn't seem to notice. Instead, she glanced at her reticule thoughtfully. "Maybe he wants his telegram back."

"You took his telegram?"

She met his gaze with a triumphant lift of her chin. "It has a rough layout of the bank on the back. I thought you might want it."

"Lorelei…" he began. Apprehension filled her eyes. He caught her waist, lifted her in the air and waited until she looked him in the eye before continuing. "You're a wonder."

Her eyes never left his once her feet made it safely to the ground. She seemed to be trying to determine his sincerity. She must have been satisfied for she tilted her head in acknowledgment of the compliment, and the most unguarded smile he'd seen yet slowly blossomed on her lips. She finally turned away to begin walking along the winding garden path. She came to an abrupt stop. "Where are we exactly?"

"The far reaches of the hotel garden." He placed a hand near her waist to guide her forward. "I think you're going the right way. It's easy to get lost in here, so stay close."

"Yes, I think that's the point," she murmured.

They ignored a few forks in the path that probably would have taken them deeper into the heart of the garden. Even so, it was a while before the path widened then abruptly opened into the main area. He glanced at Lorelei sharply when she gasped. "Look at this. Isn't it lovely?"

A long rectangular pond with a fountain stood in the center of the garden. Upon its raised stone border sat small glowing lamps. They dispelled the darkness just enough to cast golden light on everything without penetrating the feeling of seclusion. It was nice, but he was more interested in the evidence Lorelei had for him. "It sure is. How about letting me have a look at the telegram?"

She sent him a hopeless look as she dug it out of her reticule and handed it to him. "Sean, you have no sense of romance."

He carefully studied the telegram. *Wait. Did Lorelei use the word* romance *in the same sentence with my name?*

He tried to recall the comment he'd automatically dismissed as a quip. Yes, she'd used his name in the same sentence as *romance* if only to point out his lack of it. He took a second look at his setting and situation. He couldn't go shooting himself in the foot when it came to courting Lorelei. He ought to take advantage of this situation, but how? It would probably be a good start to put the telegram away.

Lorelei had wandered toward the pond. She glanced back to find him watching and smiled as she hugged her arms to her waist. "Oh, I don't think I've ever felt so wonderful! Wait. Yes, I have. Right before you found me with the Brightlys and I almost drowned. Isn't it exhilarating?"

He chuckled. "Drowning?"

"No!" She laughed. "This. Preventing crime. Protecting the people you love. No wonder you're a sheriff. You get to do this every day."

He meandered closer. "It's mostly paperwork. This is really unusual for Peppin."

"Yes, but it's important paperwork."

He considered this thoughtfully for a minute, then shook his head. "No, usually it's pretty bor—"

She stepped forward to place a stilling hand on his chest. "Sean, do me a favor. Just let me have this moment. All right?"

"Whatever you say," he murmured. Her knees suddenly seemed to give out, and he had to catch her before she slipped to the ground. "Lorelei, what happened? Can you hear me?"

She closed her eyes as though dizzy. "I don't know. I must have had a moment of delusion. I thought you said, 'whatever you say.'"

"I did," he said, then froze when she opened one mischievous eye. He released her. "I should have let you fall."

She began laughing, then couldn't seem to stop. He finally shook his head at her and headed for the hotel porch. She caught his arm to try to pull him to a stop. "I'm sorry, Sean. I'd just never heard those words come out of your mouth before."

He turned toward her but kept walking backward. "Your apology would be a lot more effective if you weren't laughing."

That finally quieted her laughter. She peered up at him as though trying to discern his facial expression in the low light. "You aren't really upset, are you?"

He tugged her closer, bringing them both to a stop. "What do you think?"

The moment lengthened after his quiet question. Her gaze searched his face, then his eyes. That close, he could watch as she raised her guard. "I think I'd better go home."

Disappointment filled him, but he nodded, realizing it wouldn't do well to push her too much, too fast. "I need to think about our next step anyway."

Her eyes widened. "Another step?"

"With the robbery," he explained when he realized she thought he was talking about their courtship. "I'd better walk you home."

"But Calhoun—"

"—is exactly why I want to walk home with you. You disappeared fifteen minutes ago. What you've done during that time is anyone's guess. If you show up with me, the only thing he'll know for sure is that we're courting. Everyone knows that." He offered her his arm. "Let's make it convincing."

"Lorelei, is that you?" her mother called from the kitchen a few minutes later.

"Yes, I'm home." She walked to the kitchen to watch her mother pour herself a cup of tea.

"Did you have a good time?"

"Yes."

"What did you do?"

Lorelei glanced up at her mother. The woman offered her a cup of tea by lifting an empty cup. Lorelei shook her head. "We went for a walk in the hotel gardens."

"That's sounds lovely."

"It was wonderful." At her mother's knowing look, Lorelei dropped the smile she hadn't known was on her face. She said good-night, then walked up the stairs to her room and closed the door behind her. She set her reticule down and pulled the hairpins from her hair. She had to admit—it had been exhilarating. She'd held her own with those outlaws and Sean had seen it all.

She wandered to the window and peered out at the stars as she brushed her hair. She had to admit, it wasn't until Sean lifted her in his arms, looked her in the eye and called her a "wonder" that all of those emotions were released. It wasn't because she was falling in love. No, she wouldn't let it be that. It was just that, after all those years of receiving his disapproval, she'd finally done something right in his eyes.

This afterglow was only the result of finally being able to create a friendship and a fledgling partnership with him. She was perfectly content with both and hoped that Sean would be, too. Surely he'd give up on this courtship once he realized he was wasting his time and efforts. Then maybe they'd be able to settle down into a warm friendship with no heartache involved. She just had to wait him out.

Chapter Sixteen

Sean lifted the open-style kitchen shelves into place and somehow managed to settle a nail into the pre-drilled hole in the back of the unit. He banged the nail through the hole into the wall, then frowned. Perhaps he should have waited for Nathan's help on this one. He was almost done fixing up the kitchen in his new place and hadn't wanted to wait. He was too far along to stop now, so he slid to the other side of the unit.

"This is not the same kitchen." The sound of Lorelei's voice made him nearly drop his hammer.

He peered over his shoulder at her. "What are you doing here? Never mind. Come over here and help me hold this shelf in place. It isn't heavy."

She set her reticule on the new kitchen table to join him near the stove. "Where did all this furniture come from?"

"I made it." With his newly freed hand, he was able to set the nails and hammer them through the wall in just a few seconds.

Lorelei hesitantly let the shelf unit go. Once it stayed in place, she turned to him in confusion. "Wait. You made the furniture? All of it? Even that cupboard over there?"

He glanced at the large piece of furniture standing by the window. "Is something wrong with the cupboard?"

She walked over to run her fingers over it. "Nothing is wrong with it. That's my point. I knew you whittled and you've talked about designing furniture, but I didn't realize you were such an accomplished carpenter."

He shrugged. "I'm not a carpenter. I just like to make furniture now and then. It's a hobby."

She shook her head in awe. "I wish I had a hobby like that."

"You do." He crossed his arms. "You're a pianist. You're dedicated to it. It's the one thing that's held your interest for years. You should focus on it and stop trying to force yourself to do other things you're only half-interested in."

"Maybe, but I like doing new things." She tried out one of the kitchen chairs. "I don't want to interrupt your carpentry. Ellie asked me to show her around. I'm sure she won't be long."

"It's no interruption. I was just doing this while I waited for Ellie." He smiled as he repeated Lorelei's exact words. "'She wanted me to show her around.'"

"What?" she breathed in confusion.

"Ellie has been overly confident in her skills as a matchmaker since she was about ten years old. If this is one of her latest escapades, she might not show up at all."

"I don't believe it. She sounded like she really wanted to see the house. I still think she's just running late."

"If you say so," he said doubtfully. Fifteen minutes later, with no sign of Ellie, they both thought it prudent to give up. "No use wasting a trip out here. I can at least show you the rest of the property. Let's walk."

Lorelei kept up with Sean's steady pace as they explored the different areas of the farm from the barn and chicken coop to the empty fields and pastures for the animals. He told her of his plans for the future of the farm. She listened intently and even smiled now and again when he was particularly enthusiastic about something. He let out a sigh of relief. Her reaction to the farm was much better than it had been the first time. Perhaps she was beginning to see the value in the land that he did. Finally, he announced, "There's only one more thing I want to show you. It's on the way back."

If she didn't fall in love with the farm after this, there would be no hope for her. The trees began to thin out until they stepped into a clearing. One large oak tree stood by itself. The trunk had to be more than seven feet in diameter. Three thick offshoots rose from the trunk high into the air while one seemed to mosey out sideways for at least ten feet before it also contributed to the maze of large branches hovering above the ground. He glanced at Lorelei when he heard her gasp.

"It's so beautiful! I've never seen anything like it." She shook her head in wonder.

Sean followed her gaze to the large wooden swing attached to the branch that hovered over the ground. He gently bumped her arm with his. "Want to try it out?"

"Of course I want to try it out." She tugged at his arm, pulling him forward with her.

"Are you ready?" he asked a moment later.

She caught the ropes on either side of the seat. "Ready."

His hands settled on the ropes below hers as he pulled the swing back, then let it go. She swung higher each time he pushed her while the wind teased and pulled at her hair, trying to work it free from the pins. The swing was starting to get pretty high off the ground. It was now or never.

"Slide to one side," Sean warned.

Lorelei quickly did as he directed then gasped as he took hold of the ropes and lifted himself onto the seat beside her. He balanced on the swing in a hunched position for a moment before he managed to lift himself into the correct position. The swing tottered along its usual path until Sean pumped his legs enough to straighten it out. Finally, he looked at her with a grin. She stared back at him in amused exasperation. "That could have ended badly. You know that, right?"

He laughed. "No, I had it all planned out. I knew it would work."

Her dark blue eyes narrowed thoughtfully. "Do you realize you do that constantly?"

His confused look must have told her that he had no idea what she was talking about.

"You plan constantly," she said. "Every time we come upon a situation that holds the least bit of uncertainty you rush in to save the day. You plan the problem away in a matter of minutes. Then you make sure every little part of the plan is carried out successfully."

"I guess I do, don't I?" He flashed a grin. "You're welcome."

She rolled her eyes. "I'm not thanking you, Sean. I'm asking you why you do it."

He felt tension begin to build in his shoulders. He tried to shrug it away. "I don't know. I guess I'm trying to control everything so it will turn out all right."

"That explains a lot."

"Like what exactly?"

She shifted in her seat to face him a bit more directly. "It explains why you bought this house without even asking my opinion. I guess it's also why you told me you were going to court me regardless of how I felt about it. And—"

"I understand."

She lifted her brow and stared back at him inquiringly. "So you realize that God is the only one who could possibly control everything in your life? That the only way any of your plans will come out right is if you surrender them to Him?"

He definitely didn't want to talk about this. What was going on with everyone lately? Was he doing such a bad job of managing his life that everyone felt he needed to listen to their advice? He was glad that Lorelei wanted to talk about spiritual things. It signified a deepening in their relationship. But, why this? Why now, when he was finally getting things in hand? He cleared his throat. "That's a lot to take in."

She left it at that to glance up at the sky thoughtfully. He should probably have done the same, but he noticed a long hairpin working its way loose from her fashionable chignon. "Your pin is falling out."

She found it but couldn't seem to fix it with only one hand free, so he reached over to do it for her. He barely touched the silly thing before it wobbled and fell from her hair. Lorelei gasped, then turned her head toward him abruptly, sending her long brown curls spilling over her shoulders. "Thank you so much for helping."

"Anytime." He grinned as the wind took complete control of her hair, tossing it across her face and teasing his cheek. At its fleeting touch, the tension immediately fled. He caught his breath. *How is that possible?*

He brushed her hair out of her face, then allowed his

hand to stray into her curls. They were soft and full and like nothing he'd ever felt before. He met her wide blue eyes. Suddenly, he recognized the girl he'd known at eighteen when past tension seemed easily buried and new possibilities were at hand. He saw the future they could have had if a misunderstanding and childish pride hadn't stood in the way. He saw the woman she was now. The woman he was beginning to care for. It scared him, and he was tempted to bring the past between them again but he didn't want to. He wanted for one day, one moment to let his guard down enough to see her as she really was—the woman he'd always longed for.

It was in that moment that he knew he was going to do something crazy, but he didn't try to stop himself. He kissed her. He kissed her gently, testing, half expecting her to send him flying off the swing for his gall. She would have had every right to do so. For that reason, he ended it nearly as quickly as it began.

Her dark lashes swept down to hide her stormy blue eyes. They were both quiet for a long moment as the swing settled into nothing more than a gentle sway. Finally, she glanced up at him again. The anger in her eyes told him he was in for a sudden squall.

Lorelei set her boots on the ground to bring the swing to an abrupt halt and pinned Sean with a glare. "I don't want to be just another one of your plans, Sean O'Brien."

He had the nerve to look confused. "What are you talking about?"

"If you made our courtship real just so you can go through the motions and check things off your list, you can just stop this silliness right now." She twisted her hair back into its normal style and used the only remaining pin in her curls to keep it in place. She stood to look around for her missing hairpins. "At least when I'm acting for the town, you still know exactly where you stand with me. Sean, the only person you're really fooling now is you."

"You don't know what you're talking about," he growled as he stood to help her look in the grass.

"Do you really think if you just plan it out and follow all of the steps, you can schedule yourself into loving me?" She took the hairpin he offered her and shifted it into place. "Buy a house. Check. First outing as a couple. Check. First kiss. Check. Check. Check. I refuse to add to that checklist you have in your head."

"Will you hush for half a minute?" He caught her arms and pulled her toward him. "I don't have a checklist, but I will admit that I planned to court you. Why is that wrong? I told you I would."

She braced her hand against his chest to push herself away, but he wouldn't release her. She forced herself to ignore the warmth that spread across her hand as it flexed against his chest. "It's wrong because you aren't telling the whole truth."

His gaze was unflinching. "What truth am I not telling you?"

Why wouldn't he just let her go? She shook her head. "The truth is you don't want to court me any more than you wanted to kiss me."

He stared at her in what seemed to be amazement. "How could you possibly think that?"

"A woman can tell when a man wants to kiss her and when he doesn't."

"Apparently not."

"Just admit it, Sean. That kiss was just like you—controlled and lacking any true emotion."

His jaw tightened, though his stare held disbelief. "Did you ever think I was just trying to be a gentleman?"

"If you were a gentleman, you wouldn't have tried to steal a kiss in the first place," she reasoned passionately. He seemed to lack the ability to respond to her well-argued logic. He would cave any second now. He'd give in and tell the truth, then she'd know she couldn't trust him with her heart.

She'd be able to weed out every little seed of hope that had taken root inside of her. She would get back to the peaceful life she'd led before he'd stormed in attempting to take control of her affections. A slight feeling of unease shifted through her. She almost questioned if that would be the best choice. She pushed the feeling away and tried again to make him admit the truth. "I could have seemed more sincere than that just by acting."

He stared at her in deep contemplation for a moment. She could feel her victory coming. His jaw flexed again, then he lifted a brow and said exactly what she would never have expected him to say. "Prove it."

She stared at him. "What?"

"I said prove it." He released her but didn't step away. "Prove that you can give me a more genuine kiss by acting than I was able to give you a minute ago when I wasn't acting."

When he says it like that it sounds crazy, she admitted to herself as she tried to think. She thought about calling on the Lord for help, but she'd gotten herself into this mess. She had a funny feeling that He wouldn't get her out of it. In fact, she had an uncanny sense that He was as interested in seeing how this might play out as Scan seemed to be.

Drat. What had she been thinking? A small flicker of a fire seemed to light his eyes with gold as he stared back at her, daring her to continue. She immediately began to doubt herself. After all, pretending to rob a bank was nothing like pretending to kiss somebody. She really didn't even have that much experience to draw from. She couldn't remember the last time Lawson had kissed her. Their relationship hadn't had much of a physical aspect to it. It hadn't had much of anything else, either.

Sean's arms slipped around her waist. Suddenly, she realized this wasn't a game because Sean wasn't playing. He was serious—really serious. She froze. "I get where this is going. I know what you're trying to prove, but I'm pretty sure that it won't work."

"I think you're just afraid it will."

Since when did he know her well enough to read her thoughts? Since now, apparently. She could make this easier on herself by stepping away from him. Of course, she didn't.

"It's time you realized something, Lorelei Wilkins." He pulled her slightly closer. "I've never hated you. I don't dislike you. I'm sorry that we've wasted so much time at each other's throats. I think it's the only way we knew how to fight against this."

"Fight against what?" she whispered.

"These feelings that have always been there and never seem to go away. I, for one, am tired of fighting against them and you. I want to see where this goes."

She stared into his sincere green eyes, but she couldn't quite believe the words he was saying. His face blurred with her tears, and she tried to blink them away. It didn't do any good. He saw her tears and wrapped his arms around her until she surrendered to his embrace by hesitantly resting her forehead on his chest. He shook his head. "I'm so sorry we've hurt each other. I do care about you, and I'm trying to show it, as unsophisticated as I may be at it."

"Sean," she breathed for lack of anything better to say. She finally glanced up to meet his gaze. "Do you really mean it—about being sorry?"

He nodded solemnly.

"Thank you." Impulsively, she rose on her tiptoes to kiss him gently.

He stared down at her in surprise. Slowly, a smile tipped his lips, and he shook his head. "We just can't get our timing right on this. Are you ready?"

"Yes." Yet, even as she spoke, his head dropped toward hers. His lips hovered over hers for an achingly eternal second before they captured hers. She could feel the sun shining down on those infernal seeds of hope inside of her, and at the moment she didn't care a whit.

He could have gone on kissing Lorelei all day, but somehow he managed to set her away from him. Only the self-control gifted to him by the Holy Spirit kept him from hauling her into his arms and doing it all over again when he caught sight of Lorelei's dazed expression. His voice came out at least half an octave lower than it normally was. "Were you acting?"

"No."

He set her away from him. "In that case, we'd better not make a habit of that just yet."

She blushed. He winked at her, then caught her hand in his to lead her through the woods back toward the house. She dragged a bit behind him. He glanced back but found her gaze already on him. He sent her an inquiring look, and she glanced away.

"You're going to be incorrigible after this. I can already tell," she muttered.

He grinned as they stepped out of the woods and walked to the front of the house. He felt like singing, but he knew better than to try. They still had a long way to go, but they'd definitely made progress. He paused at the sight of Ellie waiting for them on the porch steps. She bounced up to her feet with a smile. "I'm sorry I'm so late. Kate has been feeling poorly and everything that could delay me did. I've been waiting here about fifteen minutes. I figured you two would make it back eventually."

Ellie paused to take a breath. When no one responded, she gazed at them curiously. Her eyes widened at the sight of their joined hands. Lorelei seemed to notice at the same time because she abruptly jerked her hand from his and tucked it into her skirt pocket. Ellie tilted her head thoughtfully. A curious smile curved her lips as she sent him a questioning look. He shrugged.

"Well," she said briskly before a mischievous smile graced her lips. "It looks like you two have been having a lot of fun without me."

Chapter Seventeen

"'This is what I command you: that you love one another.'"

Lorelei sighed at the message she couldn't seem to get away from.

Reverend Sparks closed his Bible and set it on the pulpit. He looked at the congregation. "This is probably going to be the hardest thing I've had to do in my ministry."

Lorelei watched in confusion as Reverend Sparks looked at his wife who sat in the front row. The woman rose to her feet and went to stand by his side. He turned to face the congregation again. He straightened his shoulders. "Today I'd like to announce that I am stepping down as the reverend of this church."

A gasp rang through the church, leaving only silence in its wake.

"I'm still going to live in Peppin. I will still be involved in this church. I even promise to preach the occasional sermon. However, the time for me to shepherd this flock is over. God has made that abundantly clear to me and to my wife."

He smiled peacefully. "In fact, just as I was seriously

thinking of stepping down, I received a letter out of the nowhere from someone whom I would eventually regard as a son. Someone whom I am fully convinced is being called to this town."

Lorelei shifted in her seat along with half of the congregation who now craned their necks to watch the proceedings.

"I received the first letter a few weeks ago. We've been corresponding regularly since then. I have gotten to know this man and his family through the letters. He is a traveling preacher who has been looking for a place to settle down with his wife and five children."

Lorelei stopped breathing. Her eyes narrowed. *Impossible.* Lorelei frowned and shot a glance over her shoulder to Sean. He met her gaze to share a look of suspicion. Reverend Sparks's voice drew her gaze back to him.

"He heard about our little town and felt compelled to write to the church to find out if there were any open positions on staff. I told him there might be a position opening up. The rest, as they say, is history." He grinned. "James Brightly and his family will arrive in Peppin in two weeks."

"Oh," she breathed in alarm. Thankfully no one noticed because everyone started talking at once. *This is not good. If they mention anything about what happened with Miss Elmira—even accidentally—everything Sean and I have been doing will have been for nothing.*

"I hope to make the transition a very smooth one," she heard Reverend Sparks say, but the rest of his words faded into mumbles.

The congregation began dispersing, but Lorelei didn't move. She glanced up to find her mother hovering over her. "Are you all right, Lorelei? You look so pale."

She looked from her mother's concerned face to her father's. They didn't know. They didn't recognize the name, and she didn't have the strength to tell them. She shook her head. "I'm fine."

The words weren't true, but they needed to be. This was not the time to cause a scene. *Sean. Where is Sean?* She turned in search of him just as he appeared at her side. He looked just as bewildered as she felt. She saw his gaze slip to her parents and the moment he realized they didn't know that a crisis could be at hand. He slid into the pew next to her. "Mr. and Mrs. Wilkins, would you mind if I had a moment alone with Lorelei?"

Richard frowned. "I don't know. She looks like she had a fainting spell. She needs to go home."

She sent him a pleading look. "Please, Papa. I need to talk to him. He'll take care of me."

She watched indecision war across his features before he nodded. "Come on, Caroline."

Once her parents left, they had the sanctuary to themselves. Sean's arm stretched across the back of the pew, and she turned toward him. She finally felt the color begin to return to her cheeks. "I can't believe it."

"We should have told them we hated this place."

She let out a nervous laugh. She glanced up at him as amusement overcame her dread. "We should have told them how muddy the sidewalks get. How you can hear the noise from the saloon three blocks away because everything else is so quiet. How frightening it is to hear the train whistle when you least expect it."

His shook his head. "Lorelei Wilkins, we have a major problem on our hands. What are we going to do?"

"You're the one who always has the plans."

He quirked a smile at her. "I thought you hated my plans."

He coaxed an answering smile from her as she widened her eyes innocently. "Oh, no. I love your plans. They are always extremely well thought-out."

"Sure you do."

She looked him over with a measuring glance. "Are you trying to tell me that you don't have a plan?"

He shook his head slowly. "Don't tempt me. I'm trying to reform."

She sent him an unappreciative look.

"Hey, you should be proud that you made your point so well."

"I don't see how it's doing me any good."

"Where's your faith? 'None of your plans will turn out right if you don't surrender them to God,'" he parroted.

"Do you really believe that now?"

His gaze turned serious. "I don't know. I'm trying."

"Maybe our first step is to pray."

"We can do that." He caught her hand in his. They both bowed their heads as Sean began to pray. He asked God to lead them and give them wisdom in how to respond to this new challenge. Lorelei was feeling much calmer by the end of the prayer. Her mind spun with possible answers to their problem. "We should write the Brightlys a letter."

Sean pulled her to her feet but didn't move out of the aisle. He seemed to be assessing her steadiness. "What would we say?"

"We could explain everything," she said as he guided her out to the aisle and they walked toward the exit. "We can tell them that we're planning to get married. We could ask them to keep what happened to themselves."

"It might be worth a shot." He stayed close to her as they walked through the small foyer.

She glanced over her shoulder at him. "I'm not going to collapse."

He ignored her as he opened the door for her to step outside. She surveyed the milling groups of people who were gathered around either the Reverend or his wife. She gasped. Sean was instantly beside her with his hand supportively catching her arm. She turned to meet his gaze. "Forget the Brightlys. What if they told the Sparkses?"

"I'd better talk to the reverend."

"I'd better talk to his wife."

They split apart, and Lorelei managed to get close enough to Mrs. Sparks's conversation to hear what they were talking about.

"I hate to see you two step down," Mrs. Williams said. "There's a time for everything, though."

"Yes, I'm actually very pleased about it. This move has been coming for a long time. I'm especially glad that such a nice family will be taking our place."

Mrs. Stone smiled as she resettled her baby on her hip. "It's just amazing that he happened to write you at just the right time."

"It looks like Peppin is the talk of Texas," Mrs. Bradley said. "I wonder who might have told them about us."

Mrs. Sparks's gaze connected with Lorelei's. "I think we have Lorelei to thank for that."

Lorelei glanced around at the large group of women who now focused entirely on her. The question lingered in the air so loudly she wondered why someone didn't just say it. "I met the Brightlys when I ran away."

Mrs. Greene leaned forward as though she couldn't help herself despite their agreement. "Where did you have your sights set on going again?"

Her smile felt rather stiff, but she offered it anyway. "California. I have a great-aunt who lives there."

Mrs. Lettie touched her arm. "Well, what is your take on our new pastor?"

Grateful for the well-timed subject change, she met the kind eyes of the woman who had almost been her mother-in-law to concede, "He and his wife and children are wonderful."

Mrs. Lettie nodded as if that settled it. "The family should be a good addition to our town."

Lorelei stayed in the circle a few more minutes until she was satisfied that the conversation had completely moved on. She stepped away and began looking for her parents. Her mother waved at her. She wound her way through the crowd toward them.

"Miss Wilkins."

She turned to see Silas at her side. "Silas, I'm sorry but I really can't talk right now."

"When?"

She tried to think quickly. "Tomorrow at one. I'll be dropping a letter off at the post office at that time. You can meet me then."

He nodded, then slipped away.

A moment later, she met her parents. They insisted on escorting her right home, and she let them. She needed to talk to them privately anyway. It would be unfair of her to keep this from them. Yes, she'd tell them, then write one very important letter.

Lorelei held the sealed envelope tightly in her hand as she stepped onto the wooden sidewalk that ran alongside the boardinghouse. Two men stood on the sidewalk just ahead of her. One of them noticed her coming and made the others move out of the way for her. "Good afternoon, miss."

She nodded politely and tried to ignore their stares as she passed. She stiffened as one of them let out a low whistle. They made no attempt to hide their conversation from her. "I've never seen so many pretty women in one place."

"It makes me glad we'll be here a few days," the other responded.

She tried to step out onto the street, but a wagon abruptly turned in front of her so she had to step back.

"What do you think my chances are with that one?"

Lorelei dashed a glance toward them. They were still watching her. She gave them a cold stare, then lifted her chin. "Nonexistent, and I'll thank you to keep your comments to yourself."

That left them dumbfounded enough to allow her to escape across the street before their hoots of laughter echoed behind her. She stepped onto the sidewalk, then looked up to meet Silas's brown eyes. He took her arm, then speared the men on the other side of the street with a quelling glare. "Did they say something uncouth?"

"No, they were just overly outgoing," she said as she pulled her arm from his grasp. "I hope they aren't staying at Bradleys'. I would assume Mr. Bradley would be more cautious than that with his daughters working there."

"They aren't staying at the boardinghouse. They're just a couple of fools making a nuisance of themselves," he said with a bit of aggravation, then smiled politely. "I see you have a letter to mail. I was heading in that direction myself. Mind if I join you?"

"Not at all," she said as they walked. When he didn't immediately begin a conversation, she figured he must think they'd be too easily overheard on the bustling sidewalk. "How is Amy?"

His face seemed to turn pensive. "She's well."

"Are you two still spending time together?"

He nodded but wouldn't meet her gaze.

She lowered her voice, so only he could hear her. "You're going to break her heart."

He pinned her with a piercing gaze. "What about you and your sheriff? I hear you two seem to be getting pretty serious. How do you feel about breaking his heart?"

"Not nearly as bad as you feel about breaking Amy's," she guessed.

The color heightened in his face. "Leave it alone, Lorelei. We need to focus on getting the job done."

"Fine," she said as they passed the seamstress's shop. "Has that new manager come in yet?"

"He's here."

"Good. I need you to meet me Thursday at two o'clock outside of the courthouse. We'll go over a few last-minute things, and I'll let you know when we'll be ready to move." He tipped his hat and was gone almost as quickly he appeared.

He has to be one of the strangest people I know, she thought to herself as she stood behind the only other person in line at the post office. *He sure doesn't seem like a hardened criminal. Maybe he's new to the job. He needs to get rid of some of that politeness if he wants to make it as a bank robber. He seemed truly upset that those men were bothering me. I would believe those men were criminals before I would believe Silas was.*

This was not the time to worry about Silas she realized as she stared at the letter in her hand. She bowed her head and prayed, her lips barely moving along with her entreaty. *Please, God. Let the Brightlys want to help us by keeping quiet about the whole thing for now. Please—*

"Miss Wilkins, did you want to mail something?" the young man behind the counter asked.

She glanced up to see she was now the only one in line so she stepped up to the counter. "Yes, I'm sorry. I was thinking about something. How fast do you think this will get to where it needs to go?"

He took the letter and stared thoughtfully at the address. "Reverend Sparks usually hears back from this fellow in a couple of days."

"Am I sending it to the right address, then?" She handed him the money for postage.

"Yes, ma'am." He postmarked it and placed it into the mailbag behind him. "Just check back in a few days."

"Thank you." With a parting smile, she turned away breathing quietly, "Your will be done."

"Thanks, Maddie," Sean said as Maddie slid the cup of lemonade he'd requested onto the table.

"Sure thing." She straightened, then paused to peer out the window. "Why didn't you tell me Lorelei was coming?"

"She isn't."

"Sure, she is. She's right there. Aren't you going to have lunch with her?"

He followed her gaze to see Lorelei crossing the street toward the café. "I wasn't planning on it."

Maddie placed a hand on her slim hip. "Well, here's your chance. Go get her. Tell her I'll have a slice of my pecan pie waiting. That girl hasn't been in here in ages."

"Yes, ma'am," he agreed as he slipped past Maddie. Lorelei had just passed the door by the time he made it out. She was only a few feet away so he called out, "Hey, beautiful! Where are you going?"

She slowly turned around. Then, narrowing her eyes, she tilted her head at him. "I assume that means you want me to stop and talk to you."

He grinned. "Have you eaten yet?"

"No."

"Would you like to have lunch with me?"

"No."

"Lorelei."

Her dark blue eyes filled with mirth. A smile tugged at her lips, and she shook her head as she approached him. "You realize that half the people in the café have their faces pressed against the glass, don't you?"

He frowned. "What happened to the other half?"

"They already had front-row seats."

"Have lunch with me," he repeated.

She looked over his shoulder toward the café thoughtfully. "Why?"

"You're here. You're hungry. I'm here. I'm hungry. It seems like a good idea."

Her gaze lifted to meet his. "Silas said that people think we're getting serious about each other."

"That's good," he said, feeling his stomach rumble in protest of the delay. Then his eyes narrowed, and he looked at Lorelei closely. "When did he say that?"

She tugged on his arm and stepped past him. "Let's eat."

"Lorelei," he protested, but she had already walked into the café.

Her gaze met his, then danced away as Maddie showed her to his table. Maddie took Lorelei's drink order but didn't leave to fill it immediately. Instead, the woman grinned. "That was quite a hello you received."

Sean looked at Maddie in amazement. Now, how had she heard that? Perhaps the door hadn't closed behind him before he'd said it. Lorelei laughed. "I'm getting used to it. That wasn't the first time I was hallooed today."

He frowned. "It wasn't?"

She shook her head. "I think it was the third."

"Oh, my." Maddie laughed. "Sean, it looks like you may have some competition."

"Let me at them," he growled and more people in the café than just Maddie laughed.

He shook his head. That was one of the perils of living in a small town where everyone was so interconnected. There wasn't enough room to mind your own business, so you often ended up minding others'. No wonder Mr. Wilkins had been so adamant that he marry Lorelei.

"Now, what can I get you two to eat?"

They both ordered the special. After Lorelei received her drink, they were left alone for a while. Lorelei glanced up at him with a smile. "Do you know what I did today?"

Everyone seemed to go back to their own meals, but he leaned forward and lowered his voice slightly just to be safe. "You mean besides meeting Silas Smithson without so much as a word to me?"

She shook her head. "No, besides that."

"I have no idea."

"I mailed the letter to the Brightlys," she said softly. "I feel optimistic about it. After all, they're good people. They shouldn't mind helping us, should they?"

"I guess we'll find out soon enough."

She nodded. "The postmaster said it should only be a few days until I hear back."

They both stopped talking as Maddie made her way toward them with their food. After they said grace, Sean gave Lorelei a few minutes of uninterrupted eating before he pinned her with the question she should have answered long ago. "So why didn't you tell me you were meeting with him?"

She glanced up at him, then back at her food. "We arranged it yesterday at church. I told him I couldn't talk to him then, so he asked to meet me today. My parents wanted me to leave right after that, so I didn't have time to tell you."

He nodded. "I see why you didn't tell me then. Why didn't you tell me earlier today?"

She lowered her fork, admitting, "I was working on the letter but I did follow your advice. We met in a public place in the daytime just like you said we should."

"I'm glad to hear it, but next time you have to let me know so I can at least be in the general area. I mean it, Lorelei. If something happens, I need to be able to help you."

"I'm meeting him Thursday at two o'clock in front of the courthouse. He wants to go over some final details. You are more than welcome to be in the general area then."

"Thursday at two." He chewed thoughtfully for a moment. "What happens at the bank around that time?"

She glanced up curiously. "Nothing. It's usually pretty quiet."

"That's what I thought."

"You mean?"

"I mean I have a lot to do."

"*We* have a lot to do."

"That, too." He needed to go over Lorelei's role in this, but as soon as they finished, he'd head over to the courthouse and talk to the judge about swearing in as many temporary deputies as he could find. He'd put Jeff on watch at the train station. Most important, he also needed to prepare Mr. Wilkins and the new manager now that the threat seemed imminent.

His whole plan hinged on being prepared in advance. That's why Lorelei's information was so valuable. He wanted to have the tellers and the deputies lying in wait for the gang so they'd have the benefit of surprise, not the other way around. He was pretty sure he'd be able to find a lot of eager volunteer deputies. This was Peppin, after all. They wouldn't go down without a fight because they plain refused to go down at all.

Lorelei did her level best to pay attention to the book she was pretending to read and not try to scan the courtyard for Sean. He'd told her he would be in the vicinity but refused to tell her where. She sighed. *Very comforting, Sean.*

She'd been instructed to act as though she was totally oblivious to the fact the robbery might actually be happening today. She could act that way, but just the possibility of the holdup becoming a reality had her body strumming with nervousness. The waiting wasn't helping, either. *Where in the world is Silas, anyway? I've been waiting at least ten minutes already.*

She made it through the next few pages of her book before she realized someone was approaching. Silas strolled toward her bench as if he didn't have a care in the world. She closed her book and offered him a smile. "Hello, Silas."

He carefully returned her smile. "Lorelei, it's a beautiful day for a walk. Join me."

"Certainly." She slipped her arm into his, then

glanced at him curiously when he pinned it to his side. She surveyed his expression carefully. He seemed uncharacteristically lacking in emotion. "Is something wrong?"

He shook his head. "No. Everything is going according to schedule."

She allowed him to continue to lead her along the sidewalk away from the center of town. "Do you have some information you want to share with me then? Perhaps a final date so that I can be ready?"

He watched her for a long moment. A strange mix of emotions settled in his eyes. They were filled with pity, amusement and a bit of derision if she wasn't mistaken. "No, I'm afraid not."

"I don't understand. Why did you insist on meeting me today?" The sidewalk abruptly ended, causing her to stumble.

Silas caught her arms in his hands until she regained her footing, then pinned her with his stare. "You're going to cooperate, aren't you, Lorelei?"

Her eyes widened. "Yes, of course. I told you I would."

He seemed much more like the Silas she knew when he smiled his approval. "Good. Follow me."

She had little choice since he kept his grasp firmly on her arm and pulled her behind the courthouse. The rail yard stretched behind a big iron fence to the right. The sight of the large bay stallion tethered to the fence caught her attention. Waves of dread slowly filtered through her stomach as Silas made a beeline toward it. "Get on the horse, Lorelei."

She swallowed nervously. "Why?"

His voice was calm. His eyes were deadly. "If you don't, I'm going to have to kill you."

"You wouldn't—" She bit her lip as she suddenly found herself staring down the barrel of his gun. Her heart pounded in her chest. She daringly lifted one eyebrow and shrugged nonchalantly. "No need to be nasty about it. Put that thing away and give me a boost."

He put his gun away, but not before she saw a flicker of respect in his eyes. She waited until he met her gaze again. "It's happening today, isn't it?"

He gave her a hard stare, then cupped his hands for her boot. "We don't have time for this. Drape your skirt across the saddle horn and sit sidesaddle."

She did as he said. He untethered the horse and swung up behind her before turning the horse abruptly. As they rode out of town, Lorelei didn't dare look behind her to see if Sean might be following. Instead, she closed her eyes. *Lord, I've been trying to do the right thing. Please, protect me and the rest of the town. Show me how I can stop this before someone gets hurt.*

Sean waited until he felt he had a good sense of the direction Lorelei and Silas Smithson were heading before he cut through the alleyway toward the livery. Joshua Stone and Jeff Bridger looked up questioningly as Sean stepped out of the alley into the doorway of the livery. Sean gave them an abrupt nod. "Today is the day just like we thought."

"Your mount is saddled and waiting like you asked," Mr. Stone said.

"Thank you. Jeff, gather the others and get into position. Mr. Stone, notify Mr. Wilkins. Make sure everyone is armed and ready."

Jeff frowned. "Where are you going?"

He swung onto his mount, then glanced down at the

two men he knew he could count on to carry on without him. "They took Lorelei. I'm going to get her back."

As he rode out of town, he muttered a prayer. "All right, Lord, I know I haven't been the best at asking for help or advice. I reckon You must not hate my plans entirely since You let me think of them, but this one is too important for me to do by myself. The town needs You, Lorelei needs You and I need You to see to it that this plan goes off without a hitch. I'm surrendering this to You, Lord. Please, protect us all."

Chapter Eighteen

The ride was shorter than she expected. Silas reined in his horse about a quarter mile outside of town. They stopped in front of a small railroad supply shed that had obviously been built and abandoned five years ago when the railroad swept through town. She eyed the building dubiously. Silas helped her dismount before grabbing her arm in that tight grip of his and forcing her inside the shed.

Despite the bright sunlight outside, the inside of the small building was dim. The only square of sunlight in the room burst through a busted window along the back wall. Once her eyes adjusted, she met Calhoun's gaze with a smile she didn't feel. "It looks like your waiting is over, Mr. Calhoun."

He grunted around the pipe in his mouth and said nothing else at first. He just continued to watch her. It was only when she glanced away that he spoke to Silas in that rough voice of his. "The others should be here any minute."

"What others? I thought you were just waiting for your boss."

Mr. Calhoun grinned slowly. "The boss and rest of the gang, Missy."

"The rest of the gang," she echoed, wondering how many that meant. She hoped Sean was prepared for more than they'd planned. He'd refused to tell her anything about his role and what he'd done to prepare for it, so that if questioned, she could honestly say she didn't know.

Silas moved past her to stand by the window. The air suddenly filled with the sound of horse hooves and strange wild yips. Mr. Calhoun stood from where he sat on an old crate and walked toward the door muttering, "Bunch o' wild ne'er-do-wells, the lot of them."

He stood outlined in the door for a long minute while the whoops and yelps grew louder. Finally, he yelled, "All right, all right. We know you're here. Shut your traps."

The sounds only increased in volume until the first man burst through the door. She immediately recognized him as one of the men who'd pestered her on the way to mail the letter to the Brightlys. "Calhoun, you old coot, you're cranky as always, I see. Remind me why the boss keeps you around."

"Because I've got more sense than the rest of y'all put together," he said wryly, then glanced behind him. "Except for maybe Smithson here."

She knew the instant the younger man caught sight of her because he gave a slow whistle. "Who's that?"

Another man burst into the shed. He took one look at Lorelei and stopped short. A lecherous grin tipped his mouth, and he elbowed the other man. "Lookee there. You see what I see, Jake?"

Jake looked her over slowly. "Looks like a woman to me, Owen."

She straightened her shoulders and sent them a haughty glare meant to put them in their place. "That's funny. From here it looks like two fools."

Jake grinned. "You can call me whatever you want, honey, as long as I get to look at you."

Owen pinned her with his lazy smile as he sank onto a nearby crate. "Look all you want. Just don't touch her. I claimed that little gal when I saw her on the sidewalk. Ain't that right, Miss Wilkins?"

She ignored him and turned toward Silas, who was still staring out the window. "It looks like there's a lot you didn't tell me, Silas."

Calhoun hooted. "Now that's the truth."

She lifted her brows inquiringly. "Are there any other surprises, gentlemen?"

Silas suddenly turned to face her. His eyes were dark, hard and unflinching. His mocking smile sent chills through her body. "You might be surprised to know that I didn't believe your little act for a moment. I will congratulate you on your valiant effort, though."

Chills tripped down her arms. She swallowed. "What are you talking about?"

"The only reason I kept you around was to get the layouts of the bank and feed the wrong information to that sheriff of yours." He stepped toward her threateningly. "Do you really think that I wanted your help?"

"So the plans we made…"

Calhoun grinned. "That was funny. You planned a nice little robbery all by yourself, didn't you? We might have to use that plan on the next town we hit."

"I see," she said thoughtfully, then frantically tried to think of a way to get herself out of this mess. She tilted her head and gave a dry laugh. "Well, you had me fooled. I almost thought you were a gentleman."

"You thought Silas was a gentleman?" Jake laughed in disbelief. "He's just like the rest of us only he wears fancier clothes because we send him in to scout places out. I always say, you can dress up a donkey so he looks like a horse but inside he's still—"

"Shut up, Jake," Silas growled.

Jake rolled his eyes, then sat down on a crate with a thud.

"When is the boss getting here?" Owen asked.

"He's riding over now," Calhoun said from where he leaned next to the door.

Lorelei hated to bring the focus back to herself, but she needed to know what she might be up against. "If you don't mind me asking, what are you planning to do with me?"

Owen leaned forward with a leer. "Now, there's a question I'd like to answer."

She sent him a scathing glare. "I wouldn't care to know that answer. Besides, I was asking you, Silas. After all, you could have just let me remain oblivious to all this. I wouldn't have been able to tell anyone anything about your real plans. What's the point of taking me captive?"

A new man entered the shed. All of the others sat up in attention. The mood immediately became more serious as he took stock of everyone. He was tall and thin but about as well dressed as Silas. His hands rested at his holster. His light brown gaze stopped when it met hers. "You're our insurance. Your pa owns the bank. He'll be much more cooperative if he knows we've got you."

He turned to address his men. "I've been thinking. We'd better not take her with us at first. We don't want the locals to get any ideas about saving her before everything is done. Someone will need to stay behind with her, then join the rest of us in about twenty minutes. By that time, we should have what we need."

"How will he believe we have her if she isn't with us?" Silas asked.

"We'll take proof."

Calhoun frowned. "What kind of proof?"

"Something she's wearing," Jake offered.

"Her dress," Owen quietly suggested with a smirk.

"You don't have time for that," she said to the boss as she removed her hat. "You can take this. Papa knows it's mine."

He wavered for a moment, as though unwilling to accept her direction. Suddenly snatching the hat from her hand, he bellowed, "Everyone mount up. I'll go over assignments outside."

The door closed behind the last man with a bang. Lorelei knew they'd probably send Silas back in to guard her, but she didn't plan to sit around and wait while her father's bank was robbed. Her hand strayed to the small derringer Sean had insisted she strap to her leg. She sank onto a nearby crate and hid the gun beneath the folds of her skirt while she waited for her guard to come back in.

"Lord, please help me get out of here," she whispered to herself as she heard the others' horses ride away.

The door opened slowly, then closed with a decided slam. She glanced up. Instead of meeting Silas's dark eyes, she was confronted with Owen's lecherous grin. She stared back at him. She slowly rose to her feet, hiding the derringer behind her. "Where is Silas?"

Owen leaned back against the door to watch her. "The boss wanted him to go with the gang since he knows his way around town. I guess that just leaves you and me."

"Unfortunately," she murmured.

He threw his hat on a nearby crate and began to pace measured steps toward her. "The way I figure it, we've got about fifteen minutes all to ourselves. What do you reckon we could do in fifteen minutes?"

"I plan to sit right here and wait until it's time to leave," she said as her hand tightened around the gun.

"That's too bad because I'm planning on having a little bit of fun," he said, reaching toward her.

She jerked away from him, pulled the derringer from behind her back and pointed it straight at his heart. "Stay where you are or I'll pull the trigger."

He pulled his gun with a lighting-quick speed that took her breath away. Her little derringer looked awfully harmless compared to his Colt. The amusement on his face told her just how serious he was taking her threat. "That's a nice little pistol you have there, Miss Wilkins. Hold it out to the side so I can get a good look at it."

She braced herself, then squeezed the trigger. Light exploded off the end of her gun. He roared as the bullet ripped across his left shoulder. She darted past him. A sharp cry of pain rent from her lips as he grabbed her arm and twisted it behind her body. The gun slipped from her hand. He shoved her against the wall. "I'll teach you not to fool with me."

She gasped for breath as she struggled against him to no avail. *Dear God in heaven have mercy,* she thought frantically just before his filthy laugh sounded in her ear.

Sean rushed toward the shed as a gunshot rang out. He prayed he wasn't too late. Lorelei's sharp cry of pain sounded inside. He pushed through the door and saw a man pin her against the wall. Fury filled his stomach. He drew his gun.

His finger twitched over the trigger, then stalled. He flipped the gun over to hold the barrel. The man's putrid laughter filled the air as Sean walked up behind him. Without hesitation, he lifted the gun and crashed the handle onto the man's head. He dropped like a boulder in a river. Sean eyed him to make sure he was really knocked out before he glanced at Lorelei. She was still staring at the man in disbelief. Slowly, her gaze lifted to his.

Her dark blue eyes were wild and stunned. They filled with tears an instant before she launched herself into his arms. He caught her tightly to his chest. That's when he knew why he'd been fighting so hard to win the heart of a woman so reluctant to give it. He loved her. He'd been intrigued since that moment ten years ago when she'd announced their fates were intertwined. He'd hated watching her court Lawson until he'd resigned himself to it. He'd done a pretty good job of burying his feelings over the years, but they'd always been there waiting to be unearthed. With her in his arms, he lacked the will and the desire to deny their existence any longer.

"Just like breathing," he murmured.

"What?"

He glanced down at her and shook his head. He couldn't tell her. She wouldn't believe him anyway. It was best to keep his discovery to himself for now. He lifted her over the prone man to settle onto a crate close to the door with her in his lap. Her whole body seemed to tremble. Her arms clung tightly around his neck, which was fine with him because he wasn't about to let her go. He pressed a kiss against her hair. "Did they hurt you?"

She shook her head against his shoulder. "Not yet."

"I wish I could have slugged him."

She leaned back to look up at him. "Oh, Sean. It was awful. Silas knew I was pretending the whole time."

Sean placed a stilling finger on her lips. "Do you hear that?"

She was quiet for a long moment as the sound of approaching horses' hooves filled the shed. Her eyes widened. She whispered, "Someone is coming."

They hurriedly stood to their feet. Sean drew his gun again, then motioned to her. "Get behind me."

She brushed the tears from her cheek. "Don't be ridiculous. I'm not going to hide from these brutes."

"Lorelei," he chastened in frustration.

"This is my battle, too." She sent him a hard look, then picked up what he recognized as her derringer off of the ground. She spread her boots apart just enough to find her stance. Pursing her lips in concentration, she trained her gun toward the door.

They quieted in time to hear the hoofbeats come to a stop outside the shed. Someone dismounted. He tried not to let himself tense as the footsteps neared. The moment the door opened and the man stepped inside Sean commanded, "Hands in the air where I can see them!"

Silas's hands crept cautiously toward the ceiling with his right hand already holding a gun. The man's gaze swept the room quickly before returning to Sean. "What's going on here?"

"First, throw your weapon outside nice and easy. Don't give me a chance to shoot you because I'd sure like to," he said calmly.

Silas followed his directions, then lifted his hand to the ceiling again. "Is Owen dead?"

Sean shook his head. "I haven't checked but I'd say he's just unconscious for now."

"He tried to accost me," Lorelei interjected.

Silas lowered his head slightly. "I'm sorry, Lorelei. I was coming back to help you."

Sean narrowed his gaze. "Why do that after putting her in danger in the first place?"

"I had to in order to finish the job. You see, we're all on the same side here."

Lorelei shook her head. "Oh, no, we aren't."

"Yes, we are. I'm an undercover Texas Ranger."

"Prove it," Sean demanded over Lorelei's gasp.

"I have to get the papers out of my boot." At Sean's nod, he leaned over and pulled off his shoe. Using a knife he pulled from his pocket, the man wedged the heel open and removed a folded piece of paper. He dropped the knife on the ground away from him, then held out the paper for Sean to take.

Sean glanced at Lorelei. She nodded and kept her gun trained on Silas as Sean holstered his and examined the paper in his hand. He glanced up at Silas. "It looks legitimate."

"It *is* legitimate," he said as he tucked the paper in his pocket. "I've been working with this gang for almost five months. I gained their trust so I could gather the evidence I needed. As soon as they get the money from the bank, I'll be ready to arrest them. I allowed Lorelei to become involved because she would have botched the whole thing otherwise."

"Thanks a lot," she said wryly.

"I was trying to keep you safe." He stomped his foot back into his shoe.

"You left her at the mercy of one of your gang members," Sean objected. "I don't think that qualifies as keeping her safe."

Silas's gaze was defiant. "My priority was to finish the job. She involved herself in this. If something had happened, it would have been as much her fault as mine."

Sean grasped him by the front of the shirt and stared down at him. "Let's get this straight. You could have told Lorelei no in the beginning. You could have come to me, the local law enforcement, to explain your assignment. Instead, you allowed this to progress until you placed her in a position where she could have been hurt or killed. If something had happened to her, it would have been as a result of your negligence, not your duty. Do you understand?"

Silas glared back at Sean for a long moment, then shoved himself away. "I've got work to do."

"I hope that means saving my papa's bank from being robbed," Lorelei said pointedly.

"It does," he said. They followed him outside as he picked up his weapons. He stopped beside his horse. "Sheriff, you can ride along with me if you like. I'm sure I could use your help rounding up all of those outlaws."

Sean nodded. "I'll deal with the one here, then Lorelei and I will follow you into town. You and I probably won't need to do much. The whole town decided to pitch in to catch the bank robbers. We've probably got them outnumbered three to one."

Just as Sean had predicted, all of the outlaws had been bound and gagged by the time he arrived at the bank. He walked inside and was immediately met by Jeff. "It all went according to your plan."

"Anyone hurt?"

"No. Not a single gun was fired." Jeff grinned. "I wish you could have seen the look on those outlaws' faces when they burst in with their guns waving only to find themselves surrounded by half the town's arsenal. I doubt Judge Hendricks will ever swear in so many temporary deputies again."

"Where is Mr. Wilkins?"

"He's in his office with Doc. He was looking pretty pale when those good-for-nothings came in holding Lorelei's hat like a medal of honor."

Sean headed to the back of the bank and walked into Richard's office. The man stood from his chair as soon as he caught sight of Sean. "Lorelei. Is she—?"

"Fine, Mr. Wilkins. She stopped for a minute outside to talk to Amy, but I can assure you that she is perfectly fine."

Richard sank back into his chair and let out a relieved breath. "Thank God."

"Deputy Bridger tells me everything went as planned."

Richard nodded. "They hardly got past the door."

"Good," he said. "I'd better make sure those men are officially taken into custody."

Richard waved him away. Sean had barely taken a few steps out of Richard's office when Silas approached him. "I'd like to transfer these men to the jail now. They shouldn't be there long. I'll wire headquarters immediately."

"Good. I'll open the jail for you." He was walking out the door when Lorelei stepped inside.

No one could miss the glare she sent to the outlaws lined up against the wall. She grabbed her hat from where it sat on the counter, then walked over to Sean. "Is Papa in his office?"

He nodded. "He'll be glad to see you."

She glanced around, then, with half the town watching, she rose on her tiptoes to place a soft kiss on his cheek. Pausing to meet his eyes meaningfully, she whispered, "Thank you."

He might have returned her gesture with a bit more gusto if she hadn't quickly stepped past him to hurry toward her father's office. The sly knowing looks he received from the other men in the bank told him they thought he was falling hard. He smiled wryly. Lord, help him. They weren't half-wrong.

Lorelei gave a parting smile to her parents as they stopped to talk to their friends. She continued through the crowd toward the gazebo where the main Founder's Day activities would take place. It looked as if most of Peppin's citizens had turned out for the event that would begin with a picnic and end with a dance late that evening. Usually Lorelei anticipated this day for weeks, but her mind had been so preoccupied by other things lately that she'd hardly given it a second thought.

She spotted Ellie a few yards in front of her and wound her way through the crowd toward her. As she neared, Ellie caught her gaze with a smile. "Lorelei, I was just looking for you. Where are your parents?"

"They stopped to talk to Doc and Mrs. Williams," she explained, then leaned around Ellie to wave at Kate and Nathan. "Kate, how are you? Ellie told me you were feeling poorly last week."

"Just fine." Kate shared a smile with Nathan, then leaned toward Lorelei to whisper, "I told the rest of the family, so I guess I should tell you, too. Nathan and I are going to have another baby."

Lorelei's eyes widened. "Congratulations! That's wonderful."

Nathan grinned. "It certainly is. I think it's going to be another boy this time. We need to even things up."

Judge Hendricks stepped forward on the platform of the gazebo and raised his hands to get everyone's attention. "Quiet down, folks. Quiet down."

Ellie nudged Lorelei and whispered, "Did you hear that Sean is getting an award for stopping the bank robbery?"

"Yes, I know," she returned quietly. Sean had tried to convince her to let the town know about her part in apprehending the criminals, but she'd been more than appalled at the idea. Actually, she'd been more than appalled at the thought of what her father might have to say if he knew the extent of her involvement. Having caught the outlaws red-handed, there was no need for her to testify. As far as she was concerned, her foray into undercover work would remain a secret until no one cared to hear about it.

Judge Hendricks cleared his throat. "As one of the town's founders, I would like to welcome you all to the fifth annual Founder's Day celebration."

Lorelei glanced back to look for her parents, hoping they wouldn't miss the judge's speech as the hundreds of people around her cheered, whistled and clapped. She saw her parents edging forward at the back of the crowd. Richard smiled when she met his gaze and gave her a little wave. She turned back in time to see the judge hold up his hand to indicate he was ready to speak again. The cheers died down, so he continued.

"We have set this day aside to come together to show our commitment to each other and this town. We come together to remind ourselves of the ideals our town was founded upon. We come together to express our thankfulness to God for seeing our town through another year and to pray that His will is accomplished in the next.

"As we do, we remember the faith, dedication and perseverance that took us through the first fifteen years. Those same qualities will sustain us through the next one hundred and fifteen."

Lorelei joined in with the thunderous applause that interrupted the judge.

"Reverend Sparks will begin the day with a prayer. After he does, I would like to invite retired Sheriff Hawkins, who served this town for fifteen years, to come up and help me with a special announcement."

"This is it," Ellie whispered proudly a few minutes later.

Lorelei smiled as the tall but slightly stoop-shouldered sheriff from her childhood stepped forward. Judge Hendricks shook the man's hand, then turned back to the crowd. "The citizens of Peppin have long been interested in finding a way to express their appreciation to outstanding members of the community. It is my pleasure to announce that we finally figured something out."

Chuckles rang through the crowd as the judge continued, "From now on we will recognize citizens who show admirable courage, self-sacrifice, fortitude, so on and so forth by awarding them with the Peppin Award of Honor.

"I'm sure all of you have heard by now, a gang of outlaws tried to rob the First Bank of Peppin a few days ago. If they had succeeded, our celebration today would not have been quite as joyful. As it was, members of this town came together to help defend the bank and managed to put those outlaws right where they belong—in jail. Today the town would like to recognize Sheriff Sean O'Brien for his outstanding leadership in coordinating this effort and for his service to the community."

Sean stepped forward as Mr. Hawkins presented him with a fancy-looking box and everyone clapped. He faced the crowd, then held up his hand as Judge Hendricks had done. He managed to keep the applause short. "I am very grateful to all of you for finding me worthy of this award. However, this award really belongs to this town and not to me. I especially think we should recognize those who were sworn in as temporary deputies to help in the effort.

"There are about ten of you, so I didn't want to forget anyone." He grinned, then pulled out a piece of paper to read off their names. After everyone cheered for the temporary deputies, Sean put the piece of paper back in his pocket. "There is another person from our town we should thank. This person has chosen to remain anonymous but provided vital information necessary to the success of our efforts. I hope this person knows how much I truly appreciated their help."

He gave a self-deprecating smile. "Now, I think I've said about enough, so I'll leave y'all to enjoy the day."

"He did a good job," she whispered to Ellic.

Ellie nodded but tilted her head toward the gazebo with a confused look on her face. She glanced back at the gazebo to see Judge Hendricks holding his hand up to keep the people from clapping just yet. "Hold on there, Sean. I thought there was something else you were planning to say."

Even twenty feet away she could see Sean begin to redden. He whispered something to the judge, but the man just grinned. "Don't be shy, now. If a man has something to say, he ought to just go ahead and say it. Right, folks?"

Several teasing remarks rang from the crowd urging Sean to speak. Lorelei smiled and exchanged a glance with Ellie. "What in the world?"

Ellie shrugged, then cupped her hand by her lips to yell. "Speak, Sean. Speak!"

Sean laughed. "Fine. I wasn't planning to do this, but while I was waiting to come up here I realized the opportunity had presented itself."

"That and this town is too nosy to let him leave the stage without saying something interesting," Ellie whispered to Lorelei.

She giggled and nudged Ellie with her arm but had to admit, "That's the truth."

The crowd waited as Sean took the paper from his pocket and flipped it over. He read whatever was on the back of it then slipped it into his pocket. He glanced at the chortling judge and shrugged. "A man has to get this sort of thing right."

A ribbon of suspicion began to flutter in her mind about the same time that Sean's gaze met hers. His voice was loud and clear as he called out, "Lorelei Wilkins, will you come here for a minute?"

Chapter Nineteen

Her eyes widened as she felt the entire town turn to look at her. Her breath stilled in her throat. She shook her head no, but she was urged forward by Ellie and pretty much everyone else. She made it to the base of the gazebo.

"You are the most wonderful, beautiful and captivating woman I have ever met." He held his hand out to guide her up the stairs of the gazebo. A playful smile flashed at his lips for an instant, and she realized he was pulling her into their own little secret before he continued. "I have had no choice but to fall in love with you."

She covered her mouth with her hand in a gesture that appeared to be of amazement but was really meant to hold in the laughter that begged to spill from her lips. Everyone had backed away to give them their space. Now, the crowd shifted to get a better view as Sean knelt before her.

"I would be honored to spend the rest of my life with you," he said with a sincerity that might have sobered her if that playful gleam hadn't returned so quickly. "Will you marry me?"

She gave herself a moment to gather her thoughts.

Slowly, she managed to lower her hand from her mouth. A smile pulled at her lips. She nodded, then realized not everyone could see that.

"Yes," she said loudly, then bit her lip to keep from laughing at the ridiculousness of the entire situation. "Yes, Sean O'Brien, I'll marry you."

The town erupted in cheers so loud she could hardly think. Sean shot to his feet and pulled her into a warm embrace. She pulled back to meet his gaze with her mirth-filled one. She shook her head. Knowing the crowd would think she was teasing him about the proposal, she swayed toward him to whisper beneath the crowd noise. "You are such a liar!"

"Is that any way to speak to your fiancé?"

The cheers were just beginning to calm down when Ellie called out, "Give her a kiss."

Lorelei shot a glance at her soon-to-be mischief-maker-in-law as other people encouraged Sean to do the same. Turning back to Sean, she felt a blush begin to color her cheeks. He looked at her with mock seriousness. "We'd better give the people what they want. It's my job to keep the peace around here, and they might riot if we don't."

"We wouldn't want that," she breathed.

His kiss tempted her to forget all about the people watching them until he stepped away to slip the ring on her finger. She waved it at the crowd, hoping they would take the hint and move on with the festivities. She followed Sean down the steps toward his family.

Judge Hendricks regained the attention of the crowd. "That's the most exciting thing that has happened on Founder's Day yet. I hope we make it a tradition. Well, folks. That's all of the ceremonial stuff. You are free to go have fun. Enjoy each other and the festivities planned for today."

Lorelei spent the next few minutes accepting congratulations from the town as people began to disperse. The more congratulations she received, the harder it was to keep the smile from slipping off her face. Finally, her parents joined her where she stood with the O'Briens. Her father shook Sean's hand with a firm clasp. "Well done on that proposal, son."

"Thank you, sir."

Mrs. Greene stepped forward to congratulate them, but before she left she also added, "I'll be at the wedding. Don't you forget it."

Lorelei grimaced as the woman walked away, but her mother was beaming. "Why don't y'all come over to our house after lunch for dessert? I made ice cream. We can celebrate and make plans for the wedding."

Sean's family quickly agreed. Lorelei glanced around the happy faces of the two families in disbelief. *This entire thing is nothing but a farce, and they know it. How can they possibly be so genuinely happy about this?*

Sean's hand grazed her back, and she glanced up to meet his questioning gaze. "Is something wrong?"

She shook her head. "I'm fine."

It wasn't long before they were all gathered on her parents' front porch with their bowls of creamy vanilla ice cream in hand. The children sat on the porch steps in raptures at the treat. Lorelei slid onto the end of the bench where Kate and Ellie sat. Sean took a chair next to her. Her mother and father sat beside him. Nathan completed the familial circle by sitting between her father and Kate.

"Now," Caroline announced as they were all finishing with their desserts. "I think we ought to decide on a wedding date."

Lorelei's eyes widened in alarm. "So soon? I was hoping things might be able to slow down now. After all, you only gave us a deadline for the proposal."

Her father shook his head. "The sooner the better, Lorelei. Everything will settle down once you're married. Anyway, we promised Mrs. Greene."

"I guess you're right," she agreed, then bit her lip.

"How soon were you thinking, Mr. Wilkins?" Sean asked.

"I think I'll have to defer to the women on an exact time frame, but I think it should be done as soon as possible," he said with a glance toward her mother and Kate.

Kate's gaze turned thoughtful. "Ellie and I would be willing to help in whatever way we can, Mrs. Wilkins. How long do you think it will take to get everything ready?"

"Well, Lorelei already has a dress, so that should help cut down on the time considerably. I'd have to see when the church would be available."

"I'd rather not have another wedding in the church," Lorelei said. "We can have it here, if Sean doesn't mind."

"Fine by me."

"I'd like to keep things small and simple."

"Well, if that's what you want, darling," Caroline said. "That would make things easier on us. We can have a small ceremony at home. You could always have a reception later and invite more of the town. If we keep it under thirty guests, I see no reason why we can't have everything ready in two weeks."

Richard nodded his approval for the plan. "We'll set

the date for two weeks from today. Now, why don't we go back to the Founder's Day activities? I hear there is going to be a bazaar this year."

"There certainly is," Nathan said as everyone began to stand. "I brought several of my horses out for exhibition."

Lorelei let out a resigned sigh as everyone began putting the chairs back inside where they belonged. She helped gather the ice cream bowls and set them in the sink to soak before going back to the front porch to meet the others. Her breath stalled in her throat as she realized they had departed, leaving her alone with Sean. "Where did everyone go?"

"I asked them to go on ahead so we could have a moment alone," he said quietly.

"Why?" she asked, then lifted her gaze to his threateningly. "Sean, if you say 'we need to talk,' I won't be liable for my actions."

A slow smile stretched across his lips. He reached toward her, but she stepped back to avoid his touch. His hand dropped to his side as he watched her in concern. "I won't say that, but I would like to know why you're so upset with me."

She felt the tension in her shoulders ease. "I'm sorry, Sean. I shouldn't have been so harsh. I guess our marriage is just becoming more of a reality."

He frowned in confusion. "I know the proposal was a bit of a surprise, but we knew this day was coming all along."

"Yes, but I never thought you would do it so soon. We had nearly a full week before Papa's deadline. Why didn't you wait?"

She could hardly believe it, but he actually blushed.

"Honestly, I didn't plan it. I think I got a little carried away in the moment."

"Oh, that's just fine," she breathed and shook her head. "The one time you do something impulsive it's this."

He frowned at her sarcasm. "Your father wanted the proposal to be public, didn't he? What does it matter? It would have happened anyway."

"I know." She shrugged and gave him a conciliatory smile. "I guess I was just counting on a few more days of freedom."

Sean stared at Lorelei. His lips pressed together with the same agitation that filled his stomach. "Freedom? You make our marriage sound like you're going to be forced into a fate worse than death."

Her gaze dropped from his haltingly. "That isn't what I meant."

He stepped forward, then lifted her chin so that he could read the emotion on her face. "No, but it's how you feel, isn't it?"

"I don't know." She broke away from his hold but didn't step away.

Disappointment battled with panic. He'd known all along he might be faced with this moment—the moment when he knew for certain that he was in love alone. That didn't make it any easier to bear. He had to fix this. He had to prove to her and himself that the situation wasn't as hopeless as it appeared. He shook his head. "Maybe our relationship isn't ideal for two people who just got engaged, but I thought we were making progress."

"Progress?" she asked as her eyes filled with tears of frustration. "How have we made progress? We aren't any closer to loving each other than we were when we started out."

"How can you say that?" he asked in disbelief. "I thought if nothing else that kiss showed you—"

"Showed me what? That isn't love, Sean. That's nothing more than—"

"Don't," he said harshly. "Don't cheapen that moment or what we feel for each other by calling it nothing more than lust. That couldn't be further from the truth and you know it."

"Nothing has changed, Sean," she replied quietly. "We're still in the same situation that we've always been in."

He stared into her dark blue eyes. "A lot has changed. I think you're just too afraid to admit it because that means you'd have to actually allow yourself to feel something for once. That's why you're so willing to demean these feeling between us. You don't really want them to be meaningful, do you?"

She arched a brow coldly. "Are you done?"

He stepped back. "Yes, I'm done. I'm done trying to talk about love with someone who refuses to ever feel that emotion."

He started to walk away. It felt good to leave her standing there until he realized it wouldn't do for him to return to town without his fiancée in tow. He let out a deep breath, then turned to face her. "We have to go back together."

A tense moment passed between them. He almost thought she would refuse when she stepped up beside him and slipped her hand onto his arm. He met her gaze, but she immediately looked away. He narrowed his eyes as an idea came to mind. She wanted to believe that nothing had changed between them. Well, he'd just have to show her the difference.

The toe of Lorelei's kid leather boot rhythmically measured out the beats of the music as the melody coursed from the instruments in the gazebo into the heavy evening air. The sun would soon finish setting and bring a close to the endless stream of Founder's Day activities. She could hardly wait.

As soon as Sean had walked her back to the flurry of activity, they had separated. He had spent the next few hours with his nieces and nephew. She had spent the rest of the day with Ellie, Amy Bradley and Sophia Johansen. Now she was alone because they were all dancing and enjoying themselves immensely, as far as she could tell. Sean had not approached her for a dance. In fact, he hadn't approached her at all since their argument. Didn't he realize people would think it strange if he didn't even acknowledge his fiancée after proposing to her earlier that day?

"Apparently not," she mumbled to herself. She glanced over to where he stood talking with a few other men. *I'm not going to stand around waiting for him to notice me like that awkward child I once was.*

She began to thread through the crowd in an effort to find her parents so she could let them know she was going home. She heard someone call her name and turned to find Mrs. Sparks walking toward her. "Lorelei, wait just a moment."

She looked at the reverend's wife curiously. "Is something wrong, Mrs. Sparks?"

"No, no. I just wanted to give you this," she said, handing Lorelei a letter. "The postmaster accidentally put it in with our mail. I guess he saw the Brightlys sent it and assumed it was for us. I've been meaning to give it to you."

"Oh, thank you. I've been waiting for this." Lorelei glanced down thoughtfully at the letter in her hand, then back up at Mrs. Sparks. "I've been wondering something. Did the Brightlys ever mention anything about me or Sean in their letters to you?"

Mrs. Sparks smiled kindly. "One thing my husband and I have learned while in the ministry is the benefit of staying out of others' affairs unless they directly impact the ability of the church to operate as it should. Whatever the Brightlys communicated to us was private. It will stay private." Mrs. Sparks gave Lorelei's hand a gentle squeeze. "Does that answer your question, dear?"

Lorelei blinked away the tears that threatened to fill her eyes at the woman's kindness. "Yes, it does. Thank you."

"You're welcome," she said before walking away.

Lorelei slid her finger under the flap of the envelope, then stopped halfway through. She glanced over to where she'd last seen Sean. He had just as much of a right to know the contents of the letter as she did. Squaring her shoulders, she made her way through the crowd toward him. The town's blacksmith saw her first and gave her a welcoming grin. "Here comes the bride, gentlemen."

"Hello, Rhett." She flashed a smile at him, but it was Sean's gaze she sought. "I'd like to steal my fiancé away for a few minutes, if you don't mind."

"By all means, we won't miss him," Rhett said teasingly.

Sean shot him a wry look. "Thanks a lot."

She waited until they were out of the earshot of

Sean's laughing friends before she said, "Let's find a place a bit more private so we can talk."

He sent her a questioning glance but agreed. She felt his warm hand settle at the back of her waist to guide her through the maze of people. Her arm brushed his chest as they walked between a particularly dense part of the crowd, and she felt that touch way more than she should have.

She bit her lip. She hated to admit it, but he was right. She was attracted to him, but her feelings went much deeper than that. She had grown so used to being with him, laughing with him, sharing secrets with him. She hadn't planned on it, but somehow between all of their squabbles he had managed to become her closest friend. That was definitely not something she'd been expecting. Sean settled onto the church step, then glanced up at her. "Is this private enough?"

"I'd say so," she said, glancing back at the hundred or so people who talked, laughed and danced. She opened the envelope and carefully removed the letter. "Mrs. Sparks gave this to me. It's our response from the Brightlys. She said it got mixed up in her mail."

He stilled. "What does it say?"

"I don't know," she said quietly. "I thought we should read it together."

He gestured to the stairs. She carefully settled onto the step beside him. He shifted toward her and placed his arm behind her to brace himself. Awareness rushed over her. She felt the warmth emanating from his chest just inches away from her shoulder.

She glanced up toward where the moon hovered in the sky, eagerly awaiting the sun's departure as she tried to reason with herself. She didn't want to give in to the seductive feeling of hope that stirred in her chest. She didn't want to acknowledge whatever emotion spread warmly through her soul. It couldn't be love. She knew better than to give in to that, so there was no reason for her to react this way. She scooted farther away from him, then held out the letter. "You'd better read it."

He looked at her curiously but took the letter without comment. He scanned it carefully. "They say they can't promise the children won't slip and mention something, but they are willing to stay silent about it since we'll be married in a few weeks anyway. They are excited to see us again. They hope we will meet them at the train station."

"That's it?" she asked in confusion. "I wasn't expecting it to be that easy."

"That's it." He smiled as he refolded the letter. "You didn't need to be nervous after all. Now, we just have to get ready for the wedding."

She nodded slowly. "That shouldn't be too hard. It sounds like we're going to have a lot of help."

He grinned. "My sisters are going to pour themselves into it."

"So will my mother," she said with a smile. "Our families seem to get along pretty well, don't they?"

"A sight better than we do." He glanced away but not before she saw a shadow of pain in his eyes. She hated that she'd put it there. She also hated the change that seemed to have taken place in their relationship since their argument. Sean seemed less open and less like himself around her. She half expected him to get up and leave her as he'd tried to do earlier that day. Surprisingly, he seemed just as content to stay with her as she was to stay with him.

Above their silence, music from the quartet drifted softly toward them. She realized they were playing slower songs to calm folks down before the festivities came to an end. Only a few couples danced in the open field. It was hard to distinguish the identities of the couples from their silhouettes, but it looked as though her parents were out there dancing. She smiled as she watched them twirling slowly to the music. A new song started. It was just as slow as the last one.

"You've never asked me to dance," she blurted out.

He looked at her carefully. "I didn't think you would want me to."

She shrugged lightly, as though it didn't matter.

He broke the lingering tension between them with one slow, teasing, heart-stopping grin. "You want to dance with me. Don't you, Lorelei?"

She tried not to smile, but it didn't work so she met his gaze defiantly. "So what if I do?"

"Come on," he said with an enticing wink.

"We'll never make it before the song is over," she protested, even as she allowed him to pull her to her feet.

"Sure we will." He tugged her down the stairs. Instead of leading her across the field, he pulled her into his arms, then began to dance. Her gaze darted to the other couples. No one seemed to have noticed them. She wondered why he hadn't tried to move into the open where everyone would see them. She bit her lip as she was suddenly reminded of all the times he'd told her that he was no longer just pretending to court her.

Now, for the first time, she was willing to believe it. She wanted to know how it felt to be courted by the man she'd loved without endeavoring to push him away or silence her own feelings. She just wanted to enjoy the moment without worrying about what would come next or if she would get hurt or anything else. She was here with him. Perhaps that was all that mattered.

He dipped his head just enough to whisper into her ear. "I missed you today, Lorelei."

She pulled back enough to look up at him. "Then why did you stay away?"

The corner of his mouth pulled into a half smile just guilty enough to tell her he had been up to no good. "I almost wish I hadn't because I missed spending the day of our engagement with you."

She tilted her head suspiciously to repeat in a whisper, "Then why did you stay away?"

He met her gaze seriously. "I wanted to prove something."

"What?"

He stared down at her for a moment. His green eyes deepened in color, then he pulled her closer until their dancing became little more than a simple sway. She hardly noticed when they stopped dancing all together. She was more aware of the way Sean's arms slipped around her waist, the rough fabric of his shirt beneath her cheek and the way her heart seemed to respond to his. She was about to prod him for an answer when his voice rushed past her ear in a firm statement. "Lorelei Wilkins, this isn't 'nothing.'"

She let those words settle around her for a long moment as she acknowledged the truth behind them.

"I know, Sean," she agreed softly. *Yes, I know. I know, and it scares me to pieces.*

Chapter Twenty

Sean had never imagined such a large family could travel with so few pieces of luggage. He set the last large trunk onto the wagon where it joined its partner and only two other suitcases. He exchanged a look with James Brightly.

James shrugged in amusement. "It doesn't look like much to start out with, does it?"

"You couldn't carry much in that traveling wagon," Sean replied. "You should have plenty of room to spread out in the parsonage." He grinned and slapped the harried-looking man on the back. "It sure is good to see y'all."

"I feel the same way. I'm sure Marissa and the children appreciate seeing familiar faces in this new environment." James grinned. "I have a really good feeling about this town, Sean."

He laughed. "Well, don't burst your buttons yet, Preacher. This is just the railroad station."

With everyone helping, it only took a few minutes to get the Brightly family settled into the wagon. Sean gave James directions to the parsonage, then promised to meet them there to help with the unloading. The children waved at them until the wagon turned the corner. Lorelei waved back at them as they began to follow the wagon. "I thought I'd never see them again."

"They were certainly happy to see you."

"The children thought I was going to be their nanny again." She glanced away and toyed with the strap of her reticule. "I told them I couldn't because I was going to marry you."

"I hope you didn't sound that depressed when you said it."

He glanced down in time to see her press her lips together. This was not good. The closer they got to the wedding, the tenser she seemed to become. He wished he knew what to do. He'd thought about telling her the truth about his feelings for her but he was pretty sure it would just make things worse. She might even get a notion into her head to save him from a loveless marriage like she had with Lawson. At least this way she thought it was fair because they were on a level playing field.

He wanted to reassure her that everything would work out for them. He wanted to tell her that he'd be good to her. That he'd be kind and understanding while she adjusted to farm life and that he was sorry it was all he could offer her. He wanted to banish all of her fears so that she would look forward to their wedding day with joy. But who was he kidding? He hadn't been able to banish his own fears since he was ten. How could he possibly banish hers?

Lorelei slid onto the piano bench and gently brushed her fingers over the smooth keys. After helping the Brightly family unload their luggage, Sean had gone back to work while she'd slipped away to let the family settle in. She hadn't gone far. She needed the respite that the sanctuary offered. She stared at her engagement ring.

The nine days since the proposal had rushed by in a whirlwind of preparation for the wedding, leaving her breathless. Less than a week remained before she would officially become Lorelei O'Brien. She sighed. She'd just have to make the most of it. Wasn't that what people always said when they were faced with doing something they knew they would probably fail at?

A burst of sound filled the air as her fingers tripped through the scales. What had happened to that fearless girl who'd jumped on a train willing to ride all the way to California in search of a new life? She guessed that girl hadn't been running to something as much as she had been running from it. *What had Sean said? I'm afraid to allow myself to feel something for once.*

Her fingers paused abruptly. "What does he know anyway?"

Resettling her fingers on the piano, she began to play Beethoven's "Moonlight Sonata." The soft melody slowly built until she lost herself in it completely. The piece ended as softly as it began, leaving the last notes to fade into the stillness of the silent sanctuary. She valiantly tried to blink away the tears that clung to her lashes, but a few renegade drops tumbled down her cheeks. She didn't bother to brush them away. Instead she stared at the tear-blurred keys. The sound of movement in the sanctuary made her jerk to attention. She felt heat gather in her cheeks.

"Pastor James," she breathed in quiet alarm.

He stood from where he sat on one of the back pews to offer her an apologetic smile. "I didn't mean to intrude. I heard you playing and couldn't stop listening.

Mrs. Sparks said you played on Sundays, but I had no idea you were so accomplished."

"Thank you," she said, grateful that he was giving her time to recover her wits. "Reverend Sparks and his wife were gracious enough to let me practice on the piano whenever it didn't interfere with church functions."

He sat on the front row. "I hope you will continue to do that."

"I probably won't be able to come as often as I used to." She smiled briefly. "I'm getting married, you know."

"Well, I hope you'll come in and practice whenever you have the time."

She was surprised that he didn't question her about her obviously precarious emotional state. He seemed to recognize her confusion and smiled. "I am your pastor now, Lorelei. Well, maybe it isn't quite official yet, but it will be on Sunday. I hope if you ever need to talk to me or my wife, you won't hesitate to do so."

She bit her lip as she considered whether or not to ask the question that her heart begged to know. "Now that you mention it, there is something that I would like your opinion on."

He leaned forward and clasped his hands together. "Go right ahead."

"You and Marissa know more about my true history with Sean than most of the people in this town. What you may not know is that I was in love with Sean for a long time. I never told him, until recently—and at that point, I made it very clear that my feelings for him were all in the past. I carried the pain of my silly, childish broken heart for a long time." She smiled ruefully. "I've managed to forgive him and myself. Now, I think I'm falling in love with him again."

He surveyed her in careful concern. "Why do I get the feeling you think that is a bad thing?"

She bit her lip. "I had gotten to the point where I was fine without love. Now, I'm so afraid of being hurt, I think I'd rather just not feel anything at all. I don't know what to do."

He frowned thoughtfully. "I think you have the wrong idea about love, Lorelei."

"I think so, too." She turned on the piano bench so she could face him, then clasped her hands in her lap. "What is the right idea?"

"I don't mean to offend you, but the type of love you're talking about seems almost like a selfish sort of love. You're concerned with how accepting love from others will affect *you* when you should be concerned with how giving love to others will affect *them*."

"I'm not sure I understand."

"Lorelei, even if you are the only person in the world who can do without love, that doesn't mean others can. Love others as you wished to be loved. I'm not saying that you won't get hurt. We all have our failings and often end up hurting others intentionally or unintentionally. Regardless of that, we still need each other."

She glanced down and smiled ruefully. "If that's true, then it does seem like I've been rather self-preoccupied, doesn't it?"

"You were confused, hurt and trying to protect yourself. I completely understand that. It's just…" He paused for a moment as if searching for the right words. His eyes landed on something behind her, and she followed his gaze to the large wooden cross at the front of the church. She glanced back to see him step onto the platform. "We have to put it in the perspective of the cross. Wouldn't you agree that Jesus' sacrifice on the cross was the purest act of love the world has ever seen?"

She glanced up at the cross. "Yes, I would."

"Jesus was the Son of God. It was within his power to protect himself." James turned to face her and thoughtfully spread his arms out to mimic the shape of the cross. "This is how he died, Lorelei. There is nothing defensive about this position. In fact, it's probably the most exposed position a person can take. He opened up his heart. He stretched his arms wide and became completely vulnerable to show us what true love looks like."

He dropped his arms, then turned to look up at the cross. "A lot of times we only see love as beautiful and healing and restorative. Yet, sometimes love is purest when it's bruised and aching. Whatever form it takes, Lorelei, the cross proves that one thing never changes. Love is always, *always* giving."

She didn't even realize she was crying until a quiet sob caught at her throat. She covered her lips with her hand. James seemed to sense that she needed a few minutes alone because he quietly slipped away. Left with nothing but the visual reminder of his words, she allowed the tears to flow freely from her eyes. They were tears that had been held back for far too long.

Minutes later, she wiped the tears from her face. She was stronger than her fears. With God's help, she would face the future. Resolve filled her being. She was ready for her wedding.

Lorelei pulled in a deep, bracing breath as she glanced down at the clinging bodice of her wedding dress. She had made a few changes to the design since she'd last worn it, but the white satin stretched across her hips with familiar ease. She waited as her mother attached the veil to the back of her hair, then straightened it. Setting her shoulders in determination, she met her mother's gaze.

Caroline smiled as she carefully tamed one of Lorelei's wayward curls. She stepped back to survey Lorelei and nodded her approval. "You look beautiful, dear. Are you ready to head downstairs?"

"I think I'd like a few minutes alone first."

"I'll let everyone know that we're almost ready to begin."

"Thanks, Mama." She waited until her mother slipped out the door and closed it quietly behind her before she turned to face the image of a bride staring back at her in the mirror. The breeze from the open window stirred her veil and filled the room with the scent of roses.

This was it. This was the moment she had alternately hoped for and dreaded. The moment she said "I do" she would be making herself completely vulnerable. She was going to promise to love, honor and keep Sean for the rest of her life—and she was going to mean it. Despite her talk with James, traces of fear swirled through her mind.

"Perfect love casts out fear," she breathed. She'd learned a lot about love since her talk with James by studying what the Bible said about it. She opened the large family Bible that had taken up residence on her night table and flipped through the pages until she reached the verse that had been bothering her. Her finger trailed across the page. "'Love does not rejoice in iniquity, but rejoices in the truth.'"

Truth. She swallowed at the thought of all of the guests waiting downstairs. What would their reaction be to the truth?

Sean barely refrained from pulling at the high neck of his fancy white button-down shirt. He fiddled with the cuff links on his black Western-style jacket before stuffing his hand in the pocket of his black pants. He stood in the front of the parlor where the ceremony would take place and tried to make small talk with Judge Hendricks.

He glanced around the parlor at the thirty people who had managed to fit inside while still somehow leaving space for a center aisle. Some of the men stood around the perimeter to give the ladies room to sit. Judge Hendricks stepped aside to have a word with the violinist who would provide the music for Lorelei to walk down the aisle, leaving Sean to fend off his nerves by himself.

He glanced to the back of the room in time to see Caroline step in from the hall to wait with her husband. That meant no one was with Lorelei. He spotted Ellie talking to Caroline, then managed to catch his sister's attention and discreetly summon her. "What's the hold up, Ellie? I thought the ceremony was supposed to have started already."

"Goodness, you look nervous," she said in amusement. "Lorelei just wanted a few minutes to herself. That's all. Calm down."

He froze, but his heart began to race. "How long has it been since anyone talked to her?"

"A few minutes, maybe. I don't know, Sean. No one is timing it," she said distractedly. At his sharp intake of breath, she looked at him more carefully. Suddenly her eyes widened. "You don't think…" She bit her lips as if afraid to continue.

He sent her a glance that told her exactly what he thought. He tried to appear calm as he passed under Mrs. Greene's watchful eye to walk toward the Wilkinses. He met their curiosity with tempered alarm. "Did Lorelei come down these stairs?" he asked in a low voice that didn't carry past the two of them.

"Of course not," Richard said.

"She is still in her room," Caroline offered. "She just wanted a few minutes by herself."

I bet she did. He glanced up at the stairs. "Her room has a window, doesn't it?"

Caroline nodded. "Yes, it overlooks the backyard."

"Excuse me," he breathed as he stepped past them.

He walked out to the backyard, then glanced up at her open window. He expected to see a sheet hanging down the side of the house, but it wasn't there. He must have anticipated her. Any minute now he would probably see her satchel tumble to the ground beside the yellow rose bushes. Or perhaps she'd step out onto that tree branch next to her window. It was plenty close enough to afford an escape. He crossed his arms, bracing himself to wait. He heard the back door of the Wilkinses' house open and glanced over to see Caroline staring at him in confusion. "Sean, come inside."

He shook his head, then turned back to the window. "Just a minute, Mrs. Wilkins."

The woman went back inside, leaving him staring at the open window. The ground beneath him began to sway. He braced himself. He began to consider the possibility that he was too late. He should have thought of this. He should have had a plan. He'd just been so sure that she was dedicated to getting married. His only concern had been securing her love. He'd felt her tension. Why hadn't thought of making sure she was prepared to walk down the aisle? He should have planned better.

His chest began to tighten. She'd run from Lawson. Why wouldn't she run from him? It wasn't as though she loved him. She'd made that clear plenty of times. He'd thought she wouldn't want to sentence him to a loveless marriage. Maybe she didn't want to sentence herself.

He closed his eyes and tried to slow his racing thoughts. It felt as though they were swirling around just above his head. He couldn't grasp any of them. Was he going crazy? He needed to think. He needed to sit down. Maybe that would stop the swaying. He needed to pray.

His low words were interrupted by his rapid breaths. "Lord, I've been holding on to the most important pieces of life as though I could take better care of them than You. All of my plans couldn't help me hold on to the piece that meant the most to me. She's gone, but finally I'm giving my life entirely to You."

His breathing began to steady as the pressure on his chest loosened. "Your will isn't my backup plan anymore. From now on, it's my only plan. I don't just want You to be my Partner in life. I need You to be my Guide from here on out. Amen."

The swaying beneath his feet began to lessen. His mind stopped reeling enough for him to sit down on the bench beneath the crape myrtle. He buried his face in his hands and propped his elbows on his knees. A weight gradually began to lift from his shoulders.

"I thought we were getting married in the parlor." Lorelei's gently teasing voice drifted from right behind him. He froze. *Delusions? Doc never mentioned delusions.*

There was a whisper of movement, then a light touch on his back. "Doc said I might want to check on you. Ellie told me why."

The tension eased from his shoulders even as he growled. "Ellie."

She laughed. "Don't blame her entirely. I could tell she knew, so I begged it out of her. I'm pretty sure I know why you haven't told me."

"Why is that?" He managed to ask as he let his hands fall from his face so he could stare at the ground.

"You don't like showing weakness. You want me to see you as strong, dependable and controlled. Well, I've always known you were strong and dependable. Sometimes I think you're a bit too controlled. For instance, you have to be dying to see what I look like today but you're staring at that leaf so hard you're going to tear it in two."

A smile pulled at his lips, but he didn't move.

"You're building up all of that tension inside of you when turning around and sharing that moment with me would get rid of a lot of that stress. We're getting married, Sean. I need you to share your load with me and allow me to control my share of the reins. I need to know that you aren't always strong so that I have permission to be weak once in a while, too. That's the only way this is going to work."

He pulled in a deep breath. He slowly stood and turned toward her, then couldn't help staring. Her hands rested delicately on her hips, accentuating her curves, which were already embellished by the cut of the brilliant white dress. Her hair was partially pulled back from her face and gathered beneath the wreath of delicate blue flowers that crowned her head. The rest of her dark hair spilled down her back in rich curls that begged to be touched. She took his breath away, which, combined with what had just happened, left his voice sounding nothing like it usually did. "Lorelei."

Her lips curved into a tempting smile. "Better, right?"

"Much better."

"Remember that." She lifted her skirts carefully as she stepped through the grass to meet him.

"I will." She hadn't run the other way in the face of his weakness, but could he dare to upset the delicate balance of their relationship any further? He swallowed. How could he not? "Lorelei, before we do this, there is something I need to say—"

"Stop everything!' They both jumped at the sound of Mrs. Greene's voice. She burst out of the house with Richard and Caroline right behind her. "I can't make you do it."

"What?" Lorelei asked in an echo of his own confusion.

The woman fanned her brightening cheeks as she came to a stop in front of them. "Pastor Brightly called on me yesterday. We talked and he pointed a few scriptures out to me about meddling and gossip. Oh, he was gentle about it, but I got the message. I tried to ignore it, telling myself over and over again that I was in the right but seeing everyone all dressed up and ready to go…"

"You're releasing them from their promise, aren't you, Amelia?" Caroline asked as she stepped forward to place a gentle hand on her friend's arm.

"Yes. Yes, I am."

Sean's gaze shot to Lorelei. Her mouth dropped open as she looked to her father for guidance. Richard shook his head thoughtfully. "There is still the chance that all of this could be discovered. However, since there isn't an imminent danger, I think it's time we let you two decide your own fate. I believe you're fully aware of the consequences of either choice. We'll leave you to make your decision."

The relief that lowered Lorelei's shoulders told him more than he wanted to know. He turned away to gather his emotions as he heard the door close softly behind Mrs. Greene and Lorelei's parents. He shook the tension from his hands to keep them from clenching into fists. He was supposed to have surrendered his plans to God. Maybe he'd better act like it for once.

He turned to face Lorelei, then leaned back against the ashy trunk of the crape myrtle to offer a smile he didn't feel. "I guess it really is bad luck to see the bride before the wedding."

Chapter Twenty-One

Lorelei wasn't sure how she'd expected Sean to react to this news, but a careless smile wasn't it. She searched his gaze for the tension she'd seen earlier but lost sight of it in the swirl of unfathomable emotions in his green eyes. Silence hovered between them. She sat down on the bench as she tried to grasp the implications of what just happened. She shook her head. What were they going to do? They had a house full of guests waiting for a wedding. She did not want to be the one to walk away from another wedding. Who was she fooling? She didn't want to be the one to walk away from *this* wedding. She met Sean's gaze, and one thought echoed in her mind.

Love rejoices in the truth.

The truth. Her breath stilled in her throat. *The truth is I love him.*

Her heart began to thunder in her chest. With each beat came the knowledge that if she was ever going to overcome this, it would have to be now. She suddenly realized her choice would determine much more than if she said those three little words. It would determine how she would spend the rest of her life. Either she would trust God to protect her heart as she gave of it freely in obedience to His will, or she would continue on a path that would bring momentary security and lasting unhappiness. There was only one real choice.

Her heart begged to speak the truth that she'd refused to allow cross her lips. Rather than deny its request, she finally allowed the words to roll off her tongue and rest softly between them. "Sean, I love you."

That got his attention. He straightened his shoulders and stared down at her with his penetrating eyes. Some of her courage fled. She swallowed. She dropped her gaze to the tips of her white bridal boots, then forced herself to continue. "I don't think I ever really stopped. I know you probably don't return my feelings. I just thought you should know in case you are ever able—"

Lorelei was barely even aware that Sean had erased the distance between them until he guided her face upward and kissed her with a gentle reverence. Her lashes flew open to meet his gaze. He knelt in the grass in front of her with a relieved smile. "I love you, too. Now let's get married."

He began to stand, but she reached forward and grabbed his hand before he could get away. "Wait!"

"What?"

She stared at him in wide-eyed disbelief. "This is not going to be the story we tell our children, Sean O'Brien."

A confused smile tilted his lip. "What are you talking about?"

"I just said I love you—present tense, mind you." She tugged his hand until he knelt before her again, then looked at him hopefully. "Don't you have anything else to say besides 'I love you, too? Now let's get married'?"

"Should I?" At her emphatic nod, his doubtful look

turned into one of understanding. "Well, I told you everything I felt when I proposed. I meant what I said."

"You did?" She dared to ask, "What did you say?"

His shoulders slumped as though severely disappointed. "You don't remember my proposal."

She bit her lip and shrugged innocently. "I remember you proposed. Everything else is kind of blurry. There were a lot of people around and I didn't know you meant it. You acted like it was all a joke."

"I knew if I did otherwise you might not be able to say yes." He squeezed her hand. "That's all right. I remember it. It went something like this."

He cleared his throat and became all seriousness and sincerity as he captured her gaze. "Lorelei Wilkins, you are the most wonderful, beautiful and captivating woman I have ever met. I didn't fall in love with you to fulfill my plans. I fell in love with you because, as you informed me nearly ten years ago, 'We belong together. We'll always belong together. I don't know how I know it, but one day you're going to marry me and we're going to be happier than anyone who's ever lived.'"

Lorelei laughed as tears filled her eyes, and she shook her head in slow disbelief. "You remember that?"

He smiled slowly. "I never forgot it…or you. Now—" he stood and pulled her to her feet along with him "—will you *please* prove yourself right and marry me already?"

"Absolutely. I think we've left everyone waiting long enough—including each other."

They stepped inside the house a moment later to find both of their families standing in the hallway outside the parlor. Everyone waited with bated breath. Lorelei glanced at Sean. He drew out the moment by surveying each family member carefully. Finally, he spoke. "Well, what's everybody standing around here for? Someone tell them to start the music."

The hallway echoed with celebration, causing a few of the guests to peer around the corner to see what all the commotion was about. Lorelei hardly noticed. She leaned into Sean as he slipped his arm around her waist, then grinned at their families' enthusiasm. Ellie presented Lorelei with her wedding bouquet. "Hallelujah! There's going to be a wedding. Everyone get to your places and I'll tell them we're ready."

Sean was amazed at how quickly everyone was ready to go. He pulled at his choking collar and let out a relieved breath when the music began. A moment later, Lorelei started down the aisle on her father's arm. The peaceful smile on her face lasted until she was halfway down the aisle. She bit her lip. He could literally hear their family and friends sit forward in their chairs. Her steps became more halting. Her gaze met his in desperation.

Sean held out a hand to Lorelei, willing her to take it. She quickly kissed her father on the cheek, then slid her hand into his. They turned to face the judge. He could almost hear the guests let out a breath of relief behind them. Lorelei tugged at his hand as if she wanted to say something. He leaned down to incline his ear toward her. As the judge welcomed the guests to the wedding, her whisper filled his ear. "I have ants in my shoe."

He glanced at the pained expression on her face. "Which one?"

She tapped the shoe nearest him against his boot. He threw a cursory glance over his shoulder, then quickly knelt on the floor and slipped his hand under the hem of her dress. The judge abruptly stopped speaking. A gasp rent through the air.

Bracing herself with a hand on his shoulder, Lorelei used her other hand to lift her skirt. He finally found her boot and ripped it off. He brushed a few ants off of her foot, then turned the shoe over to bang it on the floor. He met her gaze thoughtfully. "You'd better take off the other one."

Her foot disappeared back under her skirt. A second later, the last shoe slid from under the white satin. He gathered the boots in his hand, then gave them to Caroline who stepped forward to collect them. Sean stood. Lorelei slipped her hand back into his. He nodded at the judge to continue.

The judge cleared his throat. "As I was saying, if anyone has just cause why these two should not be married, let them speak now or forever hold their piece."

He couldn't help it. He glanced back at Mrs. Greene. The woman caught his gaze and smiled her approval. A weight lifted from his shoulders. Once blessed silence reigned through the parlor, the judge instructed them to face each other. "Sean, will you take this woman to be your wedded wife, to live together after God's ordinance in the holy state of matrimony? Will you love her, comfort her, honor and keep her, in sickness and in health: forsaking all others, keeping only unto her so long as you both shall live?"

"I will."

"Lorelei, will you take this man to be thy wedded husband, to live together after God's ordinance in the holy estate of matrimony? Will you love, honor and keep him, in sickness and in health: forsaking all others, keeping only unto him so long as you both shall live?"

"I will," she said with calm assurance.

Judge Hendricks beckoned for the rings to be presented. "Sean, repeat after me as you place this ring on Lorelei's finger."

He took the ring, then met Lorelei's gaze sincerely as he repeated his vows. "I give you this ring as a symbol of my love." He waited for the judge to continue, then spoke. "With all that I am and all that I have, I honor you…" He slid the ring onto her finger. "In the name of the Father, and of the Son, and of the Holy Spirit."

"Lorelei, repeat after me as you place this ring onto Sean's finger."

"I give you this ring as a symbol of my love," she said confidently as she slid the ring onto his finger. Then as she glanced up to meet his gaze, she smiled. "With all that I am and all that I have, I honor you…in the name of the Father, and of the Son, and of the Holy Spirit."

"Those whom God has joined together, let no man put asunder. By the power vested in me by the state of Texas, I now pronounce you husband and wife. You may seal your union with a kiss."

Sean wasted no time in doing exactly that.

Epilogue

"Paging Mr. and Mrs. Sean O'Brien. Paging Mr. and Mrs. Sean O'Brien."

Lorelei raised her hand to attract the porter's attention before Sean even had a chance. She sent him a meaningful look as she answered the porter's call. "We're Mr. and Mrs. Sean O'Brien."

Sean grinned at her. "Sounds good, doesn't it?"

"Mmm-hmm," she agreed with an answering grin.

The porter arrived at their seats, clutching a basket of fruit. "Please accept this gift as a token of our deepest apologies."

"Well, thanks," Sean said as he took the basket. "But why are you apologizing?"

"There was a mix-up, sir. You two should have been shown to a private car in first-class when you boarded. If you'll follow me, please, your luggage has already been transferred."

Lorelei shook her head. "We didn't pay for a private car in first-class. I think we'd better stay here."

"The car has been paid for, ma'am, by a Mr. Richard Wilkins and a Mr. Nathan Rutledge."

Sean's gaze met Lorelei. "How do you like that? Our families treated us."

"I like it. Let's go."

It only took a few moments to gather their things and follow the porter up the aisle toward first-class. As they walked, a familiar flash of color caught Lorelei's eyes. She stopped abruptly. Sean ran directly into her.

"Hey," he protested, but she hardly noticed.

She narrowed her eyes, then slowly turned around. "Back up."

He watched her in confusion but walked backward as she commanded—not that he had much choice with her hand on his chest. She stopped again to stare at the traveling bag sitting abandoned on an empty seat. "That's my bag."

"What?"

She lifted the bag to look for her initials on the right handle. She found it. She turned to Sean. "This is my traveling bag. The one Elmira stole. Look, my initials are still here—*L.W.*"

He surveyed it closely. His eyes widened in recognition, but he shook his head. "Your initials are *L.O.*"

She sent him an exasperated look. "*L.W.O.* Thank you very much."

"Excuse me, ma'am," a deep voice said. Lorelei turned to find the young couple seated across the aisle was watching them closely. The man frowned. "You must be mistaken. That bag belongs to our chaperone."

She exchanged a look with Sean, who stepped toward the man. "I'm sorry, did you say your *chaperone?*"

"Yes," the young woman answered. "She just stepped out for a minute, but she'll be back and I'm sure she'll want her bag."

"*My* bag. I'm sure she'll want *my* bag. She probably stepped out as soon as she heard the porter calling us. Well, we'll wait right here until Miss Elmira comes back."

The dark-haired young man shook his head. "See? You're mistaken. Our chaperone's name is Lorrie Wilson."

"Lorrie Wilson…Lorelei Wilkins," Lorelei repeated, then looked at Sean. "She stole my name! Don't laugh at me. Do something."

Sean leaned his arm on the back of the empty seat to survey the couple. "You two seem like nice people. I guess you deserve a fair warning. Miss Lorrie Wilson was our chaperone, only back then she went by the name of Elmira Shrute. That *is* my wife's bag. Miss Elmira stole it along with my wallet. Notice I said *'my wife.'*" He lifted Lorelei's left hand and displayed it as proof. "That's just the kind of chaperone Miss Elmira is."

"Oh, heavens," the young woman breathed.

Sean grinned. "Yes, ma'am. Hiring her was the best mistake I ever made."

Their eyes met, and Lorelei smiled until he put her bag back on the seat and ushered her down the aisle. "Aren't we going to wait for Miss Elmira?"

"Nope." He took the key from the porter, who was waiting by their open door. "We certainly aren't."

"You can't be serious." She let him guide her into their room as she protested. "What about my bag?"

He closed the door and leaned against it. "You have a new one."

She tilted her head entreatingly. "My honor?"

He held up his left hand to show his wedding ring. "Protected."

She caught his hand in both of hers. "My pride?"

"Well, now." He lifted her hand to his cheek, then pressed a kiss into her palm. "That's something you'll have to take care of yourself."

She frowned. "I will. If you would be so kind as to move out of the way?"

He crossed his arms. "That isn't going to happen."

"Really? We'll see about that." She tried to reach behind him in a valiant effort to open the door. He stopped her every attempt. "Let me give her a piece of my mind!"

"No. You're not going out there. You have to let this go." He held her off with one hand and locked the door with the other, then slipped the key under the door into the hallway.

She gasped. Her eyes flew back and forth between floor and him until she met his gaze. "Do you think that's perfectly necessary?"

"Perfectly." He leaned forward to peck her on the lips.

Well, it was hopeless. She wasn't getting out. Miss Elmira was going to get away. She let out a loud disappointed sigh and caught Sean grinning at her antics before he turned away to hide it. She smiled, then crossed her arms to watch him unpack his trunk. "That's just fine. What are we going to do when we really need to get out of here?"

He had the nerve to glance around the room as though another door would suddenly appear. "There's always the window."

She laughed. "You first!"

"I am perfectly content to stay exactly where I am."

"I bet."

He caught her sly look and lifted a brow. "You ought not to insinuate such things, Mrs. O'Brien."

"Oughtn't I?"

He closed his trunk and sat on the top of it. "Come here for a minute, will you?"

Once she stood in front of him, he guided her to sit on his knee. She placed her arm around his shoulder as his went around her waist. "Lorelei, I can't let you go after Miss Elmira because she did us a favor. If she hadn't abandoned us I might never have married you."

"I know." She sighed. "It's just that every once in a while I'd think to myself that if I ever got my hands on that Elmira Shrute—"

"You'd what?"

"Well, I never got that far—probably nothing," she admitted then smiled. "You're right, though. I am thankful for everything that happened."

"Are you sure?"

She looked at him more closely. Did he honestly doubt her? "Of course, I'm sure. I love you. I wouldn't trade what we have for a thousand reckonings with Miss Elmira."

"In that case…" He reached into his pocket to pull out the key.

Her mouth dropped open. "You had it the whole time!"

He laughed. "You didn't think I'd want to be trapped in here with you for the whole trip, did you?"

She pushed away from his chest, but he wouldn't let her go. "You're a scoundrel. That's what you are."

"And you're trouble." He waited until she stopped struggling to continue, "I knew it from the moment I held you soaking wet to my side and you laughed when James threatened to kill me."

She gave him her most innocent look. "Well, it was funny."

He dipped her backward and kissed her until her arms went around his neck. When he pulled away slightly, she glanced up at him with dancing eyes but kept the tone of her breathless voice serious. "Sean, do you know what the best part of running away was?"

He shook his head. "What?"

"Getting caught."

His warm emerald eyes searched her face, then he grinned a slow heartfelt grin and she knew she was right.

* * * * *

Dear Reader,

Welcome back to Peppin, Texas! We discovered this close-knit, fictional Texas town and met the O'Brien family for the first time in *Unlawfully Wedded Bride*. In our world, it's been a relatively short period of time, but for Peppin it's been almost ten years. It was such fun to rediscover the town all these years later and find it had grown from a lazy country village into a bustling small town with modern conveniences like the railroad and telegraph.

This is the first novel I started and finished as an adult. I started writing seriously at the age of fifteen, so these characters have been with me for almost eight years now. Sean and Lorelei have very patiently waited for their turn to fall in love. As they do so, they teach us a lesson about love that I am still learning today. It's found in Colossians 3:13–14.

Ellie's story is next. She is much more impatient for her turn to find love and rightly so, since her story is actually the first one I thought of. You may be wondering who her hero is going to be. Well, let's just say he's much closer than you might think.

In the meantime, I would love to hear from you. You can find me at www.NoelleMarchand.com. I am also on Facebook, Goodreads and Twitter.

Blessings!

Noelle Marchand

Questions for Discussion

1. Sean and Lorelei are forced to marry to comply with society's standards. What do you think of this? How have society's standards changed? Do you believe they have changed for better or for worse? Why?

2. Sean often has trouble overcoming his anxiety. How does this affect his life? How does this affect his relationship with Lorelei? How does he overcome this? How can you deal with anxiety in a Godly way?

3. Lorelei is reluctant to love again. How does her history with Sean factor into this? How does she overcome it?

4. What do you think about James Brightly's perspective on love? How does it impact Lorelei? What can you do to demonstrate the kind of love he speaks about?

5. Throughout the story, Sean and Lorelei bend the truth to protect themselves and protect others. Was it right for them to do this? Why or why not?

6. Sean and Lorelei keep the truth about why they are getting married a secret from the town. Was it right for them to do this? Why or why not? At what point does a secret become a lie of omission?

7. What was Mrs. Greene's role in Sean and Lorelei's romance? Do you believe she did the right thing in the end?

8. What was the turning point in Lorelei and Sean's relationship? How did they reach it?

9. What would you say are the overriding themes in the story? Why?

10. Did Lawson's reaction to Lorelei leaving him at the altar surprise you? What about his reaction to the news of Sean and Lorelei's impending marriage? Why or why not? What do you think the future holds for him?

11. The story allows a glimpse of Kate and Nathan's life nearly ten years after they were married. What do you think of their life now? Did you notice any changes in their character or how they relate to each other?

12. Ellie still believes she is the best matchmaker in town. What do you think about her relationship advice to Sean? Was it accurate? Was it useful?

REQUEST YOUR FREE BOOKS!

2 FREE INSPIRATIONAL NOVELS
PLUS 2
FREE
MYSTERY GIFTS

Love Inspired.
HISTORICAL
INSPIRATIONAL HISTORICAL ROMANCE

YES! Please send me 2 FREE Love Inspired® Historical novels and my 2 FREE mystery gifts (gifts are worth about $10). After receiving them, if I don't wish to receive any more books, I can return the shipping statement marked "cancel". If I don't cancel, I will receive 4 brand-new novels every month and be billed just $4.49 per book in the U.S. or $4.99 per book in Canada. That's a saving of at least 22% off the cover price. It's quite a bargain! Shipping and handling is just 50¢ per book in the U.S. and 75¢ per book in Canada.* I understand that accepting the 2 free books and gifts places me under no obligation to buy anything. I can always return a shipment and cancel at any time. Even if I never buy another book, the two free books and gifts are mine to keep forever.

102/302 IDN FEHF

Name	(PLEASE PRINT)
Address	Apt. #
City	State/Prov.	Zip/Postal Code

Signature (if under 18, a parent or guardian must sign)

Mail to the Reader Service:
IN U.S.A.: P.O. Box 1867, Buffalo, NY 14240-1867
IN CANADA: P.O. Box 609, Fort Erie, Ontario L2A 5X3

Not valid for current subscribers to Love Inspired Historical books.

Want to try two free books from another series?
Call 1-800-873-8635 or visit www.ReaderService.com.

* Terms and prices subject to change without notice. Prices do not include applicable taxes. Sales tax applicable in N.Y. Canadian residents will be charged applicable taxes. Offer not valid in Quebec. This offer is limited to one order per household. All orders subject to credit approval. Credit or debit balances in a customer's account(s) may be offset by any other outstanding balance owed by or to the customer. Please allow 4 to 6 weeks for delivery. Offer available while quantities last.

Your Privacy—The Reader Service is committed to protecting your privacy. Our Privacy Policy is available online at www.ReaderService.com or upon request from the Reader Service.

We make a portion of our mailing list available to reputable third parties that offer products we believe may interest you. If you prefer that we not exchange your name with third parties, or if you wish to clarify or modify your communication preferences, please visit us at www.ReaderService.com/consumerschoice or write to us at Reader Service Preference Service, P.O. Box 9062, Buffalo, NY 14269. Include your complete name and address.

LIH11B

Finding love in unexpected places

Another inspirational tale by

DEBRA ULLRICK

It's the perfect plan—best friends Leah Bowen and Jake Lure will each advertise for mail-order spouses, and then help each other select their future mates. When the responses to the postings pour in, it seems all their dreams will soon come true. But the closer they get to the altar, the less appealing marrying a stranger becomes. Will they both realize that the perfect one has been there the entire time?

Groom Wanted

Available in August wherever books are sold.